The DreamHacker

A NOVEL BY
TIMOTHY BENSON

authorHOUSE®

AuthorHouse™
1663 Liberty Drive
Bloomington, IN 47403
www.authorhouse.com
Phone: 1 (800) 839-8640

Published by AuthorHouse 08/10/2018

ISBN: 978-1-5462-5409-6 (sc)
ISBN: 978-1-5462-5407-2 (hc)
ISBN: 978-1-5462-5408-9 (e)

Library of Congress Control Number: 2018909121

Print information available on the last page.

Dedication

To Carol, of course.

CHAPTER 1

I close my eyes and look deep inside, let the dreams that I have take flight. I lift up my head and just believe, knowing I was made to dream.

From the song *Made to Dream"* by Jackie Evancho

EVERYONE WHO WORKS FOR A living, no matter what the job, deals with something in the workplace that leads to stress. It might be an obnoxious coworker or a cubicle too cramped to be functional. It might be a manager with no clue on how to manage or something as simple as a machine that makes lousy coffee. In Dylan's case it was Monday, when his weekend was over and his work week began. Monday mornings were always tough enough to handle and the first Monday of every month was even worse. It was the monthly partner's meeting and a regular reminder that he wasn't one of them.

On those Mondays it was almost impossible for him not to think about it because his cramped, little office was at one end of the main corridor and the employee lounge and restrooms were at the other end. A cup of coffee or a few minutes in a toilet stall involved a long walk right past the elegant, glass-walled conference room where the firm's best and brightest gathered to discuss finances, caseloads and all the minutia of running Doyle and Finch, Attorneys, LLP.

Unfortunately, after six years of busting his butt and doing his job well, Dylan was still on the outside looking in.

His annual review was coming up in about a month and a half and he'd been racking his brain for ideas on how he could make sure that this one would finally bring him the partner position he'd wanted for so long. Everything seemed to be in place. His billable hours were up over last year's numbers, his clients all seemed to have favorable things to say about him and he had brought a couple of new clients, albeit small ones, to the firm.

He'd even been more careful about the little things like not playing loose with the firm's dress code the way he'd been doing from day one and by making sure he got to the office by 8:30 every morning. Of course, that was only on the days when he wasn't downtown in a courtroom trying to get some client's kid out of an underage drinking rap or another client out from under a mountain of unpaid parking tickets.

Doyle and Finch was one of the most prestigious firms in San Diego and around the state, with large corporate and institutional clients that other firms could only wish for. The partners divided up a workload that covered everything from government contracts to employment law to mergers and acquisitions. That also meant they also got to divide the lion's share of the fees and bonuses.

Dylan's role in the firm was something very different.

He was more or less the firm's blue collar lawyer, the guy who had the job of cleaning up messes and keeping their clients' names out of the newspaper and off the evening TV news. It was the kind of legal work that the partners didn't want to get involved with. They regarded it as work that was beneath them but they knew that someone in the firm needed to make those messes go away.

He had graduated second in his class and thought he was primed for a solid career in business law but somehow things took a different direction. When he'd first started with the firm Mr. William Doyle himself assigned Dylan to take care of a little problem with a client's eighteen year old son. The kid had a very strong liking for pot and had been caught in the midst of a small transaction. Maybe it was because Dylan was young and was the only man in the office who had a beard or because he'd been known to fire one up every now and then himself, but for some reason Mr. Doyle told the partners to give the case to him. Dylan had heard that Doyle's exact words were, "Let's see if this new guy, this Dylan Ward, can handle himself in the trenches."

Somehow Dylan managed to get the kid off on a procedural technicality and from then on, whenever a client had a dark, little secret or anything that smelled like a scandal, it was handed to Dylan to get rid of the stink.

When he really thought about it he had to admit to himself there was something kind of film noir about his work that appealed to him in a strange and dark way. Instead of meeting with accountants and bankers and other corporate lawyers like everyone else in the firm, he spent his time with police detectives, eyewitnesses, and the occasional unnamed source. Instead of boardrooms and posh offices most of his meetings were conducted in bars, holding cells, bail bond offices and even on street corners.

At times he felt like one of the lawyers he'd always enjoyed watching in movies and on television, the ones who sometimes had to play fast and loose with things in order to win for their clients. Somehow that style of lawyering suited him; street law, the kind of people and cases that often required a flexible take on what was legal and illegal, what was appropriate and what was over the line.

And he knew that his particular services helped to prevent the firm's clients from looking elsewhere for help from another firm so Doyle and Finch would maintain total control over all of their legal activities. Around the office the term they used for those often embarrassing, uncomfortable cases was "Ward-worthy". Dylan thought it was amusing at first but after turning thirty and after six years of doing the dirty work and looking up while standing on the bottom rung of the ladder, he was no longer laughing.

So there he sat on that Monday morning, in his windowless office reading case notes, sipping the last bit of his third cup of lukewarm coffee and feeling an urgent need to get rid of the first two. There would be no more delaying the long walk down the corridor. On the right were the glass walls of the conference room and he knew the partners would be gazing out, watching him and knowing the important restroom mission he was on. The lighting in that part of the corridor was noticeably lower, as if it were a shrine because on the left side was a twenty foot long section of wall covered with the mahogany-framed portraits of all of the firm's partners, past and present, dead and alive, their eyes riveted on anyone who walked past them. They were the twenty eight men and two women who had, over the years, made it into the inner circle.

The only things missing from the shrine were candles and incense.

The corridor felt like a gauntlet and walking it always made Dylan feel so diminished. Before he'd walked out of his office he'd made it a point to grab a stack of paperwork and stuff it all into a manila folder. He tucked it under his arm and then headed out the door, making sure to walk quickly so it would look to anyone who saw him as though he was working on something important, something with purpose. But he knew better and so did they.

When he pushed open the Men's Room door he laid the folder on the marble counter, then walked to the urinal and went about his business. Things were no sooner underway when Max Dewart walked in. The man preferred to be called Maxwell because he thought it sounded more Ivy League and important but Dylan never gave him the satisfaction. "Morning, Max," he said, looking back over his right shoulder.

"Oh, hi, Dylan," Max answered in a flat, emotionless voice. Thankfully he walked to the urinal at the far end of the row. "Good," Dylan thought, "I hate shoulder to shoulder urination, especially when the other guy is a lot taller than I am."

A few months earlier the two men would have carried on some kind of light conversation about their weekend experiences or the upcoming Monday Night Football match-up, but since Max had been made a partner he was a totally changed man. He had become a self-important asshole and had no time for Dylan now and that had only added to the level of tension between them. Despite having been with the firm three years longer than Max the managing partners had decided that Max was partner material. Not Dylan, Max.

Part of Dylan wanted to be friendly and say something appropriate to the moment but a bigger part decided to maintain the distance that Max seemed to want. Dylan finished his business and walked over to the sinks. While he washed his hands two more partners strolled in and a moment later two more. They were all engaged in conversation and not one of them gave so much as a nod of recognition that Dylan was even in the room. He stood there, ran his hand over his thinning hair, adjusted his glasses and looked into the wall-to-wall mirror.

The reflection pretty much said it all. It showed Dylan on one side of the room and the partners on the other side, standing in the porcelain with their backs to him. He dried his hands and walked out, paperwork in hand, and didn't say a word. The walk back down the corridor seemed even longer than the one before and he passed the conference room again, knowing he was being watched. He fought the urge to look in. Nope, he didn't have time for distractions. They would see that Dylan Ward was a busy man, a man in a hurry and a man with important things to do. Too bad it wasn't true.

By the time he'd reached his office he felt like he wanted to punch someone, and given his mood, Beth Chilcotte was pretty much the last person he wanted to see standing there. "Good morning," she said softly, "I was just dropping off a copy of the deposition for the McCormick hearing and I saw you coming down the hall."

From the time he'd started working right after law school Dylan had heard the age-old advice about avoiding an office romance and true to his nature he ignored it. Beth was a paralegal and Dylan's lack of professional stature within the firm made it necessary for the two of them to work closely together on his non-corporate and often colorful types of cases. She was beautiful, smart as a whip and had a self confidence that made her seem much older than twenty-seven. She also shared his cynical view on much of went on in the world.

"Oh yeah, good morning," he said. "Uh, thanks for the file, I'm just about ready to dig into that one."

Beth stood there, smiling and looking as beautiful as she had when Dylan had first laid eyes on her two years before. She seemed a little nervous and Dylan was sure he seemed the same way to her. Their year-long on-again, off-again romance had ended just three months before and it was clear that neither one of them had yet figured out what *ended* meant.

She had told him she thought he was afraid of commitment and he didn't disagree with her but the situation wasn't quite that simple. Still, he'd never come up with a better answer to her comment. He'd always thought she too showed her own subtle ways of wanting to be close but not too close.

Standing there awkwardly and after a few seconds of total silence she said, "I think it's all there, everything you need but look it over and let me know if you need anything else from me."

What perfect words to get his mind going at full speed; "Let me know if you need anything else from me." Their decision to step back from a romantic relationship was mutual but only half-hearted and the true nature of their relationship was still being defined. When they had first started to date she was just as non-committal as he was but somewhere along the way that seemed to change and she felt things had become more serious. That was when Dylan had gone into his trademark lockdown mode with the way he handled personal situations. The feelings were there but not the will to show them.

"Okay, sounds good," he answered in a careful tone that he hoped masked any hint of personal emotion. Like every other time he talked to her since the break-up he fought the urge to say anything that wasn't strictly business related.

She started to leave but hesitated at the doorway and looked back at him. "Did you trim your beard?"

"Yeah, uh, I noticed it was getting a bit shaggy and I decided I should start looking more like a lawyer and less like a hippie. Besides, all that hair on my face was making the hair on my head look even thinner."

"Well it looks nice," she said, her smile as distracting as ever.

"Thanks." It was all he could do to keep from reaching for her.

She looked as if she was going to say something else, or was waiting for him to do it. He stood there doing the same thing, hoping it would be her that said the next words, but she didn't. There was another awkward silence, they exchanged smiles and then she turned and walked down the corridor. He watched her, thinking how sexy she always looked even in the most conservative business attire. Her blonde hair was pulled back into a ponytail that swung in unison with her long legs and shapely hips.

Watching her for those few moments turned out to be the high point of his workday, a workday that lasted until six o'clock.

The early evening commute was the usual stop and go with only occasional stretches of reasonable progress. As he drove he thought about how his Monday afternoon had turned out to be just as frustrating as his Monday morning. A glass of some kind of stress reliever was his usual cure for such a situation.

Before he'd left the office he called his best friend, Lamar, to see if he wanted to meet for a drink, a little late-day ritual that they had shared as often as possible. Dylan wasn't really surprised when his friend said he was tied up. His turn-down was either because he knew Lamar's wife, Tamara, thought Dylan was a bad influence on him or because his new bicycle shop had only been open for a few months and running it seemed to consume him every minute of every day.

The two men had shared some fun and adventure in their college days, including a few things they'd both sworn to never divulge, but lately the opportunities to share some guy-time had been few and far between. Before they hung up they agreed to try again in a day or so.

He pulled into a *Subway* for something resembling dinner and when he was finally home and settled in his living room he started clicking through the channels on the television. He stared at things he didn't really care to watch and washed down his sandwich with a couple of beers. As he sat there hoping to find something even remotely entertaining he tried to decide which was worse, his stressful, stuck-in-neutral time at the office or his boring, stuck-in-neutral personal life. He came to the conclusion it was a wash.

Lately he'd been looking forward to his bedtime more than usual, not because he was more fatigued but because he'd always enjoyed the escape he got from dreaming. Everyone dreams once in a while but as far back as childhood he'd been blessed, or cursed, with a tendency to dream a lot. Early in life he'd developed a calming bedtime ritual that seemed to expand his slumbering imagination. As a kid it was wearing his lucky pajamas and downing a glass of milk.

As he got older the details of his routine became more complex but he'd always believed that those efforts helped to guarantee that he'd end up in a place he loved to be, in dreamland.

On any given night he'd have a dream, sometimes two or three or more different dreams and he could usually remember all of the details the next day. Most of them were simple, straightforward scenes of him dealing with everyday situations and the people in his life, the kind of dreams everyone has. But every now and then his unconscious mind conjured up strange and much more interesting events. Some people might even call them weird. One night it might be a romantic encounter with an unknown woman and the next night he'd find himself wrapped up in the details of a vacation he had never taken.

Every once in a while, if he was lucky, he'd dream of being in a situation where he actually came out on top at the end.

There's an old saying that the best things in life happen in the dark and, all things considered, that seemed to be the way Dylan's life had been playing out. His dreaming had become an important, maybe too important part of his life. It was recreation and adventure without leaving his bed. It was also a welcome release from the pressures of his stalled career and on occasion a sad but tolerable replacement for a less than satisfying social life. Since it happened every night and he had no control over what happened he knew that, good or bad, he just had to deal with it.

Like everyone else's dreams his were always a surprise. He couldn't predict what they would be or where they would take him. It was sort of like being in a strange car going on a long road trip to an unknown destination, traveling through a strange place without a map and with someone else doing the driving.

For the past few months the pressure to do well on his annual review had led him to bury myself in paperwork in the evenings, looking for some little clue, any hint of something that he could point to when the question was asked, "Why do you believe you have earned a partnership in this firm?" Night after night he had struggled to find the differentiator that would vault him to principal status even though the type of cases he was stuck with didn't exactly make for a clear path to partnership.

On that particular Monday night, after an hour of half-hearted review of a case file, half an hour of toying with his guitar and downing several shots of bourbon his drowsiness had begun to wrestle with his ambition. He knew from past experience that drowsiness usually won. He brushed his teeth and then did his almost nightly search in the mirror for the premature gray hairs that his father had passed on to him. After he checked the locks on the doors, set the thermostat and turned off the lights he finally fell into bed and drifted off.

FADE IN:
EXTERIOR - SANDY BEACH - DAY

The late morning sun has already changed the sand from warm to hot. A couple, wearing only swim wear and sunglasses, are sprawled closely together on a large, blue blanket, talking loudly above the noise of the waves hitting the nearby shore.

ANGELA: You seem a lot more relaxed than the last time I saw you.

DYLAN: Do I?

ANGELA: Yeah, it's like you're a whole different person.

DYLAN: Well, since you haven't seen me in over four years I guess you could say I *am* a different person.

ANGELA: I just mean you don't seem as intense as you used to be.

DYLAN: Oh, come on, on my best day I was hardly what anybody could call intense. Busy maybe, or even marginally focused, but intense, I don't think so.

ANGELA: Well whatever the change is, I like it.

At that moment they slowly turn toward each other, embrace and begin several minutes of kissing, caressing and very careful public passion. Dylan grabs the edge of the blanket and folds it up over them, concealing them from the shoulders down.

ANGELA: Whoa, slow down there, we're not the only people on the beach, you know.

DYLAN: Yeah, and that's a damn good thing for you, given the circumstances.

ANGELA: Circumstances?

DYLAN: Yeah, here I am, looking at you for the first time in a long time, feeling those old feelings but knowing I have to keep a tight grip on things or risk causing a scandal on a public beach.

ANGELA: Hmm, exactly what kind of scandal did you have in mind?

DYLAN: Well, maybe scandal isn't the right word. Let's just say it would be finishing where we left off.

ANGELA: And as I recall we left off when you were at my place and we got interrupted by a phone call from one of your clients. I think it was a woman.

DYLAN: Yeah, you're right, it was a woman, a very screwed up and very high maintenance young woman who just happened to be the daughter of one of our biggest clients. Remember what I told you at the time? My job was to put out fires and that chick had a major blaze going that landed her in a whole big pile of trouble.

ANGELA: And you were the only one who could run to her rescue in the middle of the night.

DYLAN: Well, yeah, and I was the only thing that stood between our client and the local news getting wind of what happened with his precious little girl.

ANGELA: So now you know why I remember you being so intense. Right in the middle of our love-making, when your phone rang, you grabbed it, turned off the Dylan switch and became lawyer-man.

DYLAN: Well, for what it's worth at this particular moment the lawyer man switch is turned off and Dylan is turned on.

DISSOLVE TO:
INTERIOR – MUNICIPAL COURTROOM – DAY

A small group of people is gathered around Prosecutor Michael Horvath's table, talking quietly while another group of people sits, scattered in the chairs of the public viewing area in the back of the courtroom. Seth Conant, a slender, almost gaunt young man sits alone at the defendant's table, nervously looking around at everything going on in the room. A tall, sturdily built bailiff stands near him, looking bored and frequently checking his watch for the time. Judge Patrick

McGonagle enters the room through the door to his chambers and climbs the steps to his bench. Everyone stands until he is seated and the din of conversation in the room fades away.

BAILIFF: Municipal Court of the City of San Diego is now in session, the honorable Patrick McGonagle presiding.

JUDGE McGONAGLE: Alright, let's get started here. Mr. Horvath, you will begin these proceedings and you, Mr. Ward...Mr. Ward? Where is defense counsel?

HORVATH: Your honor, it appears the Counsel for the Defense is not here to represent the defendant.

At that moment the side door of the courtroom bursts open and Attorney Dylan Ward rushes into the room. He stands behind the defendant's table, his hand on Seth Conant's shoulder and places his briefcase on the table.

DYLAN: Your honor, I apologize for my tardiness. I ran into some uncontrollable circumstances.

JUDGE McGONAGLE: Yes, I can see that. And I assume those circumstances included your inability to remove your flip-flops and put on socks and shoes like a real lawyer would wear.

DYLAN: Again, sir, I apologize. An earlier meeting with a former, uh, client had to be conducted at the beach and there was not sufficient time for me to change my attire and still be here on time.

JUDGE McGONAGLE: So that must also explain your lack of a tie and the disarray of your hair.

DYLAN: Uh, yes, sir. Again, I apologize.

JUDGE McGONAGLE: Mr. Ward, this is not the first time you have appeared before me with, shall we say, appearance issues. Is it too much to ask for you to wear an appropriate suit, tie and shoes like everyone else who comes before me? And while you're at it please get rid of the gum you're chewing.

DYLAN: Your Honor, This was just a very unusual circumstance and I assure you, sir, it won't happen again. And I'm sorry about the gum.

JUDGE McGONAGLE: Alright, Counselor, but consider this your final warning. And I mean final.

DYLAN: Yes, sir. Thank you, Your Honor.

JUDGE McGONAGLE: We are now in session, Mr. Horvath, you may proceed.

HORVATH: Your Honor, we have reviewed the defendant's written waiver of his right to a trial by jury and are in agreement. The facts of this case are quite simple and straightforward. The defendant, Mr. Seth Conant, on the night of August third of this year, willfully participated in a brawl at the Starlight Lounge and in the process, shoved the plaintiff, sitting here beside me, Mr. Jason Kovacs, against a concrete wall, causing physical injury to Mr. Kovacs. The charge against Mr. Conant is Simple Assault and we seek damages and restitution in the amount of fifteen-thousand dollars.

JUDGE McGONAGLE: Thank you, Counselor. Okay, Mr. Ward, you're up.

DYLAN: Your Honor, defense is in agreement that this is a simple and straightforward case in that Mr. Kovacs' injuries were caused by his own state of intoxication and there is no evidence that Mr. Conant was in any way responsible for Mr. Kovacs' stumbling and falling into that wall. We also object to the State's use of the word "brawl" to describe a scuffle between just two people.

JUDGE McGONAGLE: Your objection is sustained. Anything else, Mr. Ward?

DYLAN: Not at this time, Your Honor.

HORVATH: Your Honor, we have an eyewitness who will testify as to the exact nature of what happened that night. We ask that Mr. Anthony Pasquale take the stand.

A short, middle-aged man stands from his seat in the viewing area and is escorted to the witness stand by the bailiff. He is sworn in and sits nervously, squirming in his chair and pulls the microphone down and closer to his face.

HORVATH: Mr. Pasquale, you are the owner of the Starlight Lounge, is that correct?

PASQUALE: Uh, yes, sir, I am.

HORVATH: And were you on the premises on the night of August third when the, uh, when the scuffle occurred?

PASQUALE: Yes, sir. I was tending bar.

HORVATH: And will you please tell the court what happened that night and what you observed occurring in front of the Men's Room door.

PASQUALE: Well, I was waiting on a customer at the bar and it was pretty crowded, like three deep, and I heard a lot of shouting and some girl screaming. I looked in the direction of the noise and saw the defendant standing there by the door and shouting at someone, I mean at Mr. Kovacs there, who was on the floor. He looked like he was hurt.

HORVATH: You saw Mr. Conant standing over Mr. Kovacs, and he was shouting down at him as he lay on the floor.

PASQUALE: Yes, sir, and he, the defendant, he seemed really angry.

HORVATH: Thank you, Mr. Pasquale. Counselor, your witness.

DYLAN: Mr. Pasquale, it sounds like the Starlight Lounge gets very busy. That's great, good for you. Three deep at the bar means you're pouring a lot of alcohol.

JUDGE McGONAGLE: Mr. Ward, is there a point to your little compliment?

DYLAN: There is, Your Honor. The night of August third was a Wednesday. I stopped by the Starlight on Wednesday the fourteenth of this month and again on Wednesday the twenty-first. On both nights there were signs promoting "Whacky Wild Wednesday" drink specials.

JUDGE McGONAGLE: How nice. I trust you took advantage of the deals. Now exactly what is your point?

DYLAN: I'm getting there, Your Honor. Now, Mr. Pasquale, would you please tell us how tall you are?

PASQUALE: Uh, I'm five-feet six inches.

DYLAN: You're five-feet six-inches tall, you were standing behind the bar, the rear edge of which is exactly thirty-two feet from the Men's Room door. I know because I measured it. And you were standing there while a crowd of young adults, probably mostly male if the crowd was similar to the two Wednesdays I was there, was standing in front of you, three deep, trying to get waited on, and somehow you managed to see over top of them all and observe what happened at a point thirty-two feet away which also happens to be directly beyond a crowded dance floor.

PASQUALE: Uh, well, yeah, that's what happened.

DYLAN: That's strange, because the nights I was there I managed to get a seat at the bar. I guess it was because I went early. And both times I sat there and couldn't see the Men's Room door because of the people on the dance floor and the ones who were standing around me at the bar.

HORVATH: Your Honor, I believe we have established that Mr. Pasquale saw what he said he saw. What Mr. Ward saw sitting on a barstool is not relevant here.

DYLAN: No, Mr. Horvath, you're wrong. Excuse me, Your Honor, I have a little demonstration planned.

There is a murmur from the people in the viewing section as a young man enters the courtroom through a side door. He is carrying a barstool and a large, metal tape measure. The bailiff stops him and then allows him to hand the items to Dylan.

JUDGE McGONAGLE: Mr. Ward, let me guess. It's a souvenir of your nights drinking at the Starlight Lounge.

DYLAN: Well, yes, Your Honor, that's exactly what it is. This stool is identical to the ones used at the Starlight Lounge. I even purchased it at the same supply company as Mr. Pasquale used. Now, sir, if you'll please allow me some latitude I'd like to reenact what happened the night of August third.

JUDGE McGONAGLE: "Allow me some latitude", said the lawyer in flip-flops. Alright, Counselor, but get to the point, any point, please.

DYLAN: Thank you, Your Honor. Now, Mr. Pasquale, can I ask you to step down for a moment and stand right here in front of the railing?

JUDGE McGONAGLE: Mr. Pasquale, please step down, and let me remind you, you are still under oath.

DYLAN: Okay now, Mr. Pasquale, please stand there facing the back of the courtroom. Thank you. I am now placing this barstool at a point three feet in front of Mr. Pasquale exactly as it would sit in a barroom situation. Now I will measure the distance from the front of our imaginary bar to the center of our imaginary dance floor, exactly sixteen feet six inches, the same as the one at the Starlight Lounge. I know because I measured it. Okay, there is the center. I'll mark it by laying down this ballpoint pen. Now, may I ask for three or four volunteers from the public seating area to stand around that point?

A group of six people stand up and the bailiff stands nearby as they position themselves around the pen on the floor.

DYLAN: Good, thank you, folks. Bailiff, can I ask you to please escort Mr. Conant to the back of the room and have him stand about a foot in front of it? Thanks. Sir, you in the black sweater, can I ask you to stand up here behind the barstool please? Great. Now you, sir, in the gray sport coat, you appear to be the same height as me, would you please sit on the stool? Your Honor, this arrangement of people and props represents the layout of the Starlight Lounge on the night of the alleged assault.

JUDGE McGONAGLE: I know, because you measured it.

DYLAN: Exactly. Now please observe this gentleman here, who's the same height as I am, sitting on the barstool. Sir, please sit like you would if you were at a real bar and turn in your seat and look toward the back of the room. Thank you. Now I'm measuring the height of his eyes from the floor and it's exactly five-feet four inches. Great, thank you sir. Now, Mr. Pasquale, please stand like you do when you're behind the bar. I'm now measuring the height of his eyes from the floor and it's exactly five-feet two inches. Thank you. And now, you sir, on the barstool. Tell us, can you see Mr. Conant from your position?

The man moves his head up and down, then leans side to side around the man standing behind him. He shrugs and shakes his head no.

JUDGE McGONAGLE: Out loud, sir, if you please.

MAN ON STOOL: No, sir. I can't see the defendant at all.

DYLAN: Thank you, sir, and please remain seated. Now, Mr. Pasquale, please tell us if you can see Mr. Conant way back there by the imaginary Men's Room door.

PASQUALE: Well, no, I can't.

DYLAN: You just said you can't see the defendant. Please tell us what you can see.

PASQUALE: I see the man on the stool and the man behind him. And I can kind of see the people on the, well, the dance floor.

DYLAN: So our man on the barstool couldn't see what was going on at the back of the room and neither could our eyewitness, Mr. Pasquale.

HORVATH: Your Honor, I think the State has been more than patient with Mr. Ward's attempt to turn these proceedings into a circus. He has proven nothing. This courtroom is not the Starlight Lounge.

DYLAN: Your Honor, if the State's eyewitness couldn't clearly see the defendant in a well lit room with a handful of people blocking the view, I contend that he could not have possibly seen him clearly under the dim light of his bar with scores of people blocking the view.

JUDGE McGONAGLE: Would all of you folks please move back to your seats? Bailiff, please escort the defendant back to Counsel's table. Both attorneys please approach the bench.

Dylan and the Prosecutor walk up to the judge's bench and the bailiff waits for Seth Conant to sit back down. The participants in the demonstration return to their seats. The judge waits for the room to settle down and then leans forward, looking intently at both lawyers.

JUDGE McGONAGLE: Gentlemen, I don't know where to begin. This case should have been a quick in-and-out but it turned out to be something ridiculous.

HORVATH: Your Honor, the little demonstration was Counsel's idea, not mine.

JUDGE McGONAGLE: Well, Mr. Horvath, was it your idea to produce an eyewitness who couldn't possibly have witnessed the incident?

HORVATH: Well, no, sir. Based upon our interview with him at his place of business we deemed him to be credible.

JUDGE McGONAGLE: Look, if the charges against the defendant would have been more serious or the requested damages a little higher this mess would have been sorted out by a jury. But since it's a bench trial I get to enjoy it all by myself. Now please step back.

Dylan and Horvath take several steps backward. The bailiff moves to stand beside Seth Conant.

JUDGE McGONAGLE: The defendant will please stand. First of all I'd like to thank those of you in the court room for your patience in this most unusual proceeding, especially those of you who became the dancers and bar patrons in the defense's little drama. It is now time for me to render my verdict. Based upon the lack of clear and compelling evidence that the State's only eyewitness could actually see the defendant commit the act with which he is charged, and despite the unexpected and colorful recreation presented by our shoeless defense counsel, this court finds Mr. Conant not guilty. Court is adjourned.

DYLAN: Thank you, Your Honor.

JUDGE McGONAGLE: Mr. Ward, you seem to have a knack for trying my patience. I find you undisciplined and in need of professional polish. But I also must say that in a strange way you are one odd and creative son of a bitch.

DYLAN: Thank you, sir.

JUDGE McGONAGLE: That's not totally a compliment, and remember, the next time I see you I want to see shoes and socks.

.FADE OUT

CHAPTER 2

These dreams go on when I close my eyes. Every second of the night I live another life. These dreams that sleep when it's cold outside, every moment I'm awake the further I'm away.

From the song *These Dreams* by Heart

FOR THE PAST YEAR OR so Dylan's caseload at Doyle and Finch hadn't been what he could call heavy and he'd found some time to do a little moonlighting outside of the office. It was the kind of activity he had to keep under the office radar and totally secret. Since the firm hadn't yet seen fit to make him a partner and give him the chance to enjoy a better income he'd just copped a "fuck them" attitude. He did the extra work on his own time, mostly in the evening and he'd even ordered separate business cards. They were glossy black cards that read *Dylan Ward, Attorney at Law, Criminal and Business Law,* with no address but with his cellphone number and home email address.

It was just the minimal information a person would need to contact him and no more. He knew he had to keep it that way.

His office phone activity was logged for billing purposes so his moonlighting calls had to be made on his cellphone and with his office door closed. At times he'd make them from his truck in the parking lot. As far as he knew doing a little work on the side wasn't a violation of any of the firm's rules but he figured it was best to not find out the hard way.

Working in the world of criminal law was something he hadn't trained for and it had exposed him to an array of interesting people, the kind of people he never imagined he would associate with. Within that world he had somehow built a network of private investigators, bartenders, bail bondsmen, snitches and even a couple of cops. It wasn't exactly a circle of close friends but he still found a strange and uneasy enjoyment when he was with them.

At first that little community of misfits and oddballs seemed totally foreign to a guy with a white bread, middle class, northern California upbringing like he'd had. There were even a few times when he'd gotten a little nervous being around some of them. But he had to admit there was also something strangely appealing about walking and working in their world and it only took him a few months to find a comfort level with them. They rewarded him with a strange kind of loyalty and a regular supply of work that he knew he could never reveal to the people in his regular, tight-ass, corporate world.

So far it had seemed like easy money, mostly quick, in-and-out cases that he could handle through paperwork and filings instead of court appearances. The cases weren't anything too difficult but from the perspectives of the people who hired him everything they had was on the line and they counted on him to have their backs.

When he'd first started getting involved in work outside the firm he was doing it strictly for the extra income until he made partner but after a while it had become much more than a financial exercise. He'd been trained to see the law as black and white but his outside clients saw their worlds in a dozen shades of gray. To them, everything in life was vague and negotiable. Dylan's colleagues at Doyle and Finch saw him as the bearded, not-quite-accepted guy in the little office at the end of the long hallway but to those clients that he couldn't talk about he was Dylan Ward, a hero and a lifesaver.

It was a good feeling despite the fact he couldn't share it with anyone. With the exception of Beth, he'd kept it to himself and managed to make some unusual friends and a small amount of money along the way.

When he walked into the office on Tuesday morning the pile of work on his desk seemed to have grown overnight, as if a bunch of little elf lawyers had snuck into his office and dumped a large pile of folders full of paperwork, filings and general bullshit on to his desk. Before he sat down or even took off his suit coat he stood there, flipping through the first few files to see what was awaiting his attention. The first seven were labeled *Stratos Avionics*.

Stratos was owned by the Makris family and the company was the firm's newest and biggest client, a global manufacturer of high-tech aircraft navigation systems The company had numerous ties to the military and foreign governments and was a client whose day to day activities were as far removed from Dylan's role in the firm as he could imagine.

For a moment he wished that someone else in the firm had the background to represent these sadly dysfunctional people in non-business cases but he knew that would never happen. The cases were usually messy in some way, embarrassing to the clients and uncomfortable for everyone involved. From what he'd learned while doing the preliminary work on the first case, one Arlo Makris, had gotten himself into some trouble over a series of traffic violations, violations that led to serious injuries to another driver. Dylan had already helped him at his arraignment when the court set his bail and now his trial date had been set.

The clock was ticking and Dylan knew he'd have his work cut out for him if this young man was going to stay out of jail.

He flipped through two more folders and saw the same kind of bad news. It seemed Miss Sophia Makris had light fingers and had been charged with shoplifting and her cousin, Delphina Makris, liked to party and was up on a charge of drunk and disorderly conduct. There were stories floating around the office of the huge fees that Stratos had already brought to the firm and now Dylan was realizing that, because of some of the reckless members of this wealthy family, the fees for his down and dirty kind of legal work might also become substantial.

Thoughts of huge amounts of billable hours were interrupted when Anne Carter, assistant to John Finch walked in. "Good morning, Dylan. Mr. Finch asked me to tell you he wants to see you right away, like as soon as you walk in."

"I assume it has something to do with all of these Makris family files." he answered, holding one of the folders up toward her.

"You got it. He's falling all over himself trying to please the two brothers who own the company and that includes taking care of their kids' problems."

"Lucky me, I get to be the playground monitor for their spoiled brats." The words were no sooner out of his mouth when he added, "Oops, sorry. I probably shouldn't talk like that about a client."

Anne smiled, looked back at him and winked as she walked out. "Don't worry, Dylan, you're not the only one in this office who feels that way."

He hung his suit coat over the back of his chair, picked up the stack of files and walked down the corridor to Finch's palatial corner office. The old man was one of the two founding partners and since William Doyle had passed away three years earlier, Finch had consolidated his power to become the man in charge of pretty much everything the firm did. He was a brusque, almost humorless man with no time for small talk or being anything close to warm and friendly.

Dylan got to Finch's door and raised a clenched hand to knock on the door frame but Finch, sitting at his desk, cut him off. Without even looking up he said, "Please sit down, Mr. Ward."

"It looks like the Makris family is going to be keeping me busy for a while," Dylan said as he dropped into a plush leather chair in front of the huge desk. It was his small attempt at a pleasant start to the conversation.

"Yes, that's why I wanted to speak with you," Finch answered, still not bothering to look up from his desk.

Few things insulted Dylan more than when someone didn't feel he was important enough to make eye contact with him. From his very first day with the firm he'd felt a negative vibe whenever he was in Finch's presence. Despite that feeling for the first few years of his employment he'd kept his mouth shut, smiled politely and put up with everything the stern, old man threw at him. But within the past year or so he'd found himself nearing a breaking point. He sat there as Finch shuffled through some paperwork, cleared his throat, then leaned back in his chair and finally looked straight at Dylan.

He ran a hand over his almost bald head, cleared his throat again and said, "I'm sure you're aware of the Makris family's importance and value to this firm."

"Yeah, it's pretty much all anyone around here has talked about lately,"

"And starting right now it's the most important thing in your life as well. I have made assurances to the Makris brothers that, we, and that means you, will clear up these problems with their offspring."

Dylan looked at Finch, waiting to see if he had more to say. His statement sounded more like an order or an ultimatum and it had Dylan kind of rattled. "John, I've already had the arraignments for the first one and the other two are on my schedule. The son's trial is coming up and the girls will be in court week after next. I've laid enough of the groundwork to know those kids have themselves in some pretty serious trouble."

"I'm aware of that but your job with this firm is to handle these types of problems and find solutions to them."

"I know what my role around here is, John, and I have a pretty good record of success, but two of these cases involves eyewitness testimony and video footage and they also involve physical injuries to other people. Solutions won't come easy and might not come at all." He could tell Finch didn't like his tone or that he was pushing back. Finch's face was flushed and red, something that had become an almost constant part of his appearance.

Finch hesitated for a moment, his expression grim and almost confrontational. Then he leaned forward and said, "Like I said, this work is now the most important thing in your life and I expect you to focus and focus hard. I have assigned Miss Chilcotte to assist you full time and I have made it clear to her that this is also the most important thing in her world as well."

As was usually the case when he had a conversation with Finch it reached a point where Dylan wanted to punch him right in the mouth. Somehow he managed to hold his tongue in check. He took a breath and said, "I'll get on it this morning."

As Dylan gathered his files and stood up to leave, Finch wrapped up the meeting as only he could do. "And please make sure that you and Miss Chilcotte focus all your energies on the cases at hand and not on each other."

Dylan didn't bother to look at him or respond to his rude comment, he just turned and left the room feeling angry and knowing that somehow, some way he would get his satisfaction from that arrogant, old son of a bitch. When he got back to his desk it took him nearly twenty minutes to calm down enough to pick up the first of the Makris files and start to see what he'd be up against. He didn't get up from his chair for the rest of the morning.

Despite the growling in his stomach he worked through lunch and only a small swig of bourbon from a flask in his desk drawer filled the void. He was pouring over the Arlo Makris charges when Beth walked in.

It was a visit he was expecting with mixed emotions. "Hi," he said. "Looks like you also got your orders from the King."

Beth smiled slightly. "Yeah, he was crystal clear on things."

"Did he make a comment about you and me and our past?" Dylan asked as he unwrapped a stick of gum and put it in his mouth.

She looked back over her shoulder and lowered her voice. "Oh, of course, I wanted to tell him it was none of his fucking business but I need my job. I despise that old man."

"Me too, it was all I could do to keep from laying him out cold on the floor of his office. I'm so tempted to leave this place and work somewhere else but I'd have to start all over and I don't want to lose whatever amount of status I've earned here in six years."

Beth reached back and closed the door and then sat down in front of the desk. "We'd better be careful with our bitching. You never know who might be listening."

"Yeah, but given Finch's concerns about us maybe we better start an open door policy."

She looked at him with a distracting little smile and said, "Oh, stop it." She paused and then added, "And you better get some stronger gum because that one smells like alcohol."

Dylan gave her a sheepish smile and said, "Oh, sorry. Thanks."

For the next hour and a half they concentrated on the trouble that Arlo Makris was facing because his case was the most serious and had the most immediate trial date. He had been involved in a traffic accident and charged with a variety of offenses including causing serious injury to another person and leaving the scene of an accident. The rich young man was standing in a deep pile of shit.

"So what are we up against here?" he asked Beth. "Have you had time to come up with your take on things?"

"Well, when you helped him at his arraignment and got his bail reduced I think it had to have pissed of the prosecutor's office. The kid's having a rich daddy and then not having to pay through the nose to make bond is like waving red meat in front of those guys. I think you can expect them to be very aggressive."

"I agree, the costs wouldn't have been a problem for Daddy Makris, but big-dollar bails make for big headlines, and I had to do anything and everything to keep a lid on things. At least it'll be a bench trial so we won't have to deal with a jury."

Beth sat back in her chair and Dylan tried not to let on that he'd noticed when she crossed her legs. She let out a long sigh and then said, "The thing that seems to jump out at me is there were no actual eyewitnesses as to who or what caused the crash. The police report said there were three guys working on a street repair crew who heard the crash and then they all turned to see what happened. But it was after the fact so you might want to take that approach."

"That's a great point." he replied. "It should be easy to turn that into three guys speculating on what they heard and not what they never actually saw."

"And how about you?" Beth asked. "See anything in the file you can hit back with?"

"Well, I looked over the photographs the police took at the scene and then compared them to the written report, and there are a couple of things that don't seem to match up. I also had a phone conversation with one of the EMT responders. The nature of the woman's injuries seems very odd and so does the fact the guy driving the car seemed to have sudden memory problems when the cops were talking to him. Things just don't add up."

Beth looked at him with a little smirk on her face. "Come on, I know you better than you think. I can tell by your expression that you know something, or think you do, and I take it you're not going to tell me."

Dylan knew he was blushing a little when he answered, "It's just a hunch but it might be enough to help us with a plea bargain."

"Yeah, that's what happens in ninety-five percent of these cases. But even if we can plead the charges down and get everything reduced we still face the very real possibility that the victim will go out and file civil charges after the fact. If they can nail him on these charges they'll have a real solid foundation for a civil case. I'm betting the ambulance chasers are already lined up to represent the woman and get her a piece of Daddy Makris' wallet. I have a feeling this case is going to be in our laps for a long time."

Even if she hadn't noticed his blushing earlier he was sure she saw the smug look on his face when he answered, "Don't say that just yet. If I can get away with what I have in mind I think I can make both the criminal and any future civil case go away." He sat there for a moment looking at her. It was obvious she had done her homework and even some of his. "He smiled and said, "You know, you sound like you're almost enjoying this one.""

"I'm not sure *enjoying* is the right word but it's a hell of a lot more interesting than mergers and acquisitions. When my Mom agreed to put me through paralegal training she made me promise I'd eventually go on to law school but most of what I do is so boring. Your cases are actually like I'm working with people instead of balance sheets. I think I could learn to like it."

"I feel the same way except for the fact the rest of the firm looks down their noses at this kind of work, my kind of work. It's not classy or profitable enough for them and it's looking more and more like it's not a path to a partnership either." He could feel himself slowly sliding toward anger again so he changed the subject. "Okay, we'll need to get Arlo in here as soon as possible for a final run-through."

"I already spoke with him. I told him to come in this afternoon at three o'clock. I told him we'll walk through the trial process with him, tell him what to expect and tell him how to conduct himself."

"You mean, tell him not to act like a spoiled brat. No sighs, smirks or rolling his eyes."

Beth smiled and nodded. "Exactly, and I hope he can actually do it."

"Okay, it looks like we're underway with Arlo, now how about his cousin and little sister? Have you looked at their files yet?"

"Just briefly", she answered. "The charges aren't nearly as serious and that's probably why you were able to get them recognizance releases. But when we get into the courtroom we'll have the same problems with their silver spoon lifestyle and how it will play out in front of a judge."

"Yeah, that seems to be the big hurdle, doesn't it? That's why I asked the Court for bench trials for both of them too. We have to keep things like this away from juries because I doubt if these rich kids will be able to squeeze a single ounce of sympathy from all those average people who'll be more than a little unhappy about getting stuck with jury duty."

"And you have to believe that's exactly what Finch is thinking too." She paused for a moment and then asked, "So, what do you think."

Dylan looked at her lingeringly, his thoughts a mix of professional admiration and personal attraction. "Well, I think you've gotten us off to a great start. Thank you."

She smiled at him and he wondered once again if she was being flirtatious or if it was just his own wishful thinking. "You're welcome."

The rest of the workday was devoted solely to the Makris family circus. When Arlo arrived Beth met him in the lobby and escorted him to a conference room near Dylan's office. It was an attempt to keep him out of the view of John Finch but somehow the old bastard found out he was there. Finch spent fifteen minutes kissing Arlo's rich Greek ass and promising him that everything would be fine. Dylan knew it would be an uphill struggle at best but once again he held his tongue and kept his nearly constant anger toward Finch under control.

After Finch finally left, Dylan and Beth walked Arlo through the trial process and instructed him on how to dress, how to stand and how to speak when spoken to. For any average citizen in the same situation it would have been an easy thing to understand but for a wealthy young man who had rarely been challenged on anything, it was probably like they were speaking to him in a foreign tongue. His body language, his facial expressions and his audible sighs whenever they talked about the judge's perception of him combined to erase whatever small shred of confidence they had that they'd be able to achieve their goals.

It seemed clear to Dylan that before he even walked Arlo into that courtroom he'd have to work his ass off just to get him close to any kind of plea bargain.

At about five-thirty Dylan was sitting at his desk trying to decide whether to stay late or take work home with him when his cellphone rang. Thankfully, Lamar gave him a third option. After a few minutes of planning and compromising they agreed to meet for drinks at McHale's, their favorite place for happy hour. The drive from the office took about twenty minutes in traffic and Dylan managed to find one of the few remaining parking spaces in the lot behind the building.

In any big city in the country you can find a wide variety of places to enjoy a drink and San Diego is no exception. You can enjoy a beer in a microbrewery, a glass of wine in a posh wine bar or a specialty cocktail on a trendy, waterfront patio. You can go to a restaurant, a café, a grill, a loft or a bistro.

But Dylan had always thought the best place to drink was a bar, a plain old, down to earth bar. The kind of place where they only served enough food to meet the minimum requirements of their liquor license, but not so much that you needed more than a minute or two to read the menu. McHale's was that kind of place; a bar in every wonderful way you can interpret the word. It was four old, weathered brick walls, a high stamped-tin ceiling and an unassuming arrangement of small tables surrounding a huge and beautifully ornate old bar, a bar where dozens of people could sit and stand, to share a drink and stories of what was happening in their lives. You could tell that its sole purpose was to be a place for drinking and unwinding. To Dylan, it felt like a warm, comfortable home away from home.

He had no sooner walked in and reached the bar when a young couple got up and left. He sat down on one stool and was trying to come up with a way to save the other when Lamar walked up and made it unnecessary. After the stress of his workday it was as though karma, albeit a small dose, was finally working in his favor.

He grinned and extended his hand toward Lamar who had already offered his. "Hey, man, long time no see. Glad you could get out from behind the sales counter for a while." Dylan thought to himself for the hundredth time how Lamar looked like a younger, thinner Denzel Washington.

Lamar dropped down on his stool and turned it toward Dylan. "So am I. It's like that place is my new lord and master, calling all the shots and controlling my life. You know, I didn't get home last night until after eleven. Tamara and the kids were already in bed. It's fucking crazy."

"That's the wonderful world of retail. You have to work all those hours so you're available at everyone else's beck and call." Dylan scanned the bar to see if he could flag down a server but they all were tied up with other thirsty patrons.

"Yeah, that's what I thought when we opened the place but the other day Tamara came up with a great idea that should cut down on the hours we have to be at the store. She said we should switch to a boutique sales model, you know, offer specialized services to a niche market, and make it a personal, by-appointment-only kind of thing."

"You mean if I want to buy a bike from you I have to make an appointment?"

"Well, yeah, but it would be a lot more involved than that. We'd present ourselves as the premier local experts in all things bicycle. You call ahead for a day and time and then come in. We interview you about the type of riding you want to do and your fitness or competitive goals. We show you some bikes and fit you to the right model like a tailor fits you into a new suit. We tune the mechanics of the bike to match your fitness level and riding style and even outfit you in professional-grade racing apparel."

"It sounds like you'd be catering to bike snobs."

"You got it, and not just catering to them, we'll actually be creating them. We'll pamper them, train them and make them think they can't get along without us. And we'll even sponsor the events they compete in. If all you care about is price then go buy a fucking bike at Walmart, but if you're serious about your sport and your passion for it, you have to come see Lamar and Tamara at *Spokes*."

Dylan did another scan for a bartender and managed to catch the eye of Kelly, his favorite server for a variety of reasons. She smiled and signaled that she'd be right over. He waited a few seconds to see if Lamar had more to say but his friend was also looking over at Kelly. Dylan said, "So it sounds like if you make that change, your work schedule might free-up a little. Maybe we can get back to enjoying happy hour on a regular basis like we used to."

"No promises there, man. I'm a husband and a father now. Those wild, old days are behind me." He paused and then added, "But please don't ever stop inviting me."

Kelly finally made her way over to them and, as was usually the case, Dylan's attention was solely on her. "Hey, guys, where have you been lately?" She was petite and obviously in great shape. Her jet black hair was pulled back, her big, brown eyes sparkled and when she smiled it was too easy for his thoughts to travel from friendly to something more. Yes, Kelly Alvarez was a stunner.

"Well, Lamar here has been chained to his new bike shop and I've been inundated with a flood of new cases."

"Even busy men get thirsty," she replied. The idea that her smile was flirtatious was purely fantasizing on Dylan's part but he decided to believe it anyway.

"And that's exactly why we're here," he answered. "I'll have my usual IPA, a twenty-ounce."

Lamar chimed in, "And a Stoley and tonic." He noticed that Dylan was watching her walk away and said, "Man, you really have a thing for her, don't you?"

Dylan felt a little embarrassed that his interest in Kelly was that obvious. "No, not really, she's just really easy on the eyes and I'm still single so it's okay to look."

"Man, you need to find yourself a hobby or something. First it was Angela and that didn't work out, then for some reason you broke it off with Beth and now you're here gawking at a hot college student bartender. You're not getting any younger, man." His grin was ear to ear and his light hearted tone was typical Lamar.

"If telling me to find a hobby is your idea of a sales pitch to get me to buy an expensive bike, it needs some work." Dylan enjoyed his friend's humor and he also knew Lamar was concerned for him. They had been friends since their days at San Diego State and it was rare for either of them to make a serious decision without talking it over with each other. Dylan had been best man when Lamar and Tamara were married. He had given them free legal advice and helped them set up *Spokes, LLC*. Dylan knew that someday, if anything special happened in his life, Lamar would find a way to return the favor.

"Okay," Dylan added, "I know my romantic history hasn't exactly been something to brag about, but sooner or later I'll get there, to the kind of place where you are. I'm just being careful."

They stopped their conversation and waited for Kelly to set their glasses in front of them. This time Dylan went out of his way to avoid staring at her as she walked away. Both men sipped their drinks and then Dylan said, "You know, it's funny you should mention Angela because I had an amazing dream about her last night."

Lamar grinned and answered, "So what else is new? As long as I've known you, you've talked about all the dreams and adventures you have every night. I never knew anyone who was into dreaming like you are. It's strange, man."

"Well, it's not like I can control it or anything. It just happens so I go with it.

"Yeah, that's what you keep saying but you've taken it to a whole other level. You have it down to a science. You do it every night and you remember every detail. Man, that's just not fucking normal." Dylan knew his friend was just kidding but before he could respond Lamar added, "Oh, and that reminds me. I saw something online the other day and it made me think of you. Have you ever heard of lucid dreaming?"

"Dylan was surprised at the turn in the conversation but answered, "No, lucid dreaming, what is it?"

"It sounds really cool. It's when you're asleep but you're aware that you're dreaming. It's like when you're in the dream you can kind of step outside it and tell yourself it isn't real."

Lamar definitely had Dylan's attention. "I think that's happened to me once or twice," Dylan replied, "but I'm not sure if it was real and it was a long time ago."

"Well, you should look it up, man, because if you're going to be doing so damn much dreaming you might as well be in charge of what's going on. They say you can actually train yourself to do it."

The topic was fascinating to Dylan and, given his proclivity to dream so much he would have enjoyed keeping the conversation going, but it seemed like a weird thing to talk about with another guy at a bar at happy hour so he just parked it in the back of his head for call up at a later time. "Okay, lucid dreaming, I'll check it out, thanks," he said.

One of the bartenders had turned up the music system volume and Dylan noticed it was playing an old song by Weezer. He turned toward Lamar with a grin on his face. "Hey, listen, remember this song? This was the one we used to close every gig with."

"Oh yeah, the one where you said my drums always drowned out your guitar."

"Yep, that's the one, but to be honest the Martin I was playing was designed to be mellow, not loud."

"Are you still playing that thing? I remember how you practically stole it from that kid in Alpha Sig."

"I didn't steal it. The guy needed to raise some cash fast and I offered him a hundred bucks for it."

"It was worth at least five times that much."

"I know but whatever it was he needed the money for he was too scared to haggle on the price. I picked it up last night and messed around for a while and I swear it still sounds as sweet as it did back then."

"Glad to hear it. Maybe one of these days I'll find some garage sale drums and we can get the band back together." Lamar's ear to ear grin was a sight that took Dylan back to a simpler time in his life.

"Yeah, maybe, but let's get back to reality. I want to hear more about your idea for boutique bikes."

They both paused to sip their drinks and for a moment. Lamar's comment about lucid dreaming moved to the front of Dylan's mind but then he quickly pushed it aside.

They sat there talking, drinking, eating, keeping an eye on Kelly and just enjoying the chance to be two old friends hanging out again. From time to time Dylan's work at the office would find its way into his thoughts and he knew he should be burying himself in the Makris family's files but he also knew he needed to decompress for a while. Around seven-thirty they decided it was time to head for the door and go home.

It was coming up on the third anniversary of the purchase of his little Spanish-style bungalow in a seventies-vintage neighborhood a few miles from downtown. It was plenty of house for a single man, with a nice backyard and patio and a spare bedroom that served as his home office. His plan all along had been to move up to a larger house when he made partner but that goal continued to elude him.

He had spent some money on changes to his bedroom like light-blocking shades, painting the walls a darker shade of tan and a new king size bed. It seemed like more of a sleep chamber than a bedroom but that was what he wanted. Other than that, the house was pretty much the way it was when he moved in.

. When he pulled into the driveway around eight he dumped his computer bag and briefcase on to the bed, changed into a pair of sweat pants and a tee-shirt, grabbed a beer from the fridge and sat down with the Arlo Makris file and his notes on two moonlight cases. By the time the beer was gone his eyes had glazed over with boredom. He put the files back into his briefcase, poured himself a larger than normal glass of bourbon, sat down at his computer in his little office and *Googled* lucid dreaming.

He decided to forgo his nightly check in on *Facebook* and strumming his guitar. For the next hour and a half he searched sites that described the ability of a person to be in an awake-like state while dreaming and methods of learning how to do it. He even grabbed a legal pad and took notes. The training included a variety of meditation and relaxation techniques and by the time he shut down his computer and crawled into bed he had promised himself he'd try to become a lucid dreaming master.

FADE IN
INTERIOR – THE BLUE NOTE CAFÉ – DAY

Two young men navigate their way through a crowd of drinkers and diners and reach an empty table against the back wall of the casual bar and eatery. They set their backpacks on the floor beside their chairs and sit down, scanning the noisy bar room for familiar faces.

MARK BRANDON: Man, what's the deal? It's three in the afternoon and this place is as crowded as lunchtime.

DYLAN: Yeah, and half of the crowd doesn't look old enough to be in here.

MARK: Like our sophomore year when we paid all that money for those phony IDs. I'm betting the other people in the place back then were saying the same thing about us.

DYLAN: That was different.

MARK: How was that different?

DYLAN: Because it was us.

MARK: Man, for someone heading for a career in law that's one shitty argument.

DYLAN: Yeah, maybe I should think about changing my major.

MARK: I have a feeling your professors think the same thing. You know, I have to say I never really saw you as lawyer material. You seem kind of loosey-goosey when it comes to hitting the books. Lawyers are kind of tight-ass and that's definitely not you.

DYLAN: Thanks, I guess.

Their conversation is interrupted when the noise level in the bar increases noticeably. Heads turn toward the main entrance and then the crowd begins to quiet. A man walks slowly through the maze of people and tables and works his way toward the back of the room. He looks around the place and then takes a seat at the table next to Dylan and Mark.

MARK: Holy shit, man, look, that's Bruce Springsteen!

DYLAN: Yeah, I see him. Try not to act like a silly fan, okay?

MARK: Hey, Boss, welcome to San Diego. We sure didn't expect to see you in here.

BRUCE SPRINGSTEEN: Well, they serve beer here and I like beer. And now that you mention it I'm surprised to see you guys here too.

MARK: What do you mean?

BRUCE: I mean you guys don't look old enough to be served.

MARK: We have IDs that say otherwise.

BRUCE: Yeah, I had one of those when I was a kid too and all it got me was busted.

MARK: Well, Dylan here, my friend and future lawyer, knew this guy who pulled some strings and got us these perfect fake driver's licenses.

BRUCE: Wow, man, you're gonna' be a lawyer? You're gonna' stand up for the law but then you go out and break it?

DYLAN: Well, I wouldn't put it in those exact terms. It's kind of walking a fine line, but we're close to being twenty-one so it's almost legal.

BRUCE: Almost legal. Almost legal. Man, I think there's a song lyric in there somewhere.

DYLAN: You're kidding, right?

BRUCE: No, really. Let's see, something like, "Way down deep inside, uh, I know lovin' you is wrong, but baby, uh, you make it feel so right, uh, so let's not worry about that other man cause it's almost legal, so let's make love tonight."

DYLAN: Hey, I like it, I like it. And maybe somewhere you add, hmm, let's see, "Baby, sometimes, uh, following the rules is kind of tough, uh, and that means, uh, almost legal is good enough."

BRUCE: Hey, that's pretty good. I think I might be able to turn that into a respectable song. I'm gonna' work on it and see what comes out the other end. How about giving me your name and number so I can share the writing credit with you?

DYLAN: Holy shit!

FADE OUT

CHAPTER 3

When the lights go out we'll be safe and sound. We'll take control of
the world like it's all we have to hold on to, and we'll be a dream.

From the song *We'll be a Dream* by We the Kings featuring Demi Lovato

EVEN THOUGH THERE WERE JUST over twenty-four hours
before the trial of Arlo Makris, Dylan couldn't leave the house
without turning on his computer and looking one more time at the
information he'd found about lucid dreaming. It was fascinating to him
that a person could actually exist in a state that was both conscious and
unconscious. It was almost like having some kind of new kind of power.
After a life of nightly escapes into his dream world, now, all of a sudden,
he felt like he'd been missing out on something.

He sat there staring at the screen before his workday had even begun
and he was already looking forward to the night and going to bed, to sleep
and to dream.

The drive to the office was the usual mix of traffic and borderline road
rage along with his daily trip through the *Starbucks* drive-thru. Somehow
he managed to pull into the parking lot ten minutes early, at least early for
him. The lot was already packed and even though he had a reserved space
it didn't make it any easier for his four-year-old Silverado pick-up to blend
in with all the fine German machines driven by the partners.

The decision to buy a pick-up four years earlier was based solely on
his need to haul his surfboard and parasailing equipment but it had been
over two years since he last enjoyed the water. Except for the truck and
an occasional hour relaxing on the sand his beach-boy years seemed to be

behind him. He figured once he made partner he could afford to upgrade to a better ride and take on the appearance of a lawyer if not the attitude.

He had the elevator to himself and a few minutes later he was at his desk, ready to face a day full of the Makris family and their assorted transgressions. An urge for a second cup of coffee hit him around nine o'clock. Surprisingly the employee lounge was nearly empty, just Will Sutton, a senior partner, standing at the microwave. He glanced at Dylan and gave the slightest possible nod in his direction before he went back to staring at the microwave timer. It was the usual lack of camaraderie that Dylan dealt with on a regular basis. He poured a cup of coffee and left without saying anything to the man.

Despite the fact it was still early in the day Dylan's email box already had over two dozen messages. It was the one from John Finch with the subject line "Arlo Makris" that seemed to jump out at him.

"Shit," he thought, "That son of a bitch is sticking his nose in again." The list of people who were copied on the message was short, just Anne Carter and Beth. Part of him wanted to ignore it at least for a little while but he went ahead and clicked on it anyway. It was pretty much what he'd expected, another reminder of the importance of the Makris account and of Finch's desire to be kept abreast of every detail. It was the snide comment Finch had closed with that got Dylan riled up. It read, "And of course, Mr. Ward, I'm sure you have heard that I will be conducting your upcoming performance review rather than the partners committee."

His meaning was as clear as it was threatening and it triggered something in Dylan that he knew he had to keep under control. It was the feeling that Finch was no longer a colleague but an adversary.

For a few moments Dylan sat there, staring at his computer screen without actually reading anything. When he regained his focus he closed out his email, pulled up the Arlo Makris file and started to scroll through it. He felt an urge to revisit details that he practically knew by heart just to see how they matched up to the hunch he had about the facts of the crash. He tried to focus on the details but he couldn't get Finch out of his mind. Dylan was letting the old man get into his head which only pissed him off even more. It was a welcome interruption when Beth walked in.

"Good morning, Mr. Ward." she said cheerfully. Obviously, she had read the email.

"Good morning, Miss Chilcotte," he answered.

"Got a minute?" I want to talk to you about Arlo's trial tomorrow."

"Sure, have a seat. Do you want any coffee first?"

"No, I'm good, I just wanted to see if you'd tell me what your little hunch is, the one that you think is going to turn the case around. I've read the police report as many times as you have and I don't see anything out of the ordinary. I kept wondering about it last night and it's been driving me crazy."

Even given their romantic history and how comfortable he felt with her, Dylan was reluctant to respond to her curiosity. His idea, his hunch was based upon an event from his own past. He wasn't optimistic about using it as the basis for an argument in court but sometimes even longshots come in a winner. He looked her in the eye, paused, and somehow managing to restrain himself, he said, "Tell you what, come to the hearing with me tomorrow and you can have a front row seat when I unveil it."

Beth nodded slowly. "Okay, but this had better be good because we're only going to get one shot at this."

After a quick trip to police headquarters and a curbside meeting with the two officers who were at the scene of the accident, the rest of the day was a matter of going through the same case review process for the Makris women as he had gone through for Arlo. By five o'clock he he'd had just about all he could take of anything to do with that family. A thought popped into his head and he fought it for a few minutes but then picked up his desk phone and called Beth. He knew his extension number came up on her phone screen and when she answered she simply said, "Hi." There was a pause and then she said, "I hope you don't need anything from me because I was hoping to get out of here in like five minutes."

"No, I want to get out of here too. I was just wondering if you'd want to meet me at McHale's for a drink, my treat."

She hesitated for a moment. "Well, on any other day I'd say yes but Maxwell Dewart also asked me to meet him for a drink."

Dylan cringed at the idea of that asshole making a move on Beth. "Oh," he said, trying not to sound like anything but normal, "I guess he beat me to it."

"Well, he asked me first but I told him no. To be honest I think he's kind of a jerk. He keeps flirting with me and asking me out. I told him there was something I had to do with my mother which was a big, fat lie but I'm afraid to go to McHale's or any place where he might see me and be offended."

"Yeah, it sure would be a damned shame to offend good old Max."

"Can I have a raincheck?"

He had to admit those words made him feel very good at that particular moment. "Sure, count on it."

He left the office, got into his truck and pulled out into rush hour. The closer he got to his house the more he was able to leave Arlo Makris and his family in the rear view mirror. In addition to his busy workday and having to juggle a dozen details of the three cases, he also had to dig through a pile of paperwork for two of his moonlight clients. He was ready for some relief.

Postponing his dinner for a while, he managed to juggle the paperwork well enough to create several opportunities to go online and read more about lucid dreaming. Everything he'd found referred to the same things; that it was real and that it was something that could be learned. It was a type of mnemonic induction, a scientific sounding label for what seemed to be fairly simple relaxation, breathing and mind exercises. The key component to learning it was having the ability to recall your dreams and he had been doing that his whole life.

Dinner that evening consisted of a beer and a bowl of warmed over Kung Pao Chicken from the previous weekend. It passed the smell test and visible mold inspection so after he took it out of the microwave he was able to eat it with almost no fear. The only good thing about it was that it was easy and fast. After a quick clean-up he sat down with a drink and his laptop and once again slipped into exploring the world of lucid dreaming.

The research on the phenomenon was extensive and proven. It said that learning it didn't happen overnight and that it required discipline, practice and keeping a journal of your dream signs. After nearly an hour of online searches he had four pages of notes written down on a legal pad.

On the last page, he'd written in large block letters was what seemed to be a warning from one of the researchers: "It has been observed that some people in the study found lucid dreaming to be so exciting and pleasurable that they exhibited signs of a type of addiction, as if they wanted to sleep their lives away".

Given the lateness of the hour and the early start he had to make on the next day's main event, the Arlo Makris trial, Dylan headed into his bedroom. After the usual bathroom routine and a pre-sleep ritual he had developed over the years, he crawled into bed, his mind a swirling mix of his risky trial strategy, his lucid dream research and, of course, Beth. It took longer than usual to doze off.

FADE IN

INTERIOR – FRONT SEAT OF A PICK-UP TRUCK – NIGHT

Under a full moon that illuminates the highway as much as the headlights do, two men ride together in a pick-up truck, their brief bursts of conversation interrupting long periods of boredom. There is little traffic on the stretch of road as it winds through hills and farmland. The occasional clang of rolling, empty beer cans can be heard from the floor under the seat.

DYLAN: Hey, man, do you feel like stopping for coffee or a bathroom break?

LAMAR: No, I can go for a while longer but if you want to stop it's fine with me. It's driver's choice.

DYLAN: I saw a sign back there for a travel plaza. It's like three or four exits up. Let's pull over there.

LAMAR: Sounds good, my legs will probably need a good stretching by then.

There is small talk mixed with more silence as the mile-markers seem to fly by. Both men show mild interest in the mundane mix of billboards and neon that lines both sides of the road. The radio is tuned to a jazz station but the volume is turned so low the music is barely audible. A pair of headlights that has been locked in sight from the rearview mirror for miles now slowly start to get closer, until they loom close behind the men's truck. The flash of the lights in the mirror is almost blinding to Dylan.

DYLAN: What the fuck is with that guy behind us? All of a sudden he's in a big hurry.

LAMAR: Yeah, his fucking lights are shining smack in my face from the outside mirror. Why don't you slow down and let the idiot get around us?

DYLAN: Or I can just speed up a little and try to lose him.

Their truck accelerates quickly and they steadily pull away from the irritating car. After a minute or so the distance between them has returned to what it was. The two men settle back but they are no sooner comfortable when the trailing car has caught up to them and is once again dangerously close to their rear bumper.

LAMAR: What the fuck, that guy is crazy!

DYLAN: He's really starting to piss me off.

LAMAR: Why don't you try my slowing down idea?

DYLAN: Okay, here we go. Let's see what he does.

Their truck slows down, at first back to the speed limit and then even slower. The car behind them also slows but maintains its closeness to their bumper and makes no attempt to pass.

LAMAR: Well, slow doesn't work any better than fast. I'm getting a bad feeling about all this. That guy might be some kind of road rage lunatic.

DYLAN: I saw a sign back there. The travel plaza is just four miles ahead. Let's find out if this guy has the balls to follow us there.

Once again they accelerate until they reach eight-five miles an hour. After a brief lag the trailing car once again catches up and closes in on their bumper.

LAMAR: Hey, man, you can't be whipping into that travel plaza this fast. Slow it down.

DYLAN: That guy has no idea where we're heading. I'll pull off without using my turn signal and then I'll hit my brakes and he'll fly right past us.

LAMAR: I have a better idea. Let's slow way down, turn on our right turn signal and see if he follows us in.

DYLAN: Well, if we do that one of two things will happen. One, he'll just keep on driving down the road, or two, he'll follow us in and see where we park. Then what?

LAMAR: There are two of us, there are lights and cameras all over the place and your golf clubs are behind the seat. I say we take our chances.

DYLAN: I still like my plan better.

LAMAR: Why am I not surprised?

They maintain their high rate of speed and the trailing car stays right on their bumper. Finally, they see a sign that the travel plaza exit is in one mile. The seconds seem to crawl by as the two men tug at their seatbelts and prepare to make the slight turn to the right. In an attempt to mask their intentions they let their truck drift slightly to the left side of the lane, and when they reach the exit they swerve sharply back to the right, enter the exit and then hit their brakes hard. The car following them tries to react to their maneuver but the driver overcompensates in an attempt to also make the exit. His car fishtails and flips over, rolling down the long embankment on its roof. It reaches a shallow ditch at the bottom of the slope, hits a tree and then bursts into flames.

LAMAR: Holy shit, did you see that? That fucking car exploded!

DYLAN: Yeah, I guess we should have gone with your slow down plan after all. Now how about a cup of coffee?

DISOLVE TO:
McHALE'S – INTERIOR – NIGHT

The place is nearly empty and the servers are going through their late night routine of putting up chairs, wiping down the floor and the bar and taking out the trash. The music from the Pandora system has been turned off and the normal ambience has turned into dim lights and near silence.

DYLAN: Hey, Kelly, I'm sorry for stopping in so late. Did I miss last call?

KELLY: Well, yeah, you did, by like fifteen minutes, but what do you want? I'll pour it fast if you promise to drink it fast.

DYLAN: Let's go for a Maker's Mark bourbon, one cube. That won't take as long to drink as a pint of beer.

KELLY: You got it. Drinking alone tonight I take it.

DYLAN: Yeah, I worked kind of late and lost track of the clock. But then I said to myself, "You can't go home without stopping by to see Kelly for a few minutes."

KELLY: Oh, man, Dylan, sometimes you're so full of shit, but I guess if I dig deep enough there's a strange kind of compliment in there somewhere.

DYLAN: Of course there is. In fact, if you can close things down kind of fast and punch the clock, I'd love to buy you a late bite to eat.

KELLY: A bite to eat and then what?

DYLAN: I haven't really thought beyond that.

KELLY: Once again, you're so full of shit, and once again, I think there's a compliment somewhere.

DYLAN: How about a raincheck?

KELLY: How about maybe?

FADE OUT

CHAPTER 4

"Sweet dreams are made of this. Who am I to disagree? I travel the world and the seven seas. Everybody's looking for something.

From the song *Sweet Dreams* by Eurythmics

THURSDAY MORNING SEEMED TO COME way too early for Dylan. He couldn't decide if it was because of the unfinished business of Wednesday night's dreams or the uncertainty of what he would face in the Arlo Makris trial. It didn't really matter because either way, his mind was moving well ahead of his body and he didn't have much time to get them both moving on the same schedule.

Part of him wanted to roll over and go back to sleep in search of another dream but he knew his responsibility to his client wouldn't allow it.

He'd somehow managed to get through his normal workday grooming routine quickly and at about eight-thirty he pulled into the parking garage of the County courthouse and wound his way up to the third level. It was early enough that he was able to get a parking space in the section reserved for attorneys and court staff. He had no sooner stepped out of his truck when he heard Beth's voice behind him.

'Wow, you're early.'

He turned and for a few seconds he did nothing but take in the view. He had gotten so used to Beth's tied-up, pulled back, gray suit corporate look that seeing her at that moment caught him off guard. Her blonde hair was down and hanging loosely around her shoulders. The usual crisp, white blouse was, today, a flowered knit top and the usual conservative gray suit had been replaced by a black blazer and matching slacks. Beth looked more like his former girlfriend and less like his current colleague.

"Hmm," he said, "something tells me the judge is going to be distracted by the knockout woman sitting at defense counsel's table."

"Relax," she replied, seeming to share Dylan's usual need to balance the personal and the professional, "I just decided to soften my look a little. I get tired of wearing a suit as much as you do. And besides, I'm mostly an observer today. I'll be sitting at the defense table but all I'll be doing is watching the show along with everybody else."

"It's a trial, not a show."

"I told you yesterday that I had a funny feeling about what you had on your mind, or maybe I should say, up your sleeve. I just can't help thinking that I'm in for a show."

Dylan tried hard not to smirk. "Alright, let's see what we can do with "*The People-versus–Arlo Makris*", and I hope you won't be disappointed."

"I'm sure I won't be, and you better spit out your gum before things get started

They took the elevator up to the eighth floor, walked down the long, ornate corridor and entered Courtroom Four. There were still twenty-five minutes until the start of the trial but from what they could take in glancing around the room everyone who needed to be there was already in place except for the Judge and Arlo Makris.

It was as though Beth had read Dylan's mind. "Don't worry," she said, "I sent him an email last night and reminded him that he had to be here by eight-thirty and so far he's only five minutes late." The words were no sooner out of her mouth when Arlo walked in. He was dressed in a conservative gray suit, white shirt and blue tie, and looked like the solid citizen Dylan knew he wasn't. Beth waved him over to the defense table.

"Good morning, Dylan. Good morning, Beth" he said politely.

"Good morning, Arlo," Dylan replied. "Are you ready to see this through?"

"Yes, I think so. I didn't sleep much last night." He turned and looked at Beth and it wasn't the kind of look a defendant normally gives to a member of his defense team. "Beth, it's so nice to see you again."

Beth replied in exactly the right way. "Well, I'm going to take a seat here and try to see the proceedings from the public's perspective. She set her computer case on the defense table and sat down at the far end, and then Arlo and Dylan took their seats beside her.

Dylan began a brief run-through of what would happen in the next hour or so. "Arlo, when the judge comes in and things get started you'll have to follow my lead on everything. I don't think you'll be called to testify but if you are, you'll be asked to go up there, sit in that little brown chair and tell the court your side of things. And I want you to say it, word for word, just like we rehearsed it in my office. Got it?"

Arlo nodded and replied, "Got it."

"No variation, no winging it and no going away from the script, period. Got it?

"Yeah, relax, man, I know what I'm supposed to do."

Given what Dylan had observed from previous meetings with this spoiled brat over the last few weeks he wasn't even close to being convinced the man really understood, but it was show time and too late for more rehearsals. Dylan glanced over at the Prosecutor's table just in time to see him greet the plaintiffs, Michael Chalmers, the driver of the other car and his injured passenger, Mrs. Lynn Fogle. The bruising and bandages on Mrs. Fogle's head were clearly visible and Dylan was glad there wasn't going to be a jury sitting there and looking at her. Attorney Paul Moretti was handling their case. He had a reputation for winning and his confident smile told Dylan he'd be in for a battle.

The next fifteen minutes were spent looking over notes while Arlo chatted with Beth. He seemed very relaxed, no doubt something he acquired from living a life of never being held accountable for his actions. At precisely nine o'clock the Court Clerk stood from his small desk at the front of the room and said in a flat tone, "All rise. The Court of San Diego County is now in session, Judge Raymond Bailey presiding."

Judge Bailey entered the room from the side door of his chambers and climbed the five steps to his bench. "Please be seated," he said as he sat down. He paused as he settled himself into his oversize leather chair and then said, "This is the case of Chalmers and Fogle versus Makris. Mr. Makris, you are charged with, let's see here, with quite a little list of offenses. You are charged with speeding, failure to obey traffic signs, failure to obey traffic control devices in a construction zone, unsafe operation of a motor vehicle resulting in serious bodily harm and last, but not least, leaving the scene of an accident." He paused and looked directly at Arlo. "Mr. Makris, how do you plead?"

Dylan stood and answered on behalf of Arlo. "The defense pleads not guilty, Your Honor."

"Okay, let's get started. Mr. Moretti, you may proceed."

Paul Moretti was not only known for his winning record but just as much for his showboating behavior in a courtroom. He loved the limelight and was referred to as "Hollywood Paul" by his peers. He stood up, strutted more than walked to the front of the prosecutor's table and said, "Thank you, Your Honor."

He took a moment to scan the faces of the dozen or so people sitting in the public viewing section as though they were his personal audience, and then began his opening statement. With a not-so-subtle, self-confident grin he said, "You all just heard a reading of the charges against the defendant, actions that resulted in serious emotional trauma and bodily injury to the plaintiffs. We will show that these irresponsible actions behind the wheel of a vehicle present a clear danger to the community at large and that the plaintiffs are the victims of those actions."

He paused, glanced over at Dylan, then at Arlo and finally Beth. "We will present clear and irrefutable evidence that Mr. Makris is guilty of all charges." The briefness of his opening statement was evidence of his confidence. He stood there for a moment, a faint smirk on his face. When he returned to his chair and sat down Dylan knew it was his turn.

"Mr. Ward, Bailey said, "you're up."

Dylan stood up and turned briefly to face the audience, then the plaintiffs and then finally turned toward Judge Bailey. "Your Honor, there is no argument that an accident occurred, an accident that left Mrs. Fogle with injuries and Mr. Chalmers with apparent memory loss. No one likes to see things like this happen but sometimes there are circumstances that lead to unfortunate results. He turned toward the prosecutor's table. "Mr. Chalmers and Mrs. Fogle look like a very nice couple, or I mean to say, very nice people."

He paused to see if his comment changed their expressions and he was pretty sure he saw four raised eyebrows.

"The prosecutor has told you he will present evidence that shows Mr. Makris was at fault but the defense doesn't believe that will be the result. We believe the evidence will clearly show that there was no way Mr. Makris could have avoided the accident and that, in fact, the plaintiffs were at fault for what happened." The surprised look on Paul Moretti's face was priceless.

For the next forty minutes the prosecution presented its case. Each time a witness gave his testimony Dylan conducted a brief cross examination to verify the defense's understanding of the testimony. He wasn't looking to break any new ground at that point because his plan relied on presenting an entirely different line of questioning.

During the testimony Arlo carefully followed the little script Dylan had written for him. He was on his way to a dental appointment, the construction signs and activity confused him and he wasn't aware that he was driving over the posted speed limit. A construction worker said he heard the squealing tires and impact of the two cars but didn't actually see it happen. The police officer who was first at the scene talked about the amount of damage to the left rear quarter panel of Mr. Chalmer's car. A second officer discussed the length of the skid marks left by Arlo's car and how that determined that Arlo was speeding. He also described how he applied pressure to the right side of Mrs. Fogle's head until the paramedics arrived. An EMT from the ambulance told how Mr. Chalmers was so traumatized by the crash that he stammered and couldn't remember where he was going that morning.

By the time Moretti was finished presenting his case anyone watching would have thought Arlo Makris was Public Enemy Number One.

Judge Bailey had sat as still as a rock during the entire presentation of the prosecution's case, almost as if he were bored from hearing what seemed to be cut-and-dry evidence. "Mr. Ward," he said, "you offered very little in your cross-examination yet your plea is not guilty. Can we expect some kind of defense on behalf of your client?"

Dylan stood up and calmly replied, "Your Honor, the defense has no dispute with any of the testimony that was given. There were sounds of a crash. There were long skid marks. There were injuries. We recognize that, but we feel that the evidence presented is only one side of the events in this case. The prosecution did not conduct any redirect examination but defense would still request the right to re-cross the witnesses."

Judge Bailey sat there, looking at Dylan in momentary silence. Dylan took a quick glance over at Moretti. He was quietly talking with Chalmers while Mrs. Fogle hung on his every word. The smirk on Moretti's face was noticeable. Finally Judge Bailey asked, "Does the prosecution have any objection to the defense conducting a re-cross?"

Moretti looked over at Dylan, still smirking, and then turned to the judge and said, "We have no objection, Your Honor. If defense really believes there is anything more to say in this case then, by all means, let them proceed."

Dylan stood and turned and looked at Beth. She had a puzzled look on her face but also the slightest hint of a smile. He'd always had a feeling she could read his mind. He looked down at Arlo. "Showtime," he said, almost in a whisper.

He turned to Moretti and said, "Thank you, counselor." After a pause he looked at the judge and said, "The defense calls Michael Chalmers."

When Chalmers was settled into the witness stand Dylan stood off to his side so the audience could see him clearly. "Mr. Chalmers, you are a mathematics teacher at Coronado High School, is that correct?"

"Yes, sir, I teach advanced placement algebra and geometry."

"The accident occurred on a Friday morning at approximately eleven o'clock so you weren't in school that day."

"No, it was an in-service day for teachers."

"Don't in-service days usually require some sort of mandatory teacher training or meetings?"

"Well, yes. There was a series of workshops at the school district's administration building. I was running a little behind schedule."

"Yes, I guess you were because I checked and the workshops began at eight-thirty."

Chalmers looked a little nervous. He glanced over at Lynn Fogle and Moretti and replied, "Well, the sessions that we, I mean Mrs. Fogle and I were scheduled to attend didn't start until later."

"Okay," Dylan answered, "so I guess that explains why, at eleven o'clock, you were seven miles from the administration building and traveling in the opposite direction."

The look on Chalmer's face spoke volumes. He was staring at Lynn Fogle and she was staring back. "It's like I told the officer after the crash, I was kind of shaken up and didn't remember much. I still don't."

"Let me see if I understand you. You're saying that you don't remember where you were going when the accident occurred."

"Yes, sir, that's correct. I don't remember."

"Alright, thank you, Mr. Chalmers. I hope something will happen to help you get your memory back. A math teacher has to remember a lot of stuff. You may step down now."

While Chalmers returned to the prosecutor's table Dylan said, "Defense calls Officer Ben Williams." While he waited for the cop to take the stand he glanced at Chalmers. He and Lynn Fogle were practically cheek to cheek, whispering and looking down at the table.

"Okay, Officer Williams, thank you for your patience here this morning. I don't think this will take too long. Now, in your earlier testimony you stated that you were the first officer to arrive at the scene of the accident. Do you have any idea how long that was after the accident happened?

"Well, not down to the second, but a construction worker heard the crash and then when he turned and saw the wreck he called 911 right away. That call got to me in about a minute and since I was nearby I got there pretty fast. I'd say, all things considered it was about five minutes, maybe six."

"That's a great job, Officer Williams. Five or six minutes and boom, you're at the scene. He paused to choose his next words carefully. "You testified earlier that when you approached Mr. Chalmer's car both he and Mrs. Fogle were still inside the vehicle, is that correct?"

"Yes, sir. Like I said, the driver, Mr. Chalmers, was still sitting in the driver's seat and the passenger, Mrs. Fogle was on the floor of the car."

"Did you determine if either of them had been wearing a seat belt?"

Yes, the driver was still wearing his but the passenger was not."

"You said Mrs. Fogel was on the floor of the vehicle. Describe her position."

"She was lying sideways, like with her head by the steering wheel and her feet against the passenger door."

Dylan took a moment to look over at the prosecutor's table. Chalmers and Moretti seemed to be locked in a hushed conversation as Lynn Fogel stared blankly ahead.

"Okay, Officer Williams, just one last question. I checked your record of service and you've been in the Traffic Division for over seven years so I guess you have seen and learned a lot about what happens in a traffic accident. So based upon what you saw at the scene, how the defendant's car struck Mr. Chalmers car from the rear and at an angle on the left rear quarter panel, in your opinion, what direction would a front seat passenger not wearing a seatbelt be moved on impact?"

Dylan could hear the sound of a chair rolling behind him and immediately after that Paul Moretti's voice. "Objection, Your Honor. The way that Mrs. Fogel might or might not have been thrown in the car is irrelevant. Her injuries speak for themselves and the evidence shows that the defendant's reckless behavior caused them."

"Your Honor," Dylan interrupted, "Please give me another minute and I will show you how Mr. Moretti is correct in saying her injuries speak for themselves, but not in the way he suggests."

That's when Dylan saw Chalmer's reach out and grab Moretti's arm and pull him back down into his chair. There were a few moments of tense, muffled conversation and then Moretti said with a sigh, "Your Honor, permission to approach the bench."

Judge Bailey said, "Yes, by all means, and you too, Mr. Ward."

Dylan walked forward to the edge of the bench and stepped to his left to give Moretti room to be closer to the judge. The expression on Moretti's face seemed to indicate he was less than pleased with the testimony. With his hand tightly wrapped around his microphone to block their voices, Judge Bailey said, "Alright, Mr. Moretti, you can go first."

"Your Honor, defense's line of questioning is both inappropriate and out of order."

Judge Bailey looked at Dylan and then back at Moretti. "I'm not following you, counselor. Am I missing something here?"

Dylan glanced over at Moretti and before the man could answer the judge Dylan said, "Your Honor, my line of questioning only seems inappropriate to Mr. Moretti because I think he knows where it will end up."

Judge Bailey nodded and said to Dylan, "Well, at this point you're one step ahead of me so how about filling me in."

"When Officer Williams steps down I intend to call Officer Rand back to the stand. He took photographs of the damage to the car, the skid marks and the general area where the crash occurred. He showed the court everything in that big envelope full of photos that the prosecution told him to show and nothing more."

"So there is more?" Bailey asked.

"Yes, a lot more. He also took photos of the inside of the car. He's actually a pretty good photographer, one of those guys who happens to be a stickler for details. I'm talking details like Lynn Fogle's shoes side by side on the floor of the car. Like Michael Chalmers leaning against his door with some kind of wet marks on the front of his slacks. And my favorite detail was the picture of the lower part of the dashboard, the part near the driver's knees, and the car radio knob with a small blood smear on it and a few drops of blood on the carpet of the driver's side."

Moretti immediately spoke up. "Your Honor, I request that we move this conversation into your chambers."

Dylan looked straight at Judge Bailey. He was a smart man and Dylan could tell he knew exactly what the line of questioning was alluding to. Bailey nodded and announced, "Court is in recess for ten minutes."

Dylan looked over at Arlo and Beth as he trailed the judge and Moretti through the door into Bailey's chambers. When the door closed he stood in front of the judge's desk, Moretti a few feet away, waiting to follow whatever the judge demanded. "Let's make this quick," Bailey barked, still standing.

Moretti started. "Your Honor, the prosecution has presented very clear evidence that it was Mr. Makris who was speeding and driving carelessly and hit the plaintiff's car from the rear, I repeat, from the rear. There is nothing in the evidence from the scene to indicate anything else. Mr. Ward is implying something vulgar and totally without merit."

Dylan looked over at Moretti. "Counselor," he asked, "are you saying you don't want me to proceed with presenting the other photos?"

"That's exactly what I'm saying."

"Well, with all due respect you can wait for another lawyer to cave in to you because I fully intend to present the photos, the testimony and all that they imply."

"Damn you, Ward, those are two good people out there, married people, teachers, and what you have in mind can only bring needless shame and embarrassment to them."

Dylan was surprised at Judge Bailey's silence as the two men argued but he kept up his pressure. "And my client is a good person too. He was speeding, we don't contest that point and we also don't contest that he left the scene after the crash and shouldn't have. But let me ask you this.

Will you contest the fact that a man cannot maintain absolute control of a moving vehicle, in traffic, while he's receiving oral sex?"

Dylan was pretty sure that, despite their years of experience in the legal system, neither of the men had ever had a verdict hinge on oral sex. Judge Bailey had an odd, faint smile on his face as he looked at Moretti and asked, "Does the prosecution wish to go back in there and pick up where we left off?"

Moretti looked like a beaten man. He glared at Dylan and almost snarled, "I assume this is where you ask me to cut some kind of a deal."

"You assume correctly. You drop all charges related to the injuries, reduce the traffic charges to one count of misdemeanor speeding and make the leaving the scene a ninety day loss of license. In return we won't proceed any further with the fact your fine, upstanding married client was receiving oral sex from a fine, upstanding married woman and then lost control of his car."

There was an uncomfortable silence as the red faced Moretti continued his glare and seemed to be pondering his reply. Finally he said, "Your client has a rich daddy. How about in return for the reduction in charges we ask him to cover the emergency room costs?"

"How about we call Mrs. Fogle to the stand and ask her how she managed to lose both of her shoes and get her head right down next to the radio?"

"You son of a bitch, how did you ever get hired at a firm like Doyle and Finch?"

"I think it was my winning personality."

"Alright," Judge Bailey interrupted, "that's enough of that. Mr Moretti, are the defense's terms acceptable?"

Moretti practically growled his answer. "Please give me a minute to speak with my clients but yes, I think we'll have to accept them."

They all walked back into the courtroom and took their respective places. Dylan quietly explained the terms of the plea deal to Arlo who nodded his acceptance. After a few minutes of conversation all around, Moretti stood and announced, "Your Honor, the plaintiffs accept the terms of the plea agreement."

Judge Bailey responded, "Thank you, Mr. Moretti." Then he looked over at the defense table and asked, "Counselor, does the defendant also accept the terms?"

"Yes he does, Your Honor."

Bailey paused for a moment and then said, "The defendant will please rise."

Beth and Dylan stood on either side of Arlo as the judge announced the verdict and the details of the reduced sentence. Beth's surprise was obvious and Arlo's expression was almost one of shock. He turned and gave Dylan a big hug. "Oh my God, thank you, Dylan, thank you." His voice was shaking with emotion, a reaction Dylan never would have anticipated.

"You're welcome, Arlo." he answered and then added, "So how about from now on you slow the hell down and be more careful."

"Absolutely, absolutely, I will," he said. There was nothing Dylan could do but hope he really meant it.

Bailey banged his gavel. "Counsels will proceed with the revisions to the charges and findings and have them to my office no later than noon tomorrow. Court is adjourned," he barked. Then he looked over at Dylan and gave him a slight nod. Dylan wanted to think it was a sign of respect or at the very least a thank you for an interesting morning.

Dylan told Arlo that he and Beth had some business to take care of and then stood and watched him leave the courtroom. When he was gone Beth stood in front of Dylan and asked, "So are you going to tell me what in the hell went on in the judge's chambers?"

It was hard for him not to feel smug and triumphant over winning a tough case and beating Hollywood Paul Moretti, but Dylan managed to show some degree of professional cool and answered, "Let's grab some coffee across the street at Starbucks and I'll tell you every sordid detail."

It took about ten minutes to ride the elevator down to the lobby and then navigate the crowds of people and cars to get to the front door of Starbucks. After another ten minutes in line they were sitting at a small corner table. Dylan felt a little apprehensive because, despite the romantic history he had with Beth, the line of defense he had used in the case had been based on a subject most people felt uncomfortable talking about. He decided to wait for her to start the conversation or, more accurately, the inquiry, and she didn't make him wait long.

"Okay, I've been asking you for days what your defense was going to be and you wouldn't say, and now, what looked like a slam-dunk for the prosecution turns into a plea bargain where Arlo pretty much skates on everything. So what in the hell happened in that room?"

It would have been a lot easier for Dylan to have the conversation with another guy but Beth was a colleague who had worked hard on the case and she deserved an answer. He took a few moments to think about his answer and then said, "You and I talked about the case, the evidence, Arlo's recklessness, all of that, and we both saw the photos of the skid marks and the wrecked car and the police report." Beth nodded as he talked. "And everything we saw dealt with the scene where everything happened, the stuff outside."

"Yeah," Beth replied, "there must have been twenty photographs of the skid marks and the car and the caution signs and even the traffic cones around the construction."

"Yep, and they all painted a pretty grim picture of a reckless young guy and two fine, upstanding people who just happened to get in his way."

"Okay, I know all that, so I'm asking you again, what happened in that room?"

He looked at her, took a breath and said, "People make the mistake of seeing most traffic accidents as the result of external conditions like weather, road conditions, speeding and you name it. But it didn't take me long to see that stuff was all pointing straight at Arlo and if I was going to help him I had to at least try to look in another direction."

"And that direction was what?"

"I pushed aside the external and looked at the internal, the inside of the plaintiff's car."

"So you suspected something?"

"No, not at first, it was kind of like hoping to find something that I didn't really know would be there. But after I took a good close look, I mean like with a damn magnifying glass kind of look at the cop's photographs I found what I was looking for."

"And what, exactly, was that?"

"I found a reason for Mr. Chalmers and Mrs. Fogle to somehow be in Arlo's way, like not exactly in their lane or where they were supposed to be."

Beth leaned forward, her smirk slowly turning into a smile. "Okay, I looked at those photographs as many times as you did and I didn't see anything unusual. What did you see?"

For being in a conversation with a woman with whom he'd been intimate and for whom he still had undeniable feelings he was strangely reluctant to just blurt out what he was thinking. He looked around to see who might be within earshot, took a breath and a sip of coffee and answered, "I saw a woman who took off her shoes in a man's car, a woman who was injured when the car was hit from the left rear and the right side of her head impacted the radio down at the bottom of the dashboard, leaving minute traces of blood on the panel. And I also saw a man who got out of his car after the accident with some kind of wet marks down the front of his pants."

He stopped there, thinking there was no need to offer any more details.

The fact that Beth smiled but blushed noticeably was an indication, as far as he was concerned, that she was a woman with both a sense of humor and modesty. Then she shocked him with her reply. "Oh, so you just used the old blowjob defense."

Dylan was at a total loss for what to say in response. Beth had nailed it. He knew he was blushing and he tried hard to hold back a smile but it was a futile effort. After a pause he said, "Okay, let's just keep this one between us. If anyone asks just tell them it was my brilliant investigative and litigation skills that got us the plea bargain." Beth was now grinning from ear to ear and he couldn't help but reach over and briefly hold her hands in his. "Thanks for all your help," he said, "and I mean it about keeping this between us."

She held her smile and replied, "Deal, but a word of advice. You might want to send Lynn Fogle a thank you card."

They took their time with their coffee and conversation. It was as relaxing a time as he'd had in quite a while, at least it was until Beth asked, "So how are things going with your other cases, the ones outside the office that you don't ever want to talk about?"

She knew about his moonlighting and had even helped him on her own time researching case law for one of them but he still wasn't comfortable sharing that part of his world. It was the kind of work he never imagined he'd be doing, work he preferred to do discretely. But she'd asked the question and he knew he had to give her an answer. "Oh, it's the same old mix of crazy people who get themselves into crazy situations." He hoped that was enough of an answer but Beth, as usual, was like a dog on a bone.

"Anything you can talk about?" She leaned forward, her elbows on the table, with a look of anticipation that said she was expecting a more detailed answer.

Dylan looked down at the table, shook his head and then looked at her. He knew she could read his expression and she backed off. "You don't have to tell me, never mind," she said with obvious disappointment.

"No, it's okay. You know I'm just doing it for the money, until I make partner. I just think it's best if I keep it all on the down low. It's not exactly the kind of work or the kind of clients I want to put on my resume."

"Well, maybe I shouldn't say this but, however you feel about it, it seems to bring out a strange kind of enthusiasm in you, like you really get into it. But fair enough, I won't keep bringing it up." She reached over to squeeze his hand. "Just be careful." She hesitated and then added, "And let me know if you ever need help with them. They might make me feel like I'm actually helping someone."

He looked at her with a question forming in his mind that he wasn't sure he wanted to ask. It was something he had wondered about since their romance had first begun. Finally he threw caution to the winds. "Hey, I gotta' ask you something. I've always wondered, with all of the other young lawyers in our office and all the ones we work with at other firms, how do you suppose you ever got involved with me?"

Beth looked surprised and the long pause in her reply made him think he'd asked something inappropriate. Finally, she looked at him with a raised eyebrow and a faint smile. "There were a lot of reasons but the one that I think really got to me was that you're so, uh, unpredictable."

"And that's a good thing?" he asked.

"It is to me."

Through the rest of their conversation they made it clear that neither of them felt like going back to the office but they finished their coffee, made their way back to the parking garage and their cars and finally headed out into the late morning traffic.

The drive gave Dylan time to absorb the events of the morning. To him, the plea bargain was as good as a win considering the penalties Arlo had been facing, and keeping a reckless young man off the roads for ninety days was a bonus. He knew going in that his line of defense was a crap-shoot and he had to admit to himself it wasn't a particularly pleasant way to plead a case.

The rest of his day seemed to sail by and on the way home he met Lamar for a quick drink and a sandwich at McHale's. It was their usual mix of personal and professional conversation, talking with Kelly and just unwinding a little after a tough day at work. Part of the conversation was telling Lamar what he had learned about lucid dreaming and he thanked him again for telling him about it. Dylan finally realized he must have gone on a bit too long talking about it because he could see a kind of glazed look in Lamar's eyes.

He stopped and changed the subject. Dreaming was his obsession, not Lamar's or anyone else's.

That night lying in bed in the room he had tailored to the enhancement of sleep, he practiced a few of the relaxation and meditation methods he'd learned about as a way to allow lucid dreaming to happen. The notes on the legal pad that he'd been keeping since the beginning had become a notebook, almost a journal that could be used to guide a person through the world of lucid dreaming. He remembered that the key to being successful in doing it was called dream recall. He'd learned it was the absolute foundation of developing the ability to initiate lucid dreaming and operating once you were in it. He'd had a string of small successes and he was determined to learn the skills to master it.

A few tokes on a joint helped him relax and sort of set the stage for what might come next. The meditation exercises seemed to open up his imagination and lying there working on them made him feel as though he was on a journey of the mind. Real sleep itself took longer to reach but eventually he drifted off.

FADE IN
EXTERIOR - .CITY STREET – NIGHT

Two men are on a sidewalk in the middle of a brightly lit downtown commercial area of the city. It's nearly midnight and a mix of streetlights, neon signs and car headlights illuminate their route as they walk toward an intersection.

PAUL GOMEZ: Man, I feel like such an idiot. I can't believe we're actually lost. Where in the hell did I park my car?

DYLAN: And I can't believe I didn't notice where we parked either. I was too busy texting Beth and I wasn't paying attention. Sorry, man.

PAUL: Okay, let's just stop here and retrace our steps. We just left The Dog Pound right over there and before that we were around the corner on Second Street at The Ale House. I remember we walked down the hill to get there, like two or three blocks.

DYLAN: No, I think it was just one block because I remember seeing those two blondes over there. They were in the line of people trying to get into Modern Times and that's kind of kitty-corner from the Ale House. Remember? We saw those same girls when we were at Darwin's Pub.

PAUL: Wait a minute. Didn't we walk right by that billboard over there right after we parked?

DYLAN: I don't remember, I was still texting Beth for at least two blocks and besides, that billboard is like all over town.

PAUL: Well one of us better get a grip here or we'll be walking all fucking night.

DYLAN: Hey, I have an idea. Take out your key and press the alarm button and we'll just listen for the horn.

PAUL: I don't have the keys. I always lock them in the car and just use the keypad on the door to get back in.

DYLAN: Shit.

PAUL: So you're saying you were so busy texting Beth you didn't see where we were going? How is that possible?

DYLAN: Hey, I was following you. You're the driver. I thought you were paying attention, that's how it's possible.

The two men continue circling the same area of a few blocks in each direction but have no luck in finding the car. The traffic is thinning out and as businesses begin to close for the night the streets become darker. A few drops of rain begin to fall and then it turns into a light but steady shower.

PAUL: Oh, great, now it's raining. That's just fucking great.

DYLAN: Hey, what was that flash?

PAUL: What flash? I didn't see anything.

DYLAN: That big flash, I don't know, maybe it was lightning. Oh, never mind. You know, we need some kind of plan here, man. We're walking in fucking circles and getting nowhere. How about we split up? I'll go back up Second and you go over to Fourth and head up that way. We'll each go a few blocks and we should be able to see all the way down to Third at every cross street. Whoever spots the car first calls the other one.

PAUL: Well, I guess it's better than what we've been trying so far. See you in a few.

The two men separate and begin their slow, cautious search from opposite sides of the bar district. The rain lets up and eventually stops. Dylan notices that the traffic has disappeared along with every parked car along every street. Every building is closed and there are no lights on except a few streetlights. He looks at his cellphone to check the time and he realizes the battery is dead. He is totally alone and can't communicate with Paul. He pauses, takes a deep breath, looks all around him and begins to smile.

DYLAN: Ah, now I get it. Cool.

FADE OUT

CHAPTER 5

Dreams die hard when they don't come true. Dreams die hard and there's nothing you can do. Dreams die hard when they take your pride. It's hard to find a new dream with an old one in your eyes.

From the song *Dreams Die Hard* by Gary Morris

IT'S DOUBTFUL THAT MANY PEOPLE pay much attention to the ceilings in their houses. After all, the ceiling is way up there and life is lived way down below. Ceilings are just drywall, usually painted white and intended to be ignored, backgrounds to the things that play out down on the floor. But that morning, while Dylan was lying in bed with so many thoughts racing through his head, the ceiling above him had become a kind of movie screen. He laid there staring up and replaying the scenes from Arlo's trial, his time with Beth but mostly walking through the details of the dream he'd had.

It was a variation on a dream he'd had on a regular basis over the years, a dream of being lost somewhere and trying to find his way home. It was a dream that was often uncomfortable and all too familiar to him. But last night's version had been different.

Even though he had made sure the window shades would keep the daylight from intruding through the windows, the ceiling he was looking at still seemed to be a bright surface that was playing back the events that he and Paul had aimlessly walked through trying to reach their destination. It had been an unsettling dream but there was a distinct twist to the routine of the usual storyline. In this dream, while trying to find his way, there was a flash, a kind of sudden recognition that what he was going through was a dream and nothing more. Call it a kind of eureka moment or a revelation of some kind, but whatever it was, it was the point when he first realized that lucid dreaming was real.

It didn't click at the exact moment it happened but he'd reached a particular point in the dream where he stopped, looked around and realized that, "Yeah, this is just a dream. Late at night, lost our car, it's dark and scary, big deal."

For a few more minutes the ceiling continued to replay his thoughts. It seemed as though his meditation and relaxation exercises had in some way paid off. All things considered his dream had been a small one. It wasn't exciting, romantic or memorable in any way but last night something had changed. When he realized it was a dream and not reality it was almost liberating.

Lucid dreaming seemed to be a real thing and it was something he wanted to explore further. He turned toward the nightstand and the dream journal. He carefully noted the timing of the flash of light and the events that led to it. He knew it was a significant detail.

His lingering in a fog of dream analysis and fantasy had eaten up too much of the morning clock and by the time he got to his truck and headed for the office he was already late. The day before, when he had gotten back to the office after Arlo's trial, he'd had the foolish notion there would be some kind of excitement, some congratulatory response for what he had pulled off. He had assumed that Arlo would have called his father and that his father would have called John Finch or, hope against hope, he would have called Dylan personally.

"Relax", he told himself, "just wait until you get to the office and there will be lots of handshakes and pats on the back

Six years of not being taken seriously should have tempered his expectations but he still held out a small glimmer of hope that his efforts at digging Arlo Makris out of a very deep hole would be noticed by someone in the firm. No one in the lobby asked him about it and the few people he passed in the corridor either nodded or just grunted, "Dylan."

When he reached his office and sat down at his desk there was a Post-it note stuck to his computer screen. It read, "Mr. Finch wants to see you immediately." All he could think was "Finally, that old bastard is going to pay me a compliment." When he walked down the long corridor and into

Finch's office and then sat down in front of the desk, reality reached out and smacked him in the face.

Finch was sitting in his high-backed leather chair, looking like a stereotypical television lawyer in his gray suit with his wire-framed reading glasses hovering at the end of his round, red nose, His face was frozen with his usual stern and humorless expression.

"Mr. Ward," he said as he looked at Dylan over the top of the glasses, "I received a phone call from Mr. Moretti late yesterday after your trial was over. I understand that your actions in the courtroom didn't exactly bring honor to this firm and all it stands for."

Dylan shouldn't have been surprised by the comment but somehow he thought it was strange. His naïve notion that saving an important client's ass in court would impress Finch was obviously wrong. It took him a few seconds to decide how to respond and he decided that the best defense was a good offense.

"I don't know what you mean by that, but I always thought that the best way to bring honor to the firm was by winning for our clients and that's exactly what I did."

Finch's face was even redder than usual but he didn't slow down his little critique of Dylan's work. "But your win was at the expense of this firm's reputation. Doyle and Finch doesn't go in the sordid direction you chose for your defense of Mr. Makris."

That word *sordid* just struck a nerve in Dylan and as usual he reacted before he could think of the right words to use. "Hey, I didn't just choose that direction it was dumped in my lap. Arlo Makris broke half a dozen laws and his only hope of getting off was the fact the injured parties were engaged in something that shouldn't be done in a moving vehicle. All I did was point that out and it was the game-breaker as far as the verdict was concerned."

"Any other lawyer in this firm would have found a better way to build a defense, a defense that didn't require vulgarity and sexual content as its foundation."

Many times in Dylan's life his emotions had gotten in the way of good judgement and this had suddenly become another one of those times. "Any other lawyer in this firm would have totally fucked things up because they all live in a world of statutes and spread sheets and a totally different kind of law. They are so far removed from helping people in a personal way it's a joke."

"Mr. Ward, I suggest you keep your criticism of your colleagues to yourself. I don't want to hear it."

Dylan knew he had developed a reputation for being kind of a smart-ass and now it seemed to him to be a good time to draw a line in the sand with the old prick. Without taking even a moment to think things through he blurted, "Look, you pigeon-holed me into this kind of law. I never asked for it but I've managed so far to be fairly good at it. So let's do it your way. The hearings for the two Makris daughters are coming up next week. How about I withdraw from their cases and you find a hotshot attorney somewhere in one of the big offices down the hall to fill in for me. They won't win or help the clients but they'll uphold the honor of the firm, and after all, isn't that the most important thing we do around here?"

He stood up to leave, surprised at his outburst and the risky challenge he had just dropped in front of Finch. It was almost liberating to stand his ground even though he knew by the time he got back to his office he'd already be regretting it. Finch's expression was grim and the redness of his face was even more noticeable. He was a man who wasn't used to dissent or to being questioned.

All Dylan could think was that he'd really stepped into some serious shit so why not finish things up in an appropriate way. "Please let me know who to give the Makris files to so they can get started on their idea of a criminal defense." He emphasized the word criminal.

He turned and walked out the door, fully expecting Finch to roar out a demand to come back and was surprised when it didn't come. Once again he made the walk down the long corridor to his office and every step brought him a little more stress and worry. His little tirade might very well have been the end of his tenure at the firm and he couldn't decide if that was a good or a bad thing. All he could think of was finding a way to escape for a little while, a few hours or even a few days away from the fucking world of Doyle and Finch.

His thoughts took a different turn when he got to his office and saw Beth sitting in front of his desk.

THE DREAM HACKER 67

Before he could get a word out of his mouth she looked up at him and said, "I stopped by before you got in and saw the little note about Finch. I've been dying to know what he wanted."

Dylan tossed his handful of notes and files on to his desk and then half-sat and half-fell into his chair. "Well, whatever you were thinking he had to say it wasn't that. Instead of congratulations for getting Arlo out of a jam it was a criticism for the blowjob defense. He said I took a sordid direction with the firm's reputation. Can you believe it?"

Beth looked down and shook her head and then looked back at him. "You've got to be kidding. What in the hell does that old man expect you to do, ignore an obvious set of facts that got your client off the hook? That's your job."

"Yeah, that's exactly it. He thinks what I do, or really, what you and I do is just the same thing as all of the other lawyers in this firm. Traffic violations, pot busts, felony assault, it's all the same thing as corporate mergers and buy-outs. What an asshole."

"So what did you say to him? I hope you stood your ground."

"I did, or at least I think I did. I told him he should find someone else in the firm to handle the Makris daughter's trials, someone who would handle things in the oh-so-classy Doyle and Finch way, whatever the fuck that is,"

He was sure his frustration was clearly showing because Beth stood up and closed the door and then sat back down. "You have a chip on your shoulder the size of a Toyota and I have a feeling you're going to start venting any moment. Watch your temper. I don't want anyone to hear you."

"Thanks, but you know, there's a part of me that almost wishes I could vent and yell and throw shit across the room and have everyone in the office see it. I'm so fucking tired of that old fart and his narrow-minded ways. I'm sick of how he holds me back." He paused for a moment and then, in a very quiet tone said, "I wish he'd just retire or fall over dead and let this firm move on without him."

Beth nodded. "Yeah, I kind of agree, and from what I hear his health isn't exactly great so maybe you'll get your wish someday."

Talking about a death wish for a colleague wasn't something Dylan was particularly proud of. It was an awkward moment that they needed to move beyond so he said, "It'll be interesting to see what Finch does with my challenge to find someone else in the firm to take over."

"You don't think he'll actually do it, do you?"

"No, I don't. He knows damn well I'm the only attorney in this office with any criminal experience and even though he won't say it to my face he knows I'm good at it. He wants more than anything to keep this client locked in to Doyle and Finch. There's no way he'd ever let someone outside the firm get cozy with the Makris brothers."

"So what do we do now?"

"We wait."

For the next few hours Dylan went about revisiting the files of several cases that he'd been working on before the Makris family had taken over his calendar. When he felt sufficiently caught up he grabbed his cellphone and walked out to the parking lot, spending half an hour sitting in his truck looking through files of his moonlight cases and exchanging a few texts and e-mails with his outside clients

A shot of bourbon from the flask in his glove compartment was a small treat he felt he deserved, and he followed it with the usual stick of gum.

His eyes kept bouncing back and forth from the files to the phone and to the parking lot around him. His work routine had become a secretive juggling act and he hoped no one was watching him and wondering what was going on. Right when he thought he was finished the phone rang. He looked at the screen and saw the call was from Tommy Rizzo, his private investigator friend.

"Shit," he muttered, and answered the call. "Hey, Tommy, what's up?"

The voice at the other end was faint and muffled. "Hey, man, I gotta' be careful. I don't want her to hear me."

"Who are you talking about? Where are you?"

"I'm talkin' about a woman I've been tailin' for the last week. She's takin' a hot yoga class and I'm in the lobby pretendin' to be interested in a membership. Geez, even in the lobby it feels like a fuckin' oven."

"Why don't you go outside to talk?"

"Because I wanna' keep an eye on her through the big window into the yoga studio. And she looks amazin' in her tight little yoga pants by the way."

"So is this a case you need my help with or are you just calling to tell me about her ass?"

"No, this is just a divorce case, a messy one, and I know you don't like to do divorces that much."

Dylan paused for a moment and did another quick scan of the parking lot before he replied, "You're right about that. Divorces are too emotional and whether I win or lose somebody is getting screwed."

"Yeah, I've been there myself. What I'm callin' you about is totally different. I think I've got something you'll really jump at."

"Okay, fill me in but make it quick, I have to get back to my office."

"It's a woman, a rich one, and she's kind of a fence, you know, she receives some hot items, mostly jewelry, and sells them, in this case to her rich friends. I think it's how she gets her kicks."

"So have any charges been filed? I assume you've been working the case and know where things stand."

"Well, I've been keepin' an eye on her for the store's insurance company. A backroom employee has been messin' with the shipments and the books and handin' the items to this rich bitch and last week the store owner finally found out and blew the whistle. They know the employee is dirty but the rich woman claims she had no idea the stuff was stolen and only sold it because she wanted her friends to think she was all connected to the big diamond dealers."

"God, just being rich isn't enough, she also wanted to be a big shot. Is that why she works?"

"Yeah, somethin' like that. Anyway, now she's cryin' foul and I hear she's lookin' for a lawyer to get her off."

"Tommy, if she's the big, well-heeled, connected person you think she is she's probably got a bunch of lawyers she already knows."

"Yeah, she does but from what I can tell they're all the candy-ass gray suits like the guys you work with, the business shmucks. She needs somebody who, shall we say, isn't afraid to get his hands dirty."

Out of the corner of his eye Dylan noticed two men walking toward him. He turned and saw that it was Max Dewart and a man he didn't recognize. Fortunately they didn't seem to notice him. They got into Max's car and drove off. "Okay, Tommy I have to wrap this up. You've got me a little confused. You've been tracking this woman while you've worked for the people who are trying to nail her but here you are trying to find her defense counsel. What's that all about?"

"Look, my friend, I get paid no matter what happens. If she gets convicted I get my fee. If she walks I get my fee. I'm just tryin' to send a little a fee your way too, maybe even a very big one, by the way."

The entire conversation was a reminder to Dylan that his day job and his evening job were worlds apart. "Look, I need to think about it a little bit more.

"Okay, man, but don't drag your heels. I know this chick is scared and ready to hire the first guy who calls her."

"Let's meet in the morning, how about Starbucks in the Esplinade around ten?"

Tommy let out a very long and audible sigh. "Okay, and you're buyin'"

Dylan stowed his files in the compartment behind the seat of his truck and then headed back to the lobby. He managed to get back to his office without running into anyone in the hallway. It took him a few minutes to mentally shift gears and get himself back into his Doyle and Finch mode. He checked his e-mail and then tried to read his notes on a case that was due in court within a week. It was hard to concentrate on them because his confrontation with John Finch came rushing back into his thoughts.

He had no idea how Finch would handle the gauntlet he had thrown in front of him. Finch would probably take it for the insubordination that it was, but to Dylan it was also the case of an experienced lawyer standing up for the work he did, no matter how unusual his methods might have seemed to others.

It was about one-thirty when Dylan received a surprising email that he hoped would put an end to Finch's meddling. It was a message from Damien Makris, Arlo's father, and it read, "Mr. Ward, on behalf of my entire family I would like to thank you for everything you did yesterday to help Arlo. Your skill and tenacity in defense of my son are greatly appreciated and will not be forgotten. I look forward to the opportunity to meet you on my next visit to your office. Again, I thank you."

Dylan reread the message and then noticed on the copy line that it had also been sent to Finch and to Beth. He leaned back in his chair and read it again, feeling smug and more than a little victorious. While he was rereading it a message from Beth popped up, addressed only to him. It was simply a smiley-face emoji.

A few minutes later another message popped up at the top of his screen. It was from Finch and it was short and to the point. "Mr. Ward," it read, "please proceed with the defense for the Makris daughters in any manner you deem to be necessary."

He forwarded that message to Beth with the words, "Holy shit, can you believe it?" She replied, "Wow, it looks like the stars are aligned in your favor. BUT BE CAREFUL."

Surprisingly, it turned out to be a productive afternoon and around five o'clock he called Beth. "Hey," he said, "it's Friday and it seems like maybe we have a reason to feel good about the day and, if I recall correctly, I have a rain-check coming for a drink."

There was a long pause at the other end and then she answered, "How about McHale's around six?"

Dylan purposely arrived early to stake out a corner table and Beth got there right on-time. It was a comfortable, relaxing hour that felt much like a celebration. It also felt like old times. From the day they'd met he found it easy to talk with her and to just be himself. Even though there was a strong physical attraction from the beginning the romantic part had come later, long after they had developed a feeling of comfort with each other. She never blushed when he used salty language and at times she gave it back as good as she got.

Their conversation stopped for a moment when he pointed out to her that Max Dewart had just walked in. "Oh, shit," she said, "I hope he doesn't come over." Dylan looked over at Max who was staring right at them. He didn't have anything close to a friendly look on his face as he turned away and headed for the bar. "Good," she said.

They continued their rambling conversation on anything and everything that didn't include the Makris family. Dylan even got around to telling her about his discovery of lucid dreaming. Since they had shared a lot of time together and a bed on a number of occasions she was familiar with his tendency to wander off into dreamland. She had even commented that it was something she had never encountered with anyone else, so he wasn't totally surprised when she asked, "You and your nighttime adventures. So now instead of just lying there in a dream you can actually tell it's only a dream?"

"Yep, that's about it, and my goal is to actually learn how to take control of whatever it is I'm dreaming. From what I've learned it's possible to do it and even to get really good at it."

Beth hesitated then leaned forward with a look on her face that seemed to be more than a little suggestive. "So like, if you had a dream about me and you were in a lucid state you could control me?"

It was definitely a moment that required a careful response. "Well, I don't think anybody could ever control you, in a dream or in the real world, but I might be able to sort of steer the situation."

She seemed to like the words he'd chosen. "Promise you'll tell me all the details if it ever happens?"

It was another moment for a careful response but he didn't feel like giving her one. "Oh hell yes, I look forward to it."

Dylan was definitely ready for a weekend and it was with mixed emotions that he walked Beth to her car and said goodnight. When he got home and finished his evening routine and a toke on his last joint, he crawled into bed earlier than he usually did on a Friday. As much as he wanted to just lie back, look at the ceiling and replay the events of the past few days he was more focused on lucid dreaming.

The brief taste he'd had in his dream the night before just whetted his appetite for another one. He knew a dream or two would be coming soon so he looked over the pages of details he'd compiled in his dream journal. They were a list of items he'd learned about preparing himself to be aware of events and when to know precisely that it was only a dream. He still wondered if the bright flash he had seen, or thought he'd seen in the dream, was some kind of signal from his brain that he was in a state of awareness.

For a moment he wondered if it had been a mistake to tell Beth about it. Was lucid dreaming something weird, something he shouldn't talk about in case people would look at him and think he was some kind of sad, pathetic man who was living a life halfway between a fantasy world and a real one? That thought passed quickly.

He took a few minutes on his guitar to strum a song he and his old band had played many times. When he finished it dawned on him that his increasing dream activity had sadly cut into the time he spent staying connected to his music. He leaned the guitar against the wall beside him, swallowed the last bit of bourbon from the glass on the nightstand and turned off the lamp.

In a matter of minutes he'd begun to drift off, somewhere between awake and asleep, ready and eager for his next slumbering adventure.

CHAPTER 6

Yeah, runnin' down a dream that never would come to me. Workin' on a mystery, goin' wherever it leads. Runnin' down a dream.

From the song *Runnin' Down a Dream* by
Tom Petty and the Heartbreakers

THE SUN WAS BARELY UP and the first thing Dylan noticed was the warmer than normal breeze coming in from the slightly open window beside the bed. The shades were swaying with the light wind, making the little bit of daylight coming in appear as though it was being turned off and on in the rhythm of the wind. Autumn in San Diego was usually a very temperate time of year with warm days and cool nights, but for the past couple of years it had also included a couple of warm spells that moved the daytime temperature well into the nineties. All things considered it wasn't anything to complain about compared to most other parts of the country.

It was Saturday and he pulled back the covers and let that breeze wash over him as he looked up at the ceiling.

The journal was on the nightstand, but even though he knew that writing down his dream details was critical to the lucid dream training, he felt a need to lie there and revisit them first in his imagination. He'd had three dreams, three nighttime adventures and, from what he could recall, three successes at being aware and lucid for parts of all of them. They weren't big, exciting dreams or even ones that were particularly interesting. They were ordinary, almost mundane little mind-plays like everyone has and immediately forgets but in each of them he'd experienced a degree of freedom and control that was exhilarating.

In one of them he was in a very crowded and boring meeting at the office and he reached a point where he got up from the table and before he left the room he turned and asked the group, "How can you people just sit there and listen to all of this shit?" In another dream he was on a dirt road in a huge field riding a bike with Lamar beside him on his own, and when Lamar turned and asked, "How does the new bike feel to you?" Dylan sped up and literally jumped over a ten-foot high hill.

But it was the third dream that seemed to stick in his head more than the others. He was in his truck heading out of the parking lot after work and John Finch was walking beside him on the way to his car. Dylan slowed down, lowered his window and when Finch looked over at him Dylan gave him the finger. He just held out his hand, stuck up his middle finger and waved it in Finch's flushed, wrinkled old face.

For being just a dream that little moment was somehow very satisfying. Like the other dreams there was a moment, a sort of flash or brightness that seemed to signal that he was lucid and aware of what was going on in the dream. It was just a small taste of what lucid dreaming could be like and to Dylan it tasted great. And it was enough incentive for him to keep trying to master it in some way.

He grabbed the journal and entered the descriptions of his three dreams, making sure to include exactly when he had seen the flash of light and how it related to what was going on at the time they occurred. He had come to realize that it was critical for him to recognize the flash in order to be ready for lucid involvement in whatever came next. As he laid the binder back down on his nightstand a strange thought came over him.

In a way, he was writing a handbook, an owner's manual for dreamers. He wondered if there was any value to it. The idea only made it harder for him to get out of bed.

For the past few months his weekends had settled into a routine of house cleaning, lawn work and running errands. He felt like any average suburban guy going through the weekend rituals of life-maintenance but he was doing them all without a partner. All of his old friends had gotten married and were busy with lives of their own, lives that didn't have a lot of room for a bachelor friend. In addition to that, after years of playing golf he had drifted apart from his old golfing buddies when an old back problem reappeared and kept him off the course.

Weekends didn't hold the pleasures they had in the past.

For some period of time bachelorhood is a part of every man's life but he was learning that eventually the appeal wears off. At times the freedom of being single just felt like a different kind of being lonely but whenever thoughts of a committed relationship and marriage crossed his mind he quickly brushed them away.

He had always assumed that came about because of his parent's long and unpleasant divorce back when he was in high school. He had a ringside seat to watch the two people he loved the most and who he thought loved each other slowly turn into angry, bitter combatants. It was a tough thing for him to go through at a time when he was just learning how to navigate his own boy-girl relationships. And with no siblings to lean on for support he had to deal with it on his own.

At the time he'd tried hard to avoid listening when his mother made harsh, emasculating comments to his father but in their small house it was impossible not to see and hear almost everything. There were several times when he'd wished his father would show more anger and yell back at her but it never seemed to happen. Instead the man just seemed to sit in quiet acceptance of his situation.

When his father died of cancer four years after the divorce, his death had added a level of bitterness to the whole marriage/relationship topic that just hardened Dylan's resistance all the more. His mother's refusal to attend the funeral had led to an estrangement between them and a hardening of his skepticism toward any kind of romantic commitment.

Except for her phone calls on his birthday and Christmas and an occasional appearance in a dream they'd had no contact for years.

After that he'd had his share of romances and flings but he'd never let himself get too close to any of his love interests. If things started to feel like they were turning into anything resembling monogamy he backed off. A part of him wondered if there was more to his desire to maintain boundaries than his parent's divorce but he never allowed himself to probe the subject too deeply. "No rush," he told himself, "you have lots of time for that later, just enjoy your life for now." So far he'd been able to buy into his own excuses but he wondered how long that could last.

On his way to the kitchen to make a pot of coffee his cellphone vibrated. It was a text from Lamar. "Call me when you can, have a business question." Dylan thought for a moment and then texted him back, "Downtown later for a meeting at ten, how about I stop by after?" Lamar responded, "Cool."

The early part of the morning flew by quickly and he met with Tommy as planned. After a lot of talk and soul searching he'd told Tommy he would have to pass on taking on the rich woman as a client. The money was tempting but Dylan knew it would be next to impossible to keep the case out of the headlines and himself out of the courtroom for extended trial sessions. Someone from Doyle and Finch was bound to find out and he couldn't risk the consequences.

Tommy was disappointed and silent as they walked to their cars in the parking lot and when they reached them he said almost in desperation, "Listen, it's the weekend so maybe this chick won't be makin' any decisions. How about you sleep on it until Monday?"

"I doubt that I'll feel any different then, but okay."

Tommy opened his car door and then turned back toward Dylan. "Hey man, there's one last thing. Do you still want a bag of stuff like we talked about? You said you were gettin' low and this is some of Mexico's finest by the way."

Dylan hesitated and then said, "Sure, why not?" He pulled out his wallet while Tommy sat down on the driver's seat and reached over into the glove box. They made the exchange as casually as they had so many times before, said goodbye and drove off.

Around eleven-thirty Dylan found himself a parking space within view of the front door of *Spokes*. When he walked in Tamara greeted him with a lukewarm smile and a quick handshake. "Hi, Dylan, Lamar said you'd be stopping by." There was an uncomfortable pause and then she added, "I haven't seen you since the grand opening."

"Yeah, I know. I've been meaning to stop by but you guys seem to be slammed all day and all night and I didn't want to get in the way."

"I know what you mean but Lamar said he told you about the boutique sales idea and we're hoping that will make life a lot easier. That's what we wanted to talk to you about. It's the liability insurance thing, the amount of coverage we'll need if someone crashes his bike and tries to find a way to put us at fault."

Dylan looked over toward a display of pricey Yeti mountain bikes and saw Lamar talking to a man about them. From what Dylan knew about those bikes they were state-of-the-art carbon fiber construction, had the most sophisticated gear engineering in the world and sold for over ten thousand dollars. Lamar was smiling and so was the potential customer so Dylan turned back to Tamara and said, "It looks like he's ready to close a deal so let's not interrupt him."

They sat down in a small lounge area at the edge of the sales floor and Tamara poured him a latte, a part of their new sales approach. They talked for a while and got caught up on each other's lives. She was bright, warm and engaging, the kind of person you meet and instantly like. Despite whatever differences she had with Dylan he still thought Lamar had found himself a winner. They shared small talk and the recent events of their lives.

Finally Lamar walked over to them, his customer trailing a few feet behind. In a very measured and professional tone he said, "Tamara, Mr. Kinter here is ready to become a Yeti owner. Would you mind taking over?"

Tamara looked at Dylan and with a sheepish smile said, "I'm the detail side of this team." Lamar handed her a clipboard with a sizable stack of paperwork clamped to it and she and the customer walked back toward the sales counter.

"Wow," Dylan said, making sure to keep his voice low, "you sold that guy a Yeti! Isn't that like five figures?"

"Yeah, and I hope I made it clear to him that it's the kind of bike he could ride in the Tour de France and to respect it and use it enough to justify the cost."

"Is he a serious rider?"

"I'm still trying to learn what a serious rider is, but spending over ten grand on a bike definitely separates him from the average Joe."

"So what happens now? Is this where you try to sell the guy all of the add-ons and clothes and shit?"

"Well, I guess the answer is yes, but there's really more to it than that and that's why I wanted to talk to you. Tamara and I got to talking and we realized that making the jump from being a traditional retailer to a boutique service provider might come with some legal problems and we wanted to run it by you before we go any further."

"I'm not sure what you mean. I thought we did a pretty thorough job when we set up your LLC and set the whole thing in motion."

"Yeah, we think everything you did and everything we talked about covered our ass as a retailer. But now we're going way beyond that. Before, if a guy came in and just bought a bike and he crashed it, there wouldn't be much he could do but blame himself. Now here we are, analyzing the guy's fitness level, his riding goals and even measuring and fitting him into the freaking frame itself. So now if he crashes his expensive bike, it seems like he'd have more recourse to come after *Spokes* to get his compensation. I was hoping you'd check things out for us so we're not hanging out there like a sitting duck for a lawsuit."

Lamar's potential vulnerability was just another reminder of one of the parts of Dylan's legal career that he'd always found distasteful; trying to find an honest defense to counter someone else's self-serving offense. His friend was a straight-up good guy trying to make a living but sooner or later some accident or circumstance could open the door for some predatory personal injury lawyer looking for a payday. That lawyer would put the bike manufacturer at the top of his hit list because the checkbook would be bigger, but Lamar and Tamara would still get caught in the shit storm and quite possibly lose everything they owned.

"I see your point," Dylan said, "and I agree. You're in a totally different level of customer involvement here."

Lamar turned and looked back over his shoulder at Tamara and the still-smiling customer. "Yeah, and as nice and friendly as that guy is right now, if he goes balls up in a wreck and gets hurt, the first thing his ego is going to tell him is that it's not his fault and to find someone to point the finger at. And the Black guy who sold him a God-awful expensive bike would be the obvious place to start."

"Yeah, you're probably right. I'll need a little while to dig into the personal injury statutes that are in place now and then check on a few other things. Give me a week or so, okay? I've got a couple of fucking rich kids to rescue first."

Lamar smiled. "Okay, man, whatever it takes. I know you've got my back even though I'm not rich and I'm not a kid."

"You know, if I could push everything else aside and jump on this for you I'd do it in a heartbeat, but I can't." Saying that reminded him that if he was a partner he'd have some degree of control over his workload and the ability to help someone he actually cared about.

"Relax, man, we'll be careful about what we promise and what we sell. Just keep us on your calendar, okay?"

As Dylan got up to leave, their friendship and history led them to a mutually-initiated man-hug. "Don't worry," Dylan said, "I'll take care of it."

On the way home from some errands he stopped at McHale's for a beer and what amounted to a late lunch or early dinner. Since it was too early for Happy Hour he managed to have his pick of barstools and took one at the end where the beer taps were located. Kelly was tending bar which was the only reason it took him two and a half hours to finish his chicken sandwich and three beers. It was way too easy for him to flirt with her or at least that's what he thought he was doing. There was no way to know if she saw it as flirting or just some older, single guy trying to be charming. Either way, he enjoyed every minute and hoped that he hadn't looked foolish

He drove home and by nine o'clock when the three beers had worn off the thought of having a nightcap or some other form of a dream-inducer popped into his head. His years of being a dedicated social drinker had taught him that what he drank and when he drank it were big factors in the way he slept. In college he'd found that pot was a great unwinder and he usually kept a small bag on hand for those moments when he wanted it. But his tastes had changed a bit since then. He still enjoyed a toke but a double shot of bourbon had become his go-to relaxer.

He stretched out on the bed and ran through a quick mental checklist of the relaxation techniques that he hoped would lead to another lucid adventure. He made sure his journal was on the nightstand, finished the bourbon and eventually dozed off while he was staring at the ceiling.

FADE IN
EXTERIOR –GONDOLA OF A HOT AIR BALLOON – DAY

Sunlight illuminates the huge red, yellow and blue balloon as it seems to strain against the thick ropes that keep it moored to the ground. The early morning breeze tousles the hair of the three passengers and the pilot and the blast of the propane tank feeding the flame that heats the air in the balloon drowns out all other sound. All three passengers appear to be nervous as the pilot goes through his pre-launch checklist, shouting to his ground crew.

DYLAN: Hi, I'm Dylan Ward, and you are?

JOSH: I'm Josh Warren and this is my wife, Kim.

KIM: Hi, Dylan, nice to meet you.

JOSH: Is this your first time in a balloon like it is for us?

DYLAN: Yeah, it's my first too. I have been telling myself for years that I had to try it once and for all. I'm not crazy about heights but they always say, the best thing to do is confront your fears. So this morning I'll be confronting my ass off.

KIM: I'm the same way. Josh has wanted to do this for years but I was always afraid to try it, but he finally talked me into it.

JOSH: And you just wait. When it's all over and we're back on the ground you'll both say it was an awesome experience.

The pilot finishes his conversation with the ground crew and as they unhook the lines tethering the gondola to the ground he turns towards the controls of the propane tank. The passengers find places to stand at the edge of the basket and grip the rail tightly as they feel the upward movement begin.

PILOT: Good morning, folks, I'm Cal Dykstra. I'll be your pilot and tour guide today, and when I look around at your faces something tells me this is your first time aloft. Am I right?

DYLAN: Yep, I'm a balloon virgin.

JOSH: It's our first time too. So how high are we gonna' be flying today?

CAL: Well, at some point we'll reach our maximum altitude of three thousand feet but we'll be moving up and down along the way so we can catch the good wind flows.

KIM: Oh, my God, three thousand feet!

CAL: Miss, I guarantee if you don't like heights you won't feel any difference between three thousand feet or three hundred or even thirty, so just get comfortable. Find a place you want to stand and please don't lean over the edge. We'll be up in the air for about an hour and a half, maybe a bit longer."

The balloon climbs slowly and steadily as the wind pushes them eastward. In a matter of minutes they are at three hundred feet and the ocean becomes visible to the west. The pilot turns down the propane until there is barely any sound from the flame. There is almost total silence as the passengers, still nervous and maintaining a tight grip on the gondola railing, look out over the landscape below. The flight continues for a few more minutes when, suddenly, the pilot drops to his knees and then collapses on to the floor of the gondola. As he falls his hand hits the control of the propane tank and turns up the flame. The balloon begins a rapid climb as the passengers turn around to see what is happening.

JOSH: Holy shit, Cal, what happened? Are you okay?

Dylan moves toward the fallen man and as he bends down to check the situation a flash of sunlight reflected from his watch crosses his face. Dylan lifts the man into a seated position but he is unresponsive and Kim kneels down to assist.

DYLAN: I don't know what's wrong with him but if you know anything about CPR or first aid now would be the time to try something.

KIM: Oh my God, we're going to die! How can we land without him?

JOSH: Relax, honey, we'll be okay. Let me help you.

Dylan stands up and, remembering what he'd observed earlier, begins to adjust the valve on the propane tank. Their steady climb begins to slow and eventually the balloon starts to level off. There is still no movement or sign of consciousness from the pilot as Kim and Josh try to give him CPR. Their look of panic is in contrast to Dylan's calm smile. After several tense moments Josh looks up and notices Dylan's surprising expression.

JOSH: What's up with you, man, aren't you scared.

DYLAN: No, not really. It's pretty simple, really. Turn up the gas to go up and turn down the gas to go down.

JOSH: But you don't know anything about steering and landing.

DYLAN: Sooner or later we'll find a wind current and it'll take us where it wants us to be. Just relax and enjoy the ride.

JOSH: But what about Cal? There's something really wrong with him and we can't do anything to help him up here.

DYLAN: Exactly, so stop wetting your pants. Look down there at that white pick-up that's kicking up all that dust behind us. That's the chase crew and they'll stay pinned to our ass until we touch down. The best you two can do for Cal is to take his walkie-talkie off his belt, call the crew and tell them to have an EMT or an ambulance head out to meet us when we land.

JOSH: For a guy who's afraid of heights and never went ballooning before you sure seem chill.

DYLAN: No problem, just another day in the sky.

DISOLVE TO:
INTERIOR – HOTEL DEL CORONADO – NIGHT

A large group of people has gathered in the festively decorated banquet room of the luxurious hotel. A band is playing in the background, a handful of people are dancing while others mingle at a small bar at the rear of the room. A man walks carefully through the array of crowded tables along the right side of the room, making his way to the bar.

DYLAN: Bartender, can you make me a perfect Manhattan?

BARTENDER: Absolutely sir. You'll like it so much you'll never drink anyone else's mix.

DYLAN: I like a man with confidence.

As he scans the room and waits for his drink a voice behind him calls out.

TOMMY RIZZO: Hey, Dylan, how in hell did you get in here? I thought this bash was for bigshots only.

DYLAN: Hey, Tommy, I could ask you the same thing. Unless being a private investigator qualifies as being a bigshot.

TOMMY: Well, over the years I've sat in my car and watched the comings and goings of about a dozen people in this room. I think they put me on the guest list just so I'll keep my mouth shut.

As Rizzo sips his drink Dylan turns and once again scans the crowd. Out of the corner of his eye a blonde woman in a short, white dress catches his attention. She is walking toward him and he quickly realizes it's Beth. He is surprised to see her and even more surprised when he notices that she is not alone. A tall, dark-haired man in a blue suit, his arm around her waist, is walking with her. The three of them all make eye contact at the same time.

BETH: Oh, hi Dylan. I didn't know you were going to be here.

DYLAN: Likewise. And I see you have a, what is that, a date with you?

MAX: Easy, Dylan. I asked her to this event weeks ago.

BARTENDER: Your Manhattan, sir. I hope it's to your liking.

BETH: Well, this is awkward to say the least.

DYLAN: No, don't worry about it. I'm sure Max wanted to impress everyone by having a beautiful woman on his arm. After all, isn't maintaining an image what the partners are all about?

MAX: That was totally uncalled for.

TOMMY: Hey, Dylan, is this that blonde lawyer you were telling me about, the one you're so hot for?

DYLAN: Tommy, how about we change the subject?

BETH: Yes, please, let's change the subject.

TOMMY: Let me introduce myself. I'm Tommy Rizzo, a professional associate of Dylan's. You must be Beth, and let me say, in my humble opinion, you are every bit as lovely as Dylan has described you. And you, sir, who might you be?

MAX: Maxwell Dewart. I'm a partner at Doyle and Finch, and Beth is with me.

TOMMY: Geez, Dylan, this is awkward. Maybe you should have asked me to keep an eye on things for you. So, Maxwell, you look too young to be a partner. What'd you do, catch the boss banging some chick and now he owes you one?

DYLAN: Come on, Tommy, that's crude even for you.

MAX: What the hell kind of remark is that? Come on, Beth, let's let this tacky pair drink in peace.

BETH: Dylan, please, let's talk tomorrow, okay?

TOMMY: Hey, Mr. Partner-in-a Law-Firm, who the hell are you calling tacky?

DYLAN: I was wondering the same thing.

Just then a flash from the mirror ball over the dance floor washes over the bar area. The couple begins to walk away but Dylan steps in front of them. Rizzo takes a step toward Max but Dylan raises his arm to hold him back.

DYLAN: Relax, Tommy, this pompous ass is all mine.

MAX: Oh gee, I'm so scared. The two-bit ambulance chaser is mad at me.

DYLAN: Max, I don't get mad, I get even.

Without another word Dylan takes a swing and lands his right fist square on Max's jaw. Max is stunned and falls backward, landing on a table full of plates and glassware. People scatter, the table tips over and as glasses fall to the floor one of them empties its contents all over Max. He rolls on to his back obviously stunned, his lower lip bleeding, and he looks around at the crowd of people staring at him.

DYLAN: Max, you should be ashamed of yourself, a partner in Doyle and Finch lying on the floor at a party like some kind of low-life.

TOMMY: Yeah, that's really tacky. Hey, Dylan, that was a nice right cross by the way.

DYLAN: Thanks, Tommy, I thought I executed that little maneuver perfectly.

BETH: Dylan, was that really necessary?

DYLAN: You know something, I think it was. Yes, it was definitely necessary.

BETH: Now what am I supposed to think? You just got into a fight in a public place and embarrassed everyone involved.

Without responding to Beth's comment, Dylan steps toward her, puts his arms around her and kisses her on the lips. She wraps her arms around him and they lock into a long and passionate kiss.

TOMMY: Good job, Dylan, good job. I'll be at the bar if you need any more help.

FADE OUT

CHAPTER 7

So long ago, was it in a dream? Was it just a dream? I know,
yes I know. It seemed so very real, seemed so real to me.

From the song *#9 Dream* by John Lennon

I N JUST OVER A WEEK Dylan's foray into the world of lucid
dreaming had turned out to be everything he'd hoped it would be.
His dreams were still happening at the same, steady rate as they always
had but now, instead of being in the audience he was up on the stage. He
had cracked through that imaginary fourth wall that actors and audiences
talk about and was smack in the middle of the action.

It was exciting and fun and, in a strange way, almost addictive. Since
he'd had more free time over the weekend he had spent a few extra hours
in bed, enjoying every possible minute of his newly acquired skill. Along
with that came a sense of guilt that he should be doing something more
productive with his free time.

He made a quick entry in his journal which he had decided to call
Dreamware and then began his morning get-ready-for-work ritual.

As much as he was enjoying his expanded dream world, the pressure
in his real world had been building daily. The trials for the two Makris
women were just days away, a hearing for another client's wayward wife
had been moved up on the calendar and a moonlight case involving an
exotic dancer was scheduled for six days down the road. And to add to his
stress his annual review with John Finch was just a week away and he'd
been wracking his brain for ways to outmaneuver the old man. He was
hoping the fact he seemed to be in the good graces of the Makris family

might help him but Finch's obvious dislike for him was an obstacle that might end up being just too big to overcome.

It was another stressful Monday and he sat at his desk with his first cup of coffee, keeping one eye on the Doyle and Finch emails on his laptop screen while he scrolled through his personal email on his phone. Judging by the volume of messages on both screens it looked like he'd be doing a lot of juggling in the week ahead. If he could continue to keep his moonlight cases from going to court, that part of his activity would be easy to keep under wraps, but he figured that sooner or later he'd have a case that would require his presence in front of a judge. That bridge would only be crossed if and when he came to it.

When Beth walked into his office around nine o'clock he was ready for a little diversion. "Morning," she said, "am I interrupting anything?"

"Nothing that can't wait for a few minutes. Have a seat."

She sat down, perched at the edge of a chair in front of his desk and said, "I can't stay long, I just wanted to give you this." She laid a flat, gift-wrapped package on his desk.

"What's this? he asked, surprised and a bit confused. "Is there a special occasion I missed?"

"No, it's no big deal, just something I found at the Balboa Flea Market over the weekend. Tracy and I spent the day shopping for junk.

"So you bought me some junk?"

"No, go ahead and open it. It's just something that made me think of you."

He carefully tore back the wrapping paper then put it aside, and saw the book. It was titled *Dream Legends–A History*. He thumbed through a few pages and looked at the chapter titles. "Ooh, very cool," he said, "this looks like a fun read."

"Like I said, it made me think of you and all of your dreaming. There was another book there called *Freudian Dream Analysis* but I figured you already knew about how he related everything in dreams to sex." She made no attempt to hide a smile.

As tempted as he was to respond in kind he just returned her smile and held back. "Well, thanks. I'll dig into this tonight before I go to bed."

Beth seemed to hesitate for a moment before she stood up. "Well, back to work. I have to make sure we have everything ready for the Makris girls."

"Yeah, me too. I think I'm ready at my end." Then he added, "And thanks again for the book, and also, thanks for thinking of me."

She smiled. "Sure. I just hope it doesn't give you any crazy ideas."

"If it does you'll be the first to know."

He set the book off to the side of his desk and even though his workload kept him chained there for most of the day he couldn't resist an occasional urge to pick it up and flip through the pages. There was a chapter on an ancient Japanese legend about Baku, a monster who devoured dreams. Another chapter studied the Ojibwe Indians and their dreamcatchers that let good dreams through the net but captured the nightmares. He remembered having one of those hanging over his bed as a kid, a gift from his father, and believing that it actually worked. And there was the legend of the benevolent Sandman, who snuck into bedrooms at night to sprinkle dust on the eyes of sleeping children to help them dream. That had been another part of his growing up.

It was just after five o'clock when he finished the last inch of bourbon in his flask, popped a stick of gum into his mouth, clicked off his computer and leaned back in his chair. He picked up the book again and scanned the index.

The title of Chapter Eleven caught his eye. It read *Dream Transfer – Sharing Other People's Dreams.* The basic premise of the legend was that when a person lies awake at night unable to sleep, it's because that person is actively taking part in another person's dreams. Even though his dreams were an unusually big part of his life they were just his dreams and no one else's. His newly acquired skill in controlling his dreams was exciting but he had to admit this idea of taking part in other people's dreams had a strange appeal to him, like some kind of guilty pleasure. Since he could now control his own dreams it was impossible not to wonder if he could find a way to enter and control someone else's.

He knew at that moment that he'd be buried in Chapter Eleven before the evening was over. But first there was a stop he had to make on his way home.

When it came to entertainment, strip clubs were not exactly familiar territory for Dylan. He had been to one when he was in his early twenties when a friend had decided it would be a good place to have a bachelor party. When a guy is that age he feels almost no embarrassment in ogling nude and semi-nude women. In that situation the biggest concerns are maintaining your self-control and having a sufficient number of dollar bills to properly reward them for their efforts. In Dylan's case his one night of practice didn't exactly lead to proficiency in doing it well or a comfort level in being involved.

. *Vibrations Gentlemen's Club* was located at the far end of a 70's-era shopping plaza that had seen better days. It was only six-thirty but there were already half a dozen men waiting in their cars in the parking lot. Dylan parked and had no sooner reached the front door and pushed it open a few inches when it was jerked out of his hand. A tall, muscular man with a goatee and two arms full of tattoos blocked his way and snarled, "Read the sign, man, we open at seven."

"I saw the sign but I have an appointment with Misty, I'm her lawyer."

The man looked him up and down and said, "You don't look like no lawyer."

Dylan tried to hold back a smirk and said, "Thank you, I appreciate that."

The man spent a few more seconds looking Dylan over and then said, "Wait here, I'll see if she can talk to you." He closed the door in Dylan's face and made him stand there for a couple of minutes before the door opened again and the same man said, "Okay, come on in."

He led Dylan toward the hostess stand and said, "Just wait, Misty knows you're here," then he walked away and for about five minutes Dylan got to see what a strip club looked like when it wasn't full of rowdy men and before the spotlights went on and the music was cranked up. The smell of cigarettes was obvious and he guessed the odor had become a permanent part of the walls and carpet. The faint smell of air freshener didn't do much to mask the tobacco.

He couldn't help but notice when three beautiful and barely dressed young women entered the main room through a curtain-draped doorway near the end of the bar. He had never met Misty. So far she had just been a soft but frightened sounding voice at the other end of the phone. He had pictured her as a blonde but the women walking toward him were a redhead and two brunettes.

When they got a little closer he noticed the large bruise under the right eye of the redhead that her make-up didn't begin to hide. He knew right then she was Misty. She smiled and said, "Hi, Mr. Ward, I'm Misty, thanks for coming over."

"Hi, Misty, it's nice to finally meet you, and please call me Dylan."

The two brunettes stood nearby, both dressed in skimpy dance attire similar to Misty's. There wasn't much to the typical dancer's costume; just a shiny, sparkling bikini top and an equally shiny matching thong, stiletto heels and a colorful wristband that more than likely was never even noticed by the admiring audience members.

Misty turned to her friends and said, "It's okay," and as they walked away she said, "Let's go over to that corner booth where we can talk."

Dylan let her lead the way, partly out of courtesy but mostly so he could enjoy the view. They sat down at opposite sides of the table and he started the conversation. "Okay, tell me what's going on. You sounded nervous on the phone." He made a concerted effort to keep his eyes on hers.

Misty looked around the room and answered in a low voice, "I'm so scared. I was going to go to your office this morning but the business card that Tommy gave me doesn't have an address so that's why I called."

"Well, the work I do at my office is a different kind of law. It's kind of just business stuff so I do your kind of cases from my home. It's best that you don't come to my office, okay?"

"Sure, I understand, but like I said I'm scared. You said the restraining order would keep Tony away from me for ninety days but he was parked outside my house when I got home from work last night and the order is only like three weeks old."

"Is that all he did, just sit in his car?"

"Yeah, and he sat there for like an hour and then he drove away. I kept checking the locks and I was afraid to turn off the lights and I couldn't fall asleep. Isn't he supposed to stay like three hundred feet away from me or something like that?"

"Yep, the Protection from Abuse order states that he can't get closer to you then three hundred feet and he isn't allowed to call you, speak to you or contact you in any way, including via email."

"Well, what do I do? He was parked less than three hundred feet from my front door so it seems like he doesn't care about the law, and I don't need another black eye."

"There are a couple of things we can do to drive home the message and maybe even scare him a little. Give me until noon tomorrow. I'll send a message to your phone, and in the meantime you should probably spend tonight with a friend. Can you do that?"

"Yeah, I told Caitlyn about all this, she's the brunette over there in the pink outfit, and she said I could stay at her place." He turned and looked across the room and made eye contact with her friend. He smiled and nodded toward her and she gave him a little wave. "By the way," Misty added, "she has a little problem of her own and asked me to get one of your cards. Is that okay?"

He pulled a card from his wallet and handed it to her. "Sure, I'm always glad to help someone in need."

"Oh, you're so sweet. Your girlfriend is so lucky, that is, I assume you have a girlfriend because you aren't wearing a ring."

"Let's just say I'm between girlfriends right now."

Misty smiled and said, "You just wait, some girl is gonna' grab on to you. I can introduce you to a couple of my friends if you want."

"Well, I'll think about it but for now let's just worry about you."

She slid herself to the edge of the booth and stood up. "Oh, one last thing, the boss gave me a couple of private parties to work this weekend so I'll get some extra money and be able to pay the retainer I promised you."

Dylan stood up and smiled at her as they walked toward the door. "Relax, I know you're good for it."

When he was back in the car and heading for home it took a while to get the image of Misty off his mind but eventually the thought of the dream legend popped back into his head. For as fixated as he'd been on that idea, the three beautiful, underdressed women had taken his mind in a whole other direction for a while.

The drive-through window at a Chinese restaurant was his source for dinner and by nine o'clock he had finished eating, returning emails and catching up on the day's news on television. He even took a few minutes to play his guitar and check out Facebook. His social media activity was mostly playing the role of a voyeur gawking at the things his online friends posted. He never felt comfortable sharing the details of his life with a group of people he hadn't seen in years and might never see again. His viewing only lasted about ten minutes.

For the rest of the evening his focus was on the dream legend and trying to determine if there was a way to plug into other people's dreams. After a double shot of bourbon he went to bed and stared at the ceiling for a while, then closed his eyes and replayed the things he had read.

The story in the book was based upon historical as well as clinical research and seemed to indicate that the legend was found in many cultures and countries. There was a lot of anecdotal evidence from people who claimed to have found themselves in the dreams of other people.

Some of them described being in a state halfway between wakeful resting and sleep. Others claimed that the feeling was more like being intoxicated or high on some kind of drug. A woman from Japan said she dreamed that she was walking a path with someone who was vaguely familiar to her and who was telling her what to do but without actually speaking to her. A man from New York said he'd found himself in a dream where he was naked in a room full of well-dressed strangers when a woman he'd dated five years earlier walked in, acting as though everything was normal, and asked him to dance.

The part of the legend that struck him most was the fact that anyone he had ever known: childhood friends, teachers, co-workers, Facebook friends and anyone else he'd ever had any relationship with, could potentially have a dream that involved him. The fact was he had probably been in other people's dreams hundreds of times over the years without knowing it. So, if the legend was true, he could have been lying awake in bed while his old college friends who lived on the east coast were already asleep and dreaming things that he was a part of.

The possibilities seemed endless.

The legend's description of people being in a state halfway between resting and sleeping was eerily similar to the state he had learned to reach in order to induce lucid dreaming. Were they the same state? How did a person recognize when he reached the point where he was in that state and not just resting, and how could he keep from falling asleep? Was it possible to navigate between the two states? The adventures that could result if he could find a link between lucid dreaming and dream sharing were almost too much to comprehend. The potential for fun, adventure and pleasure could take his dreaming to a level he'd never imagined. It was both enticing and unnerving.

He laid there with his eyes closed and followed the pattern of breathing and relaxation exercises he'd been going through every night and finally fell asleep.

FADE IN
McCALE'S – INTERIOR - NIGHT

It's a Friday night and the place is surprisingly uncrowded. Dylan sits on a stool enjoying a beer and watching Kelly as she goes about her routine behind the bar. She glances over at him several times and smiles. After a few minutes she walks over to him.

KELLY: So, what are you doing in here on a Friday night? Shouldn't you be out someplace dancing and partying and having a good time?

DYLAN: What makes you think I'm not having a good time right here?

KELLY: Well, I know you like this place but it's not exactly Party Central.

DYLAN: Yeah, but it has you.

KELLY: Man, you sure know how to lay it on, I'll give you that.

DYLAN: I'm not laying on anything, I'm being totally sincere.

KELLY: You know, I seem to recall you offering me a raincheck on dinner and tonight is the night I can get off early. Did the offer expire yet or can I still take you up on it?

Before Dylan can answer, Kelly gets called away by the other bartender. As he sits there looking around the barroom he sees Angela walk in. She is wearing jeans and a white, form-fitting top. She notices him and walks over, flashing a beautiful smile.

ANGELA: Well hello, stranger. I see you're still hanging around this place.

DYLAN: Yeah, it's still my favorite bar, and if I remember correctly, you always loved it when we came here.

ANGELA: That's why I came tonight. Mind if I join you?

DYLAN: Of course not. Here, sit down.

Angela sets her purse on the bar and places her cellphone beside it and then sits on the stool next to Dylan's. She turns and faces him, their knees touching.

ANGELA: Do you remember my favorite drink?

Dylan hesitates for a moment as her cellphone rings. She picks it up and turns away to answer it just as Kelly returns. She looks over at Angela with a surprised and curious expression.

KELLY: It looks like your Friday plans have changed.

DYLAN: Well, my only plan was to come here for a drink and as of right now that's the only thing I'm sure of.

KELLY: What is your pretty friend drinking?

DYLAN: I think she wants a Bombay Sapphire and tonic, with two cubes.

KELLY: Wow, a lady with good taste. She has good taste in men too.

DYLAN: Why, Kelly Alvarez, if I didn't know better I'd say you were flirting.

Kelly gives him a lingering smile and walks away to mix the drink as Angela clicks off her phone and turns back toward Dylan.

ANGELA: Sorry about that. I should probably turn off my phone before that happens again.

DYLAN: No problem. When we were together I must have let a hundred calls interrupt us.

ANGELA: Yeah, and they interrupted a lot of fun stuff as I recall.

DYLAN: Careful there, I blush easily.

ANGELA: So, I couldn't help but notice how the bartender was flirting with you. You must be a big tipper.

DYLAN: Why, is that the only reason a pretty woman would flirt with me?

ANGELA: I didn't mean it that way. It's just that she looks young and I'm sure she knows the value of a kind word and a big smile. I was a server once myself.

Just then Kelly returns and sets Angela's drink in front of her. The two women exchange a quick and not-so-subtle glance at each other.

KELLY: Is there anything else I can do for you, Dylan?

DYLAN: Not right now, but you never know what might happen.

Kelly gives him the same lingering smile and walks away without a word or a look in Angela's direction. Angela sips her drink and then turns her stool toward Dylan again. She pushes her glass aside and places her hand on Dylan's.

ANGELA: So, do you think our running into each other like this was a coincidence or do you think it was meant to happen?

DYLAN: That's kind of a loaded question.

ANGELA: Well, we haven't seen each other in a long time and you're out alone and I'm out alone and here we are having a drink together.

DYLAN: Well, it might be karma or it might just be that we were both thirsty.

ANGELA: I was hoping to hear something more romantic.

The front door opens and a group of people walk in. Dylan looks over at them and a beautiful redhead catches his eye. It's Misty and they make eye contact. She smiles, waves and starts to walk toward him.

MISTY: Hi, Dylan, how are you?

DYLAN: I'm fine, Misty. You know, this is my regular hangout and I've never seen you here before.

MISTY: I've never been here before but I got a night off for a change and decided to come along when my friends invited me. But hey, it looks like you have a date and I'm interrupting. Sorry.

DYLAN: No, it's not a date. Misty, this is my, this is Angela. Angela, this is Misty. She's a client of mine.

The two women exchange an uncomfortable nod as Dylan squirms on his barstool.

ANGELA: Nice to meet you, Misty.

MISTY: Likewise.

DYLAN: Well, this evening has gotten interesting in a hurry.

MISTY: I think I better join my friends. I'll be at that big table over in the corner in case you need to talk to me about anything.

The two women exchange another glance and Angela stares at Misty while she walks away.

ANGELA: Wow, she sure doesn't look like an average client. Please don't tell me she's a banker or a business tycoon, not with that outfit and that body.

DYLAN: Well, she's not a Doyle and Finch client. She's someone I'm sort of helping out on my own time. I've been doing some moonlighting lately.

ANGELA: Well I have to say her little visit sure broke the mood for me. I hope we can get it back.

The side door of the main barroom opens and the flash of headlights momentarily sweeps over the bar. Dylan takes a long, slow sip of his beer. He looks at the door and sees Beth approaching him. He looks at the corner table and watches as Misty walks toward him and from the corner of his eye he sees Kelly coming over. Within seconds the four women seem to surround him.

DYLAN: Ladies, I want you to know there are about a hundred fun thoughts going through my head right now but I think it would be best if I don't share them. I'm in the middle of every man's dream and I want you to know this is tough for me. It could turn out to be my best fantasy or my worst nightmare and. to be honest, I'm afraid to find out which it will be. I think I just better say goodnight.

ANGELA: You know, Dylan, nobody said you have to choose just one.

FADE OUT

CHAPTER 8

Until my fantasy becomes reality, I'll keep on
dreaming until my dreams come true.

From the song *Until my Dreams Come True* by Jack Greene

THERE'S AN OLD SAYING IN the business world that if
you want to get a job done, give it to a busy person. Somehow,
in the past week Dylan had accomplished more than he'd ever
imagined he could even though his workload hadn't decreased. That was
because too many of his business clients seemed to share a propensity for
bad behavior in their personal lives. It was as though there was a direct
relationship with the amount of money they made and the amount of
trouble they got into. He had learned that the Makris family troubles were
typical of the rest of the firm's client roster.

With help from Beth he had done some intense, last-minute review of
the evidence in Sophia Makris' shoplifting case and it paid off. There was
extensive videotape from the store's security camera that showed Sophia
trying on the jacket, removing the tags and then wearing it as she started
to walk toward the front of the store and the exit.

To anyone watching the video it was an obvious attempt at theft. But
Beth noticed that the store's security guard had made a big mistake. As
Sophia nonchalantly walked toward the front of the store she reached the
intersection of the aisle toward the check-out and the aisle toward the front
door. If you looked closely at her right hand you could see she was still
holding the price tag from the jacket. That was the point where the guard
stepped in front of her, blocking her path. But what Beth had pointed out

was that Sophia was not only blocked from leaving the store but also from the register where she could pay for the garment.

In court they played the videotape and stopped it at the exact moment the guard stopped Sophia. Their argument was that she, like many people, liked to put on a new item of clothing as soon as they buy it. She made no attempt to destroy or conceal the price tag and, as she approached the front of the store with the intention of turning left toward the checkout, the guard blocked her path and prevented her from doing so.

Deep down inside a part of Dylan believed that Sophia was really planning to steal the jacket but their argument for her acquittal seemed logical and believable. That was what the judge determined as well and young Sophia went home happy and without a criminal record.

The other Makris case was a bit more work. Cousin Delphina was known to be a partier. Arlo had referred to her as the "wild child" of the Makris family which was saying a lot. This case wasn't the first time she had been asked to leave a bar or nightclub but it was the first time she had been involved in any kind of physical altercation. Once again there was security camera video involved and Dylan had also interviewed a dozen eyewitnesses. Everything seemed to point to the intoxicated Delphina losing her temper and getting into a shoving, hair-pulling tussle with another female patron causing the other woman to fall backward. Delphina landed on top of her and the woman's head hit the concrete floor.

When Delphina was deposed she had accused the other woman, one Caitlin Carter, of grabbing her hair and pulling it, and when Delphina screamed for her to let go Ms. Carter yelled back "I'm not doing it!" and the tugging just continued. That was when Ms. Carter started to fall backward and Delphina couldn't stop her momentum and wound up on top of her. And just as in Sophia's case it had been Beth that had seen something in the video that turned things in favor of the defense.

There was enough light in the bar area to clearly show that Ms. Carter wasn't actually holding on to Delphina's hair but her bracelet was. It was caught in the hair on the right side of Delphina's head and the video made it obvious. With her hair so completely entangled in the bracelet there was no way that Delphina could pull away or do anything to separate herself from the other woman. Delphina did not "aggressively and maliciously knock Ms. Carter to the floor" as was stated in the charges. She was merely a victim of gravity as Ms. Carter tripped over her own feet and dragged Delphina down with her.

The eyewitness testimony wasn't worth much because most of the patrons had been in some stage of inebriation when the trouble started or they simply weren't in a good position to see things clearly. But when the video was shown in court, with Dylan giving the play-by-play description and slowing and stopping the tape for emphasis, it was clear that Delphina, the party girl, the wild child and the borderline drunken defendant, had no control over what had happened. In a strange way she had been shown to be the victim. That was how the judge saw things too, and Delphina became the third, spoiled, troublesome Makris kid to go free.

The morning after Delphina's trial Dylan received emails from both Sophia's father, Damien and Delphina's father, Constantine. The sentiments were similar to the message Damien had sent him after Arlo's trial; thanks for everything he did to protect the family name and an expression of their wish to meet him and continue the association. The main difference this time was that while Beth had been copied on the message, John Finch hadn't.

Part of Dylan wanted Finch to know that his biggest clients continued to praise his work but another part was just as glad that he had been kept out of things. He decided right then to save the e-mails in case he'd need them in the future.

Those two cases, along with getting through a stressful half hour in a closed door meeting with Misty's angry and threatening boyfriend leading to him being charged and fined for his violation of the Protection from Abuse order had made for a damned good week for Dylan. He'd even managed to come up with new language for Lamar's sales agreement that he was certain would keep his friend out of liability trouble.

All of it should have been enough of a reason to slow down and catch his breath. He and Beth did manage to get out for a celebratory drink at a café near her apartment but that was the extent of it. He had a few other things on his Doyle and Finch plate and his moonlight workload was growing faster than he could handle. One of Misty's fellow dancers hired him to help her with a dispute with her landlord, Tommy Rizzo had referred two juicy-sounding divorce cases to him and, despite his usual misgivings about that kind of work, he'd reluctantly agreed to take them on. The other case involved the owner of a small bar on the strip in Mission Beach who wanted help with a zoning dispute with the city. Nothing too complicated and certainly not glamorous but the extra money was welcome to someone still waiting to make a partner-level income.

Somehow, while he was juggling all of the cases and all of the meetings he had also found time at night to work on his lucid dreaming skills and to experiment with dream sharing. He had gotten the lucid part down well enough that he was able to be aware and in control during some part of almost every dream. That alone made his nights more than a little interesting even though he felt he had yet to scratch the surface of what he could do in his dreams. The part of his journal that dealt with lucid dreaming had almost become a course for teaching it.

But now the dream sharing legend had made him far more interested in tapping into other people's minds.

He had decided to keep his lucid dreaming activities to himself so people didn't think he was an oddball, and it was even more important to keep the dream sharing just as secret. It was hard to imagine a person not feeling threatened if he ever talked to them about his interest in invading someone else's dreams, including theirs.

That evening he practiced his normal relaxation techniques but tried to stop at a certain point just before he felt himself falling asleep. He had no idea if that was a path that would lead him to another person's dreams. The chapter of the book on dream sharing was fairly vague. It was clear on the fact that, for many years, people believed that it happened but there was almost no information on exactly how.

He was in totally uncharted territory.

As he got closer to sleep the room had become totally dark. He was lying on his back, arms folded across his chest and he felt completely relaxed. For some reason he thought back to a *Philosophy and Religion* class he had taken in college, and a particular section of the course that dealt with Buddhism and the search for nirvana. He remembered learning that nirvana referred to the stillness of the mind after all feelings of desire and delusion had been overcome. The thing that struck him at the time was that everyone held some kind of delusions and they weren't always negative ones. And having feelings of desire wasn't something he ever wanted to give up. It just felt too damned good. All in all it was an interesting class but he'd decided then that reaching nirvana wasn't for him. Maybe he'd find an acceptable alternative.

For about an hour he laid there in the darkness enjoying a doobie. When he finished it he cleared his mind, alternating between relaxed awareness and a near-sleep level. Sleep finally took over.

FADE IN
INTERIOR – McHALES – NIGHT

It's about seven o'clock, the happy hour crowd has left and the evening crowd hasn't yet arrived. Many of the tables are crowded but there are only a few people sitting at the bar. Dylan sits on his favorite stool drinking bourbon and looking through the menu for what will be his Tuesday night dinner. A well-dressed couple approaches the bar, looking around the room as if they are unfamiliar with the place.

GARRET LEWIS: Excuse me, we aren't from around here and we were wondering if the food is good in this place.

DYLAN: Yeah, it's very good, nothing fancy, just good, old fashioned pub-grub but still really tasty.

GARRET: Thanks, I guess we'll consider that an endorsement.

The couple sits at the bar two stools down from Dylan. They look through the menu together and when the bartender approaches they order two glasses of Cabernet. The bartender gives them an odd look, nods and walks away to pour their drinks. Garret turns toward Dylan.

GARRET: Excuse me, I'm Garret Lewis and this is my wife, Anne.

DYLAN: Nice to meet you both, I'm Dylan Ward.

GARRET: This seems like a great place, kind of a classic pub or tavern feel to it.

DYLAN: Yeah, it's sort of my regular spot. It's not fancy but then, neither am I.

ANNE: I love this classic old bar. It looks like it's a hundred years old.

DYLAN: Good guess, it's been here since right after World War One. It was built in San Francisco and shipped here on horse-drawn wagons. They literally built the walls of the building around it.

ANNE: Fascinating.

GARRET: So, Dylan, what do you do for a living?

DYLAN: I'm an attorney at Doyle and Finch here in San Diego.

GARRET: Oh, I've heard of them, a first-class firm, very impressive reputation.

DYLAN" Yeah, they're a good bunch of people, the best business lawyers anywhere.

Anne looks over the small menu and the bartender returns with their wine. As he places it in front of the Lewis's the glare from a light over the bar hits their glasses and flashes across Dylan's face.

GARRET: Listen, Dylan, if you don't mind talking shop for a few minutes, what's your background in helping clients with major real estate investments?

DYLAN: What do you mean by *major?*

GARRET: Oh, let's say fifty million and up.

DYLAN: Interesting, that's pretty much in my wheelhouse. I've been doing that kind of deal for going on six years.

GARRET: So, if I was here in San Diego and I was looking to find a local attorney to represent my interests on a potential acquisition, you would be someone who could help me.

DYLAN: Oh, hell yes. Pardon my French. Since I joined Doyle and Finch most of my work has been handling REITs and pension fund investments. I can't really call it glamorous work or anything like that but I really get a lot of satisfaction from bringing people into situations that will give them security and a solid financial future.

GARRET: Very interesting. How well do you know the local market?

ANNE: Excuse me, honey. Have you looked at the menu? I'm not seeing anything too healthy. Maybe we should just finish our wine and go somewhere else for dinner.

GARRET: Give me a few minutes, okay? I'll check out the menu after Dylan and I are finished. So again, Dylan, how well do you know the local market?

DYLAN: Well, I have three of the major office brokers on my go-to team, along with the best apartment and condo guy in town and my retail guy always gives me the first look at whatever he comes up with.

GARRET: It sounds like you and I should meet and talk while I'm in town.

DYLAN: That'd be great, but I always like my first meeting with a client to be somewhere besides my office. It's just so stuffy and, you know, *lawyerly* there. I sometimes feel like that office just holds me back. I like to meet a potential client someplace where he or she feels comfortable.

GARRET: I like the way you think, and truth be told, I always feel a little uncomfortable in a lawyer's office. No offense intended, but lawyers are usually too tight-ass for me.

DYLAN: Me too, and I have to work with those guys every freaking day!

GARRET: Okay, we'll be here for a couple of days. Here's my card. Call me and we'll set up a place and time.

DYLAN: Sounds good. Here's my Doyle and Finch card but I'm also going to give you this one. This is my cellphone number and my personal email address. It's the card I use for client's that demand something extra in privacy and talking to me without all of the Doyle and Finch background noise. And also it's a way to streamline the fees.

GARRET: Dylan, I gotta' say, you sound like my kind of lawyer.

DYLAN: I'll be whatever kind of lawyer I need to be.

FADE OUT

CHAPTER 9

You can get me high, you can get me low, but you can't tell
me how to live my life you know. As certain as it seems,
I think you might agree. Well, is this real life or is this
just another dream? Yeah, it's just another dream.

From the song *Just Another Dream* by Stick Figure

HOW MANY PEOPLE HAVE DREAMED of turning a hobby into a career? Like the guy with a wood shop in his garage who dreams of becoming the next big thing in the furniture business. Or the woman who gives interior decorating advice to her friends and neighbors with the thought that she deserves her own show on *HGTV*. Or maybe it's the guy who tinkers every night in his basement trying to invent the new kitchen gadget that no home in America will be complete without.

It was a very interesting moment, a moment with more than a little angst and even embarrassment, when it just hit Dylan that he was a man whose hobby was dreaming. And that realization wasn't really all that far from thinking that he was a man whose hobby was sleeping. He had a good education, he worked hard all day and beyond that, much of his time was spent lying in bed sound asleep. As much as his lucid dreaming had provided him with pleasure and satisfaction, it wasn't something that produced any kind of tangible by-product, at least not yet. He'd wake up in the morning, look around and see nothing he could point to and say, "Hey, look what I did."

If someone asked him, "So, what do you do when you're not being a lawyer?" how would he respond? Maybe he'd say, "Oh, I dream about chasing women." Or maybe, "I dream about having a real personal life." And probably the saddest answer of all would be, "I dream about being in control of my life." Whatever answer he could come up with would be a bit sad and even pathetic. And if he was able to figure out a way to learn dream sharing what would his answer to that question be? Maybe he'd say, "I intrude into other people's dreams because mine aren't interesting enough."

It was obvious that, given his current life circumstances there was no good way to answer that question.

But despite the mixed feelings that came with his dreaming he couldn't stop thinking that his sleep skills had some kind of value, something that could lead to some kind of monetary gain if he could find an audience for it. His journal carefully documented everything he'd tried and learned, everything that had led to his mastering lucid dreaming. The more he flipped through the pages the more he realized it was an owner's manual for dreamers that could teach others how to control their dreams.

Maybe what had seemed like a poor excuse for a hobby could turn into something he'd be proud of, something he could profit from. It was something worth looking into.

He had a gut feeling he was getting close to figuring out dream sharing and he fought the urge to roll over and go back to sleep. He'd have to put it off for a while.

Sitting in traffic on his morning commute gave him time to look around the inside of his truck and realize once again that it wasn't exactly an example of modern automotive technology. While everyone he knew was driving a car with touch-screen navigation or voice-activated features his Silverado was pretty much just basic transportation.

Beth often talked about how she could synch her cellphone to her car to get her messages on the screen in the dash. Dylan's version of that feature was half a dozen yellow Post-It notes stuck to various parts of the dashboard, carefully placed where they wouldn't block the gauges. He had to wait until he was stopped at a traffic light or parked somewhere before he could reread the messages and punch the numbers into his phone. It was a crude, low-tech system that worked in the most rudimentary way but it was also a reminder of how much he needed to make more money.

He got to the parking lot at the office and before he got out of the truck he checked his phone. There were three old messages from the previous day that he hadn't yet answered and, surprisingly, another four messages that were left during the twenty-five minute drive from his house. All four were from moonlight clients.

That was the moment when he realized he needed a better way to categorize those odd but still important people. Calling them moonlight clients was a label that made them seem of secondary value when, in fact, they were people who mattered, people who, despite the way society might view them, were still people who needed his help.

Given his personal dislike for many of his Doyle and Finch clients, his other clients, the ones on the outside, were actually becoming more important to him.

It took him nearly half an hour, sitting there in his truck, to return the calls and emails. In doing so he pretty much committed most of his upcoming evenings to one kind of meeting or another. Full days at the office would be followed by hours of discussions and strategizing with Tommy Rizzo and the diverse cast of characters he had sent Dylan's way. Even though relaxing evenings at McHale's or at home would be his preference he knew the week ahead would offer some very interesting times. And he had to admit there was a part of him that was looking forward to it.

A very busy morning gave way to a take-out sandwich lunch in front of his computer and then a long afternoon of reviewing testimony and evidence in half a dozen different cases. By five-fifteen he was ready to shut things down and head out to meet with Tommy. While he was packing up his files and pulling on his suit coat his computer chimed with what he told himself would be the last message he'd read for the day. It turned out to be a big one.

Anne Carter had marked the message *Urgent* and it said, "Dylan, we have to reschedule this Tuesday's meeting to complete your annual review. Mr. Finch isn't feeling well and will be taking next week off. I will contact you to reschedule when he returns. Sorry for the inconvenience."

Despite the craziness of his schedule and the time he'd been spending on his dream experiments, he had built a solid presentation to give to Finch about his qualifications for partnership. He had a well-reasoned, detailed argument that he felt was so good Finch would have no way to respond with anything less than making Dylan the newest Doyle and Finch principal. Now he was back to waiting. Six long years of working hard and priming himself for success and now he was back stuck in neutral because one old man was feeling ill. Finch had never given him an explanation as to why the partners committee wouldn't be conducting his review and Dylan regretted that he never asked him for a reason.

It was too late for that now and he was stuck with the circumstances. His frustration would last at least another week.

Dylan's taste in restaurants and bars wasn't limited just to places like McHale's. There were several places he enjoyed visiting when the food selection was important or if he was meeting a Doyle and Finch client. Tommy Rizzo, on the other hand, had tastes that were, to put it kindly, more basic. Their last restaurant meeting had been Dylan's choice and they ate at *Driftwood,* a nice but reasonably priced seafood café near Balboa Park. Tommy complained that it was too fancy so Dylan had agreed to let him pick their next gathering spot. Now Dylan was on his way to meet Tommy at *Cal Zone,* a small diner that gave new meaning to the term "greasy spoon".

It was a twenty-minute drive and a fifteen-minute search for a parking place somewhere he could be halfway certain his truck would be safe and sitting there when he got back to it.

Tommy was already sitting in a booth at the back of the cramped dining room and waved to Dylan as he stood by the entrance, looking around and trying to take in what passed for ambience. The black and white vinyl tiled floor had seen better days as had the red vinyl chairs and booths that covered most of it. "Hey, Dylan, glad you could make it. Welcome to my favorite place."

They shook hands and as he sat down across the table from Tommy, Dylan said, "So this is where you're sitting half the times you call me."

"Yeah, nice, huh? It's not fancy like the places you prefer but it reminds me of when I was living in Philadelphia. The pizza and calzones are great and the beer is cheap. And tonight is sausage night."

"Yep, I knew that the moment I walked in."

"And the best part is you won't have to worry about runnin' into any of those snobs you work with at your office."

Dylan looked over at the patrons who filled every barstool and around him at the people sitting at the tables. "You're right about that."

Tommy leaned forward, his elbows on the table, glancing left and right like a man who had spent a lifetime making sure he hadn't been followed. "So, did you get a chance to read the stuff I sent you?"

"Yeah, I read through it kind of quickly and I'll dig into it deeper when I get home, but from what I could tell both of your clients have pretty good cases on their husbands but there are a couple of loose ends you'll need to tie down before we can file anything."

"Loose ends!" I thought I came up with two pretty good trails of evidence for you to follow. And the pictures, I got the best pictures of those guys anyone could ask for. The one of the guy reachin' down and checkin' his zipper outside the hotel lobby, that was detective Hall of Fame shit." When Tommy got the least bit upset his voice went up a couple of octaves and he'd wring his hands like he was washing them. His slick, drugstore-dyed black hair framed a round face that always seemed to show a slight shine of nervous perspiration when he got excited.

"Relax," Dylan replied, "I'm just talking small stuff here, nothing major. You did a great job at logging movements and activities that are definitely not part of their normal routines and that's always important in raising red flags to a judge. But I have to present the facts of the case in a way that makes sure there is no room for their attorneys to see one thing and call it something else."

"Okay, there's a whole lot of fee ridin' on these two cases so tell me what you need."

"I'll do that and get back to you tomorrow. What I'll need first is a little more background on the wives. We need to make them look like loving and loyal partners to their neglectful, philandering husbands. If either of them has a skeleton in the closet I need to know that going in."

"Look, they each called me sayin' they suspected their husband of having an affair. I met with them, taped our conversations, wrote up a whole bunch of notes on their husband's backgrounds, habits, hangouts and that kind of shit. It's what I do. I spent a lot of time with my binoculars and my camera and I think you'd agree by the size of the files I gave you I got some great shit to use against them. And by the way, did you get a good look at the pictures of Mr. Brainard's girlfriend? Woof. He's riskin' his marriage and his money on that dog?"

Tommy's enthusiasm for the sometimes slimy work he did was strangely admirable. He was a man who was comfortable dealing with things that made most people squirm and, whether Dylan cared to admit it or not, Tommy's work usually led to better days for his clients and money for the people he chose to work with him.

"Yeah," Dylan said, "I saw them and all I can say is love, or maybe in this case lust makes a man do strange things."

"Right, so what do you need on the wives? I can't just go to them and ask them if they've ever screwed around on their husbands. The wives aren't my targets, the husbands are. I'm a professional and I have to conduct myself in a certain manner."

Dylan managed to stifle a smirk and said, "I realize that and don't worry. Before we go to court I'll be sitting down with each of them and I'll ask some questions, very carefully I might add, for the sole purpose of keeping the opposing attorneys from blindsiding us. I just wondered if you knew anything that could be a starting point."

"I don't think there's much there for you to worry about. Joanna Brainard is a class lady and to tell you the truth I was thinkin' that, once you get her a nice settlement I just might try to get together with her and ease her pain a little, if you know what I mean. And Lauren Cox seems really solid. She even teaches Sunday school so you should bring that up in the conversation someplace. A little of that religion crap goes a long way."

"Religion crap? Why, Tommy, I'm shocked to hear those words from a good Italian Catholic boy like you."

Tommy flashed a smile that was both snarky and sheepish. "Yeah, it's funny, but after all those years of parochial school and nuns and bein' an altar boy, not one piece of that stuff ever stuck to me. Lucky me, huh?"

They ordered dinner, if a sausage and pepper calzone could be called a dinner, drank a few beers and went through the rest of the details they'd be using to build the cases for the two women.

Despite having the outward appearance of being a flake, Tommy had a way of methodically building an evidence file. Every note, voice recording and photograph was carefully marked with an electronic time and date stamp. He didn't go out of his way to get salacious or explicit photographs of his targets, although Dylan knew he had still managed to get his share of them. Tommy was more concerned about documenting a pattern of behavior, a pattern that was foreign to the target's normal routine and lifestyle. A long list of small things that were out of place in a person's life could be as damning as any lewd photograph if the lawyer was willing to work it that way.

Dylan was willing, and it proved to be very successful. In an odd way, Tommy had become a great partner to him.

They ended their little meeting around eight o'clock and when Dylan got back to his truck he was relieved to find that nothing had happened to it. A half an hour later he was home and settled into a chair in front of the television, With the help of a quickly wrapped doobie he'd begun working on another night of trying to shed himself of the stress of the office so he could welcome the almost certain adventure of sleep.

With lucid dreaming now a regular part of his sleep pattern he had to keep working on a way, if there was one, to master dream sharing. The key, he had come to realize, was reaching the exact point where the mind relaxation that might allow him to be drawn into another person's dreams and then maintaining that state without going further into actual sleep.

His normal bedtime ritual had evolved into an elaborate series of tasks and mind exercises all of which he'd written into *Dreamware*. It started in the living room with a couple of tokes of weed or a double shot of bourbon and sometimes both. He'd step into the hallway and set the thermostat at exactly seventy-four degrees, no more and no less. In the bathroom he brushed his teeth and stripped down to his underwear. Then things moved into the bedroom where he pulled down the shades, put the ceiling fan on a low setting that made a quiet, soothing rhythm, set the alarm clock for six-thirty and arranged the four bed pillows into a tight arc around the area where he laid his head.

When everything was set he crawled into bed and laid on his back, his head buried in the pillows, the sheet and blanket neatly pulled up to his shoulders, his hands folded across his chest and his legs fully extended with his feet crossed, right on left.

When his sleep environment was exactly the way he wanted it he laid there and began the careful, regular breathing pattern he had practiced so many times. With his eyes closed he focused his mind on the image of a small, white flower. Nothing else mattered. Nothing else was allowed to intrude on his thoughts. That flower was everything, the only thing that mattered. He could feel the day's tension draining away, replaced by a deep calmness and serenity. The flower floated above him as if locked in place by his mind.

Time passed but there was no drowsiness, just a quiet and focused relaxation. Somehow it felt like a whole new state of mind.

FADE IN
DOYLE AND FINCH OFFICES – INTERIOR – DAY

A group of three attorneys, a financial advisor, a client and an assistant are seated around a large conference table, staring at their laptops and discussing a plan to market and sell Maquina Corporation, the client's large and valuable manufacturing company. The meeting has already lasted more than two hours and the frustration on the part of the participants is becoming increasingly clear as the clock continues to tick.

MAXWELL DEWART: Okay, we've been talking and studying and talking some more and we're stuck in neutral. Dave, I'll say it again. You've got what I see as a very solid offer from Hastings and based on everything I've been able to dig up on the other potential buyers this is the best deal you're going to get.

DAVID MONTOYA: I know you feel that way, Maxwell, you've said it a dozen times but it still seems to me that something is missing here, something we've left out of our trophy case to make our CIM look a lot shinier. I refuse to leave any money on the table when I accept an offer.

MAXWELL: Believe me, I've put together enough Confidential Information Memorandums to know what to include and I can't imagine anything that's not on the list. I know your operation top to bottom and front to back. If there is anything of value to Hastings it's already in the CIM.

DAVID: The Hastings offer isn't substantially different from the other two we got back and of the three companies, Hastings has by far the deepest pockets. The way I see it their offer is light by at least fifteen to twenty million.

MAXWELL: I disagree. We ran comparisons to the valuations of your four main competitors and, surprisingly, all of you are very close in every criteria we use to make a pitch to a buyer.

DAVID: And we've run our own numbers as well, and I'm telling you the offer is light.

MAXWELL: Dave, I don't know what else we can do to convince you to take the deal.

There's a pause in the conversation as the conference room door opens and Dylan Ward steps in. He stands by the door for a moment, smiling and scanning the room. The lawyers at the table appear to be surprised as Maxwell looks up and sees him.

MAXWELL: This is a private meeting, Dylan. You've got the wrong conference room.

DYLAN: No, this is the right room.

The large, ornate light fixture hanging above the table flickers slightly and then flashes a bright beam of light across the gleaming, mahogany table top.

MAXWELL: We're working on an acquisition here and that's hardly your kind of case. Please leave now.

DYLAN: Don't be so quick there, Max. I think Mr. Montoya deserves every possible bit of advice we can offer him.

MAXWELL: What do you mean by we? You're out of your element here. This is business law not traffic court.

DAVID MONTOYA: Maxwell, at this point in the process I'm ready to hear just about anything that will make me feel that we haven't missed something. So, young man, may I call you Dylan?

DYLAN: Of course, David.

DAVID: Then have a seat and tell me what you have that the rest of the group has somehow missed.

Dylan takes a seat at the far end of the table and ignores the stares and unfriendly looks from Max and the other lawyers. He opens his laptop, punches a few keys and then leans forward, looking straight at Montoya.

DYLAN: Okay, I've looked over your file. From what I can see Max and his team have done a fairly good job putting together the CIM and I've seen the IOI that came back from Hastings. It's a good offer but not a great one and I think we can do better.

MAXWELL: And when you say *we*, does that include you?

DYLAN: Let's not get territorial here, Max. We need to focus on David's deal. He has put his entire life into building Maquina and it's our job to get every possible dollar into his pocket.

DAVID: You have my attention, Dylan, let's hear what you've come up with.

DYLAN: Okay, let's get one thing clear. I tend to look at things through a different prism than Max and the rest of his team. I tend to look for things that are, shall we say, hiding in plain sight.

DAVID: And you found something hiding in Maquina?

DYLAN: Yes, I did. The value of the IOI from Hastings is based on the CIM that Max's team gave them. Since that was all they were given that's all they could use for the valuation. But I believe there's something hidden inside your Leisure Products Division that could be a game changer.

MAXWELL: Oh, come on, Dylan. We dug really deep into Leisure Products. It's a secondary piece of Maquina that's been steady but unremarkable for the past five years. There are tons of other companies making sporting goods and camping equipment.

DYLAN: Yes, that's true, but there's something hiding there and you guys didn't find it.

DAVID: Okay, you keep saying that. How about getting to the point.

DYLAN: Okay. Let's all think about what goes into making all those tent frames, backpack frames, fishing poles and all the other outdoor equipment that you guys sell. The common denominator is they all include composites. When everyone else was doing G10 fiberglass and FR4 extrusions you guys had already moved on to carbon fiber and carbon fiber reinforced polymers. And you didn't just use the stuff, you designed the machines that extruded it and you even spit it out of 3-D printers. David, am I correct in saying you have all the proprietary rights to your processes?

DAVID: Yes, they are ours and ours alone and the patents are airtight. Everything is sitting in our Coachella plant.

DYLAN: Bingo, there it is.

MAXWELL: What do you mean? Where what is?

DYLAN: If Hastings wants to make fishing poles with your factory, God bless them. But your equipment patents have an enormous value unto themselves. Anyone who's in the drone manufacturing business would pay a fortune for them.

MAXWELL: How did we get from fishing poles to drones?

DYLAN: It's all hiding in plain sight, David.

DAVID: We aren't in the drone business, Dylan.

DYLAN: I know that, and neither is Hastings, but sooner or later someone in their R&D group is going to see what's there. Drones have to be strong and lightweight, and Maquina has been doing strong and lightweight longer and better than anyone. You do frame extruding and flat sheet extruding and you do custom forming. Some aerospace company or even the military will be willing to pay a lot of dough for what's sitting there in Coachella.

DAVID: So what do you suggest?

MAXWELL: David, let's slow down here, I…

DAVID: Hold it, Maxwell, I asked Dylan, not you.

DYLAN: In a nutshell I'm saying fuck the fishing poles. I suggest that you regroup and stall on Hastings' offer until you can get an accurate take on what you have and what it might be worth. Then you lay it on them and say, "Put up or shut up."

There is silence in the room as everyone around the table looks at Maxwell for his reaction. David Montoya's expression is particularly intense and his glaring eyes are an obvious counter to Maxwell's dazed expression. The other lawyers turn toward their laptop screens, feigning interest in anything other than getting involved in the uncomfortable conversation. Maxwell clears his throat, looks at David but says nothing.

DAVID: Well, Dylan, this meeting sure changed course when you walked in. Why is it I haven't seen you around the office on my previous visits?

DYLAN: Oh, that's probably because they keep me on a short leash down the hall.

DAVID: Well from now on I'm going to insist they let you work off the leash and on my behalf.

The expression on Max's face in reaction to David's comment is a mix of confusion and rage. The light fixture over the table flickers again and Dylan sees the flash reflected on the gloss of the wood table. He feels a slight dizziness.

FADE OUT.

CHAPTER 10

Dreamers live on dangerous ground. They speak their
feelings right out loud. They talk about love when hate is
strong. They keep the faith when all hope is gone.

From the song *Can't Stop a Dreamer* by Cyrill Neville

THERE ARE SO MANY MEMORABLE things that occur in
a person's life, especially those "firsts" that you never seem to
forget. You make a mental list of things you know you'll always
remember, like your first kiss and your first broken heart. You can't ever
forget your first car, when you move into your first apartment or your first
day at your first job.

Dylan had his own share of memorable firsts but as he lay in bed that
morning, staring at the ceiling he struggled to decide if his previous night's
dream activity should be added to his list. Something about it felt totally
different from every one of the thousands of dreams he'd enjoyed in his life.
It was hard to comprehend but somehow it was as though he had been in
on something that happened to someone else, like he was both the audience
and the actor. It wasn't really sleeping or at least he didn't think so.

As much as his mastery of lucid dreaming had taken him to a different
level while he slept, what happened in the previous night's dream seemed
to be every bit as profound in its effect on him.

Ever since he'd read about dream sharing it had intrigued him as
much as it made him uneasy. There were so many legends and so much
anecdotal evidence that it could actually happen but there wasn't one
shred of scientific research or clinical data that proved it was real. His
professional life had been built on a foundation of facts and precedence,

of decisions based upon previous events and things that came before. By comparison, dream sharing was like pulling something out of thin air and declaring it to be real.

But the feeling he had that morning seemed very, very real and he couldn't quite decide how he felt about it.

He was running a bit behind schedule and given what had transpired in his dream he shouldn't have been so surprised when he made it to the office and nearly got knocked over in the lobby by a very manic and distracted Max Dewart.

"Geez, Dylan, watch where you're going."

"I could say the same thing to you, Max. What's your hurry?"

The expression on Max's face had changed from his normal aloofness to one of obvious irritation. "It's none of your concern."

Even though the two of them had learned to keep their distance and maintain a minimal level of civility Max's behavior seemed to shout that something had changed. "Have a nice day." Dylan said, not even trying to mask his sarcastic tone.

During the workday Dylan had many clients to think about and many things to juggle, but not so many that the previous night's dream didn't intrude on his thoughts frequently and intensely. Before he'd left the house it was easy to be skeptical about what might have happened. He'd almost convinced himself it was all just wishful thinking. But when he walked through the front door of the office and Max acted the way he did, Dylan suddenly was convinced he had something that seemed connected to his dream. Maybe it was a coincidence. Max had always been an asshole and Dylan had learned to never really expect much from him in the way of anything beyond basic common courtesy.

But what if it was something more? What if there really was a connection to the dream, and what if the connection was that it was really Max's dream? Dylan was almost afraid to think about it.

It was around four-thirty when Beth walked into his office. Despite his desire to see her at numerous times during the day his workload had boxed him in and he'd split his time between his office and his truck. Lunchtime was only a visit to the restroom and a walk through the lounge to grab a leftover cupcake from someone's birthday celebration, one which apparently didn't include him on the invitation list. Seeing Beth immediately lifted his spirits.

She hesitated a moment before she said, "Hey there, I wasn't sure if I should stop by or not. It's like you've been hiding out here today." She sat down in a chair in front of my desk. "Is everything okay?"

"Yeah, everything's cool, I'm just trying to keep all the balls in the air."

She reached back and closed the door and then leaned forward. Her smile was almost a smirk and her raised right eyebrow hinted that he was about to hear something interesting. "Did you hear the news about Max Dewart?"

"No. I literally, physically ran into him in the lobby this morning but that was it. Why, did something happen?"

"Well, you've probably heard he's been working on this humongous sale of Maquina Corporation. It's like the only thing he's had on his plate for the last three months."

"I only know what I've read in the news and from some talking in the men's room. Max likes to get on his phone and conduct business while he sits in the stall. I know they have a plant in Mexico and two in California and the owner wants to divest himself of the whole thing. I also heard a rumor that somebody made him an offer."

That part was kind of a little white lie because Dylan knew it was more than a rumor. He had a strange penchant for going out of his way to track what Max was involved with. It was mostly on-going water-cooler chatter and keeping his ear to the ground as a way of understanding why the guy had been made partner ahead of him.

Beth continued her little piece of gossip. "From what I heard, Maquina had an offer from the Hastings Group and it was a done deal until this morning when Max pulled some eleventh hour move and told Hastings he had put the deal on hold. He never told the client, he just did it all on his own."

"Why did he pull the plug?

"I don't know all the details but I heard some scuttlebutt from Sarah because she helps out in Max's office. She said Max told Hastings they had to up their offer because Maquina's leisure products plant had the capabilities to build drones and that was worth a whole lot of money."

Dylan's mind began to race and he tried to keep his face expressionless. "Drones! How in the hell did he come up with that? From what I know all that division of Maquina makes is fishing poles and tents."

"I know, that's what Sarah said, and when the owner heard what Max did he hit the roof. He was all set to accept the Hastings offer and when Max told the people at Hastings about the drones they laughed him right out of the deal. They pulled their offer, Maquinas is back to square one and our management committee is pissed. Max is in some deep doo-doo on this one."

Dylan leaned back in his chair and stared at the ceiling. Somehow he managed to maintain an appearance of calm control while he thought about how he should react to the news. What Beth had told him couldn't be anything less than proof that he had invaded Max's dream. The details were identical to his dream. Somehow he'd gotten into Max's head and steered the events every step of the way. It couldn't be anything but proof that dream sharing was possible and that he had actually done it. Damn, it felt so amazing.

"Hey, earth to Dylan, are you okay?"

"Oh, yeah, I'm sorry. I guess I was just trying to imagine how that all went down today. I wish I could have been a fly on the wall." The answer seemed to satisfy her. He leaned forward and looked her straight in the eye. "So did anybody say how Max came up with the drone idea? That's just so way out of left field."

"All Sarah said was that Max came into the office early this morning and he was all excited about some big idea he'd come up with last night and he was strutting around the office like he owned the place. Sarah heard him tell someone on the phone his idea was going to be worth like twenty million to the client."

Dylan must have been smirking because Beth paused for a moment, staring at him with a sort of suspicious look, and then she asked, "Okay, what is it? You have that same little knowing expression that you had when you came up with your idea for Arlo Makris. I've seen you look that way before and it always meant you had something up your sleeve." She paused again and then asked, "Come on, you had something to do with this, didn't you?"

He knew he had to dodge her question somehow. "Me? Hell no. Hey, until I walked into the lobby this morning and he almost ran me over I hadn't talked to him all week, except for a quick hello and a few words of small talk in the men's room yesterday. He must have had some kind of big brainstorm idea that he thought would work for his client. Besides, he looks down his nose at me. To him I'm just the traffic court lawyer down the hall."

"Yeah, I know, but I thought I was dropping a bombshell and you just don't seem to be all that surprised, that's all."

"Look, you know how I feel about that asshole. He's smug and arrogant and I've always figured sooner or later he'd get himself into a jam and it looks like this is it. I can't wait to see how it all plays out." It was definitely time for him to change the subject. "Hey, it's going on five, how about getting a drink with me on the way home?"

Her suspicious look returned along with the smile that always got to him. "Okay, but I reserve the right to bring up this subject again." She reached across his desk, grabbed his wrist and squeezed it. "I've been telling you ever since we first met. I can read your face and I can tell when there's more to the story than meets the eye."

He smiled back, with a feeling of closeness to her that he had missed since they'd stepped back from their relationship. He also felt a palpable nervousness about revealing anything specifically related to the previous night's dream and about dream sharing in general "Fair enough," he answered.

They decided that they needed a change of scenery from their usual McHale's meeting spot so they met at a place she suggested that was near her apartment, *Gastrique*, a small bistro with a beautiful patio bar. She got there ahead of him and from the way the staff treated her he could tell she was a familiar face to them. They managed to get the last available table on the patio.

"Wow, this is a really nice place. How come you never brought me here before?" he joked.

"It's only been open for a month or two, and besides, you were always the one who wanted to pick the places we went to. I guess I was just too accommodating." Her smile and tone told him she was trying to make a larger point without actually saying the words.

The next hour or so was a total juggling act on Dylan's part. He was trying to focus on Beth and their conversation while his mind continually drifted into the realm of lucid dreaming, dream sharing and what he had managed to pull off with Max Dewart. In just one night his dreaming had changed from being innocent recreation to a way of manipulating another person's life. What had been a sort of pathetic hobby for him now seemed to be something more edgy, even dangerous and it was hard not to think about it.

It was even harder to quell his urge to do it again.

Between appetizers and sharing a bottle of a very nice Pinot Noir, he and Beth managed to have the kind of relaxing time they used to share. But he knew he could only juggle things for so long and when he was sipping the last bit of his second glass of wine she finally called him out.

"Okay," she said, her smirk back and firmly planted on her face, "let's have it."

"Have what? What do you mean?"

"I mean I know your caseload and everything you're working on and even most of what you have going on with Tommy. None of it seems like it's a big deal or anything to worry about but I've been sitting here with you, watching you and it's like only half of you is here. There's something churning behind those eyes, something that has some kind of hold on you."

He thought how it was both comforting and unsettling that she could read him so well. Under any other circumstances he probably would have enjoyed the feeling. "Holy shit, I'm just trying to put my workday behind me and relax. What are you talking about?"

"I'm talking about things like you've made the exact same comment about the wine three times. I'm talking about how you've complimented me on my new haircut twice and said how good the shrimp skewers are more times than I care to count. Come on, what's going on in that head of yours?"

He knew he was in a face-off with someone who could read him like a book. "Okay," he started, pausing to choose his words carefully, "you're right, I'm more than a little preoccupied with this deal about Max. In fact, last night I actually had a dream with him in it and it kind of creeped me out. I mean I can't stand the guy and when I hear that he's in trouble I feel like celebrating."

"You had a dream about Max?"

"Well, don't make it sound weirder than it is. You know I'm a big dreamer and the timing of the two things just seems like one strange, fucking coincidence." That little explanation didn't begin to tell her what actually had happened but it was as far as he was prepared to take it.

Beth took a small sip of wine and looked at him over the top of her glass. "I have to tell you I'm not exactly surprised that there's a dream involved."

"Why do you say that?"

"Because you're a dreamer like nobody I've ever known and sometimes I wonder if you ever take things from your dreams and inadvertently mix them into your real world."

Beth knew nothing about the success he'd been having with lucid dreams or his fascination with dream sharing, and he knew that telling her more about his new obsession would make him look pathetic, odd or scary. His only option was to deflect the conversation toward another topic.

"Okay, I know my dreaming is unusual and you know from being with me that it's simply a part of my world that I've learned to accept. This dream and the situation with Max is just something that struck me in a very strange way. I'm sorry if I've been in a fog tonight." He paused, trying to get a read on her mood and then blurted out, "I have a strange urge to kiss you right now."

His desperate attempt to change the subject couldn't have been more successful. Beth was silent, staring into his eyes with an expression that was both accepting and cautious. "What, now? Here?"

"Well, yeah. I'm sure the manager wouldn't kick us out for a small public display of affection. That is, if you wouldn't mind."

She smiled and asked, "Do you remember the last time we kissed?"

He paused, caught off guard with her question, and after a few seconds he answered, "Yeah, it was at your apartment. We were standing by the front door and I was getting ready to leave after we decided to take a breather."

"Right, and I'm glad you didn't say it was after we decided to break up because I never looked at it that way."

"Neither have I." Almost as if on cue they both leaned forward. Their lips met and neither of them tried to pull away, even after the kiss had lasted long enough for a woman at an adjacent table to stare at them. Finally they leaned back in their chairs and just smiled at each other.

"I've missed that," Beth said softly.

"So have I, along with a lot of other things." He wondered if she got the meaning of his comment but if she did she didn't offer any sign. Her lack of a response told him to drop the subject.

As they finished their bottle of wine they made small talk, mostly work-related, and Dylan tried to be more focused on their conversation but the dream he'd shared with Max broke into his thoughts more than once. With the hectic workday he'd had that had immediately shifted into Happy Hour with Beth, he hadn't had much time to really absorb what he'd done or what it all meant.

Part of him wanted to linger at the table, look into her eyes and see where the mood might take them. But another part of him, a bigger part, wanted to be alone to, sit back and figure out exactly what he'd done to gain access to Max's dream and how, once he was in, he managed to control the outcome.

Whatever the little sign was that his mind was wandering again was big enough for Beth to notice and she shrugged and said, "Okay, I guess we should wrap things up and call it a night."

He could tell from the tone of her voice that she knew his concentration was once again getting fuzzy. He felt embarrassed and he hoped he hadn't hurt her feelings. He hesitated for a moment as he looked into her eyes, and then said "Beth, I know I'm usually better company than I've been tonight but please see it for what it is. I love every minute I spend with you, every single one. But I'm juggling stuff at the office and with my moonlighting and on top of that John Finch will be back at the office tomorrow so my review will be happening soon."

The things that he told her were distracting him didn't begin to equal the distraction of his dream sharing.

Beth looked at him, moved the empty bottle of wine to the side and reached to hold his hands in hers. She didn't say anything for a moment and Dylan felt a nervousness that seemed foreign to their usual laid-back relationship. Finally she said, "Dylan, when we kissed tonight it kind of re-lit the flame for me. I know you're going through a lot right now but maybe you should think about not going through it alone."

"I felt the same thing, like kissing you was the most normal and natural thing I could do."

Beth smiled and squeezed his hands. "So, like I said, let's call it a day, but I think we need to clear our calendars and find some time to talk and see where we stand and where we want things to go. It's like you told me once, you're tired of just dancing."

Dylan leaned forward, Beth followed his lead and they shared another lingering public kiss. They paid their check and walked to Beth's car with their arms around each other. After another long and more passionate kiss they each headed for home.

The evening's events and the rekindling of his feelings for Beth hadn't really come as a surprise to him. They had always been there, clumsily buried beneath a pile of excuses. Like she had said at dinner, she never viewed their split as a break-up, merely a breather.

He'd felt the same way. He felt a strange sense of relief that they'd finally recognized something that should have been obvious. Maybe, he hoped, he could stop worrying about a relationship that was more real than he'd dared to hope for and he could concentrate on his career and his future advancement, like any of hid colleagues would.

Those thoughts faded quickly, replaced by his near-obsession with dream sharing.

Half an hour later he was in his bedroom leafing through the pages of *Dreamware.* He'd made an ongoing effort to keep the contents organized and the result was impressive. It read like a textbook. It was clearly the framework for a course, maybe something online like a website or a podcast.

He carried the binder back into the living room, sat down and spent the next half hour reading his previous notes. He also made sure to add his observations related to the dream that Max had and that he successfully invaded. Even though it had been his one and only experience with dream sharing he was convinced he was on to something very real and he started to create a separate section of notes to cover it.

He leaned back and stared up at the ceiling, trying to get his head around where his dreams had led him. *Dreamware* had grown from countless nights of dreaming and countless days of thinking about them. The old country song *Wasted Days and Wasted Nights* popped into his head. But the possibilities of marketing his idea seemed endless. Who wouldn't love to control his or her dreams? Who wouldn't jump at the chance to get inside someone else's mind and share a dream?

The potential for finding pleasure and adventure were very real. But so was the potential to do harm.

When he reached a logical point to end his notes he walked back into the bedroom and went through his nightly ritual. Finally he got into bed and laid there in his usual dream-inducing position, feeling relaxed and receptive.

The swirl of emotions and increasingly blurred events of the evening slowly transitioned back to thoughts about how he had invaded Max's dream. He knew it was Max who'd initiated the dream and the one who'd ended it. It seemed clear that in dream sharing it was the dreamer who got a person into the dream and then got him out of it. Max had simply thought of Dylan at the precise, right moment and that was when he brought him into the action. After Dylan was in it was easy for him to control things with his lucid dreaming skills. The dizziness he'd felt at the end of the dream was a new wrinkle. He wondered if it was his cue that Max's dream was ending.

He tried to remember every detail of what he had done the previous night to get his mind into the proper state of readiness to be drawn into another person's dream. As buzzed as he felt from wine and bourbon he knew it was the lure of dream sharing that had him spinning. He went so far as to recount, word for word, what the dream legend book had said about preparing oneself for the journey. Then he began the deep, rhythmic breathing that was part of the preparation.

It didn't take him long to once again find himself in the strange place between being awake and being asleep.

FADE IN
INTERIOR – A SMALL, TRENDY APARTMENT – NIGHT-TIME

A young woman clad in short pajama bottoms and a tank top, walks carefully from room to room, turning off lights as she talks on her cellphone.

BETH: I know, Sarah, I really want to go but I still don't know if I can afford it. There's the hotel and rental car and we'll have to eat every meal in a restaurant and you know how expensive they are in that area.

SARAH GAVIN: Yeah, I know, but we're talking Wine Country, Sonoma, Pasa Robles. It's like a magical place and we really need to see it. We have to commit to the reservations by tomorrow or we lose the discount.

BETH: I know. Let me sleep on it and I'll call you tomorrow, okay?

SARAH: Okay, but remember this is supposed to be our Girls Weekend and if you back out Michelle and Amy might too.

BETH: I'll probably go but I just want to think about the money again, that's all.

SARAH: Okay, talk to you tomorrow. Night-night.

Beth clicks off her phone and walks into the kitchen. As she takes a bottle of water from the refrigerator she hears a knock on the front door. She looks at the clock above the sink and sees that it's ten-forty-five, way too late for visitors. She nervously walks to the door, peers through the peephole and sees Dylan standing there. She sighs and turns the deadbolt and then opens the door.

BETH: Let me guess, you were just in the neighborhood and decided to stop by.

DYLAN: Yeah, something like that.

BETH: It's kind of late, don't you think?

DYLAN: Well, I won't stay. I just wanted to see you for a minute.

She smiles and steps back to let him enter the room. He looks at her and notices the flash of a neighbor's headlights through the window blinds as he closes the door behind him.

BETH: You must have had a busy day. I walked by your office a bunch of times but you weren't around.

DYLAN: Yeah, I was downtown at the courthouse all day. I had two pre-trial motions to file and I needed to talk to some people before I did it.

BETH: So what was it you wanted to see me about?

He steps toward her and puts his arms around her. She looks up at him with a curious expression as he pulls her tightly to his chest and kisses her square on the lips. She returns his embrace and their kiss becomes intense and passionate. Finally she pulls away, smiling, and stares into his eyes.

BETH: Is this what you wanted to see me about?

DYLAN: It's part of it.

He turns and steers her down the hallway to her bedroom. Neither of them speaks as they walk. They enter the bedroom and he begins to remove his shirt, then his shoes and jeans. She takes off her top and slips her pajama bottoms down to her ankles and kicks them to the floor.

DYLAN: This is what I wanted to see you about.

They embrace again and fall on to the bed. In moments they are both naked. He is on top of her as she looks up at him with a smile. They make love in a slow but intense way.

BETH: What took us so long?

He catches another flash of headlights out the window as he kisses her. He feels slightly dizzy.

FADE OUT

CHAPTER 11

Don't fall in love with a dreamer because he'll always take you in.
Just when you think you really changed him, he'll leave you again.
Don't fall in love with a dreamer because he'll break you every time.

From the song *Don't Fall in Live with a Dreamer*
by Kenny Rogers and Kim Carnes

WHEN DYLAN AWOKE THE NEXT morning he found himself staring at a bedroom ceiling that seemed different somehow. Even though the night had brought him a dream that he knew he would never forget he couldn't shake the feeling he'd done something wrong.

The dream had felt different. It wasn't just a dream about Beth. Given the way he had felt when he realized he had shared a dream with Max and actually controlled it the dream about Beth made him feel the same way. He was almost certain it had been her dream but he had slipped into it. And he'd felt the same dizzy feeling when Beth ended her dream. He figured it must be the key to making his exit.

Dream sharing was exciting but it also felt strangely perverse, as though he was violating other people by getting inside their minds. He lay there awhile, struggling to understand exactly how it worked and what it meant. And how he should feel about it.

It was his invasion of Max's dream that had led to the events at the office and Beth's curiosity about it. And it was her curiosity that had led to their sharing Happy Hour and that led to a kiss that might have meant nothing or everything. He and Beth had made love in her dream. He'd fully expected that sooner or later something like this would happen in reality. So much of their relationship had been undefined or unspoken. They were two people who had been in love before but never said the words, two people who wanted more from each other but couldn't say exactly what. In the nearly four months since they'd decided to step back from each other it had become clear that it was just a matter of time before they stepped forward again.

But that didn't justify his taking over her dream and the feeling that gave him was more than a little unsettling.

Dylan's dreaming had always been a big part of his life and now it looked as though it was actually steering it. It was as though he was going through the motions of his life just so he could get to the events of his dreams. Despite the pleasure he'd had with Beth in the dream he felt a sense of guilt for hacking the most personal thing another person can possess: the privacy of what goes on in the mind during sleep.

He sat up in bed and looked at the alarm clock. It was seven o'clock and he had such a huge workload he'd planned on getting to the office early. Most of the work was for his moonlight clients and he needed to use the firm's online library to research case law. That was definitely the kind of work he had to do with the office door closed. The rest of his workload consisted of a DUI, disorderly conduct and insurance fraud for three different Doyle and Finch clients. It was easy, almost formulaic kind of defense work but it still took time to do it right.

Despite his need to get into the office he closed his eyes and, for a moment, actually considered going back to sleep.

Reason prevailed and after a quick shower and combing through his closet for the last clean shirt from the drycleaner he got dressed, grabbed a banana to eat on the way and got into his truck. He'd forgotten to close the driver's side window and an overnight wind had blown his dashboard Post-It notes on to the floor. Any sense of organization had disappeared from his front-seat office.

About half an hour after he'd sat down at his desk a message popped up on his office e-mail. It was from Anne Carter and all it said was "Dylan, Mr. Finch has scheduled your annual review for 10:00 AM on Monday the eighteenth.

So there it was; an appointment that seemed more like a gauntlet that had been thrown down in front of him. He had been as prepared as he could be for the meeting but when Finch had taken his short leave of absence Dylan had put partnership things on the back burner and moved on to more immediate matters. Now it was back on his calendar for a few weeks down the road and he could already feel the stress returning.

A cup of coffee and a few minutes away from his computer seemed to be in order.

On his way to the lounge Dylan walked past Max Dewart's office. The lights were off and he couldn't help but wonder what was going on. Was Max being disciplined or was he simply taking some time off? Or had he been fired for his boneheaded handling of a very important client? Whatever it was, Dylan suddenly felt the same rush he'd felt when he'd first realized he had invaded Max's dream and orchestrated the entire mess. It was a large feeling of power mixed with a small feeling of guilt. Whatever it was he was eager to feel it again.

When he got back to his office Beth was sitting on a chair in front of his desk. She smiled as he walked in but her expression also seemed to have a sense of urgency to it. The lustful dream popped back into his mind. His years working in criminal law had helped him develop skills at masking his emotions and his real thoughts and something told him it was time to use those skills again. "Well, good morning." he said with a careful smile. "I was going to call you in a little while."

"I wasn't sure if I should barge in on you like this or call you but my feet kind of made their way down the hall." The urgent expression was still apparent.

"Well let me just say thank you to your feet." He paused a moment and then said, "I really had a nice time last night."

Beth leaned forward. "So did I, a very nice time, like we used to have before, well before." She hesitated for a moment and then leaned back and closed the door.

"Uh-oh," he said, "is that a sign there's something private coming?"

She seemed nervous and he smile had faded a bit. "Well, I had a dream last night, a very personal one and on my way to work this morning I decided to tell you about it."

"Why, because I'm the big dreamer?"

"Well, not just that but also because you were in the dream. In fact it was like you were in charge of the whole thing and it was romantic and sexy and, well, I dreamed we made love in my bed."

It was confirmation of what he'd suspected while he was still lying in bed earlier. The feeling of power he'd felt when he realized that he had hacked Max's dream came over him again but this time it was different. He hadn't intentionally tried to enter Beth's nighttime world any more than he had Max's but had been drawn into it nonetheless. He realized right then that he might have developed a power to control other people's dreams once he was in them but who the dreamer would be at any given time seemed totally random and beyond his control.

He knew that he had to respond to Beth in some way so he said, "Wow, I'd love to have a dream like that."

Her smile returned and her expression seemed more relaxed but she still seemed like she had something important to say. "It's just so weird that you had a dream about Max and then he got himself into trouble. And when we were talking about it you seemed so matter-of-fact with the whole thing, like you knew all about it. Then I had a dream last night after I got home and it was like a continuation of our evening together and you were sort of like controlling the whole thing."

She leaned closer and looked him straight in the eye. "Dylan, you have to tell me if there's something more to your dreaming than I realize, something more than just what you think about when you're sleeping."

When Beth had shown her curiosity about the dream involving Max, Dylan had managed to get himself off the hook but now that her own dream had involved him it would take more than a glib comment to satisfy her.

"No," he answered, paused and then continued," I think you're letting your imagination get the best of you. I dream a lot. You know it and everyone knows it. So something happens in a dream that kind of ties to things in real life and it's a strange coincidence. But that's all it is, a coincidence."

"That's what I told myself when I woke up from my dream this morning. But then I remembered what you told me about something you called lucid dreaming, where you could control a dream."

"Yeah, my own dreams, not yours or other people's"

She looked down at the desk and then straight at Dylan. "Look, I don't want you to think I'm being strange with all this. It's just that I know how big dreams are to you and when things in dreams start to happen for real I just get kind of creeped out, that's all."

"Fair enough. I'll tell you what, from now on I'll keep my dreams to myself and not talk about them. Deal?"

"Deal. And I'm sorry if I sounded like I was suspicious or something."

"Forget about it. No more dream talk from either one of us. Oh, and by the way, I have something for you. He stood up and pulled a key from his pocket. "I gave you this once before but you returned. It seems like it might be worth another try." He handed the key to her and she stood up and took it from his hand."

She smiled and said, "Wow, your house key. That's almost a commitment." She turned toward the door but before she opened it she smiled and said softly, "But just this one last comment. I really liked my dream last night."

Before he could reply she opened the door and headed down the corridor.

There was a wide variety of tasks on his calendar, both with firm-related cases and his moonlight clients. And of course his annual review was back on the front burner even though it was still two weeks out. Despite it all, he leaned back in his chair and allowed himself the luxury of a few minutes of personal thoughts about his dreaming and nothing else.

His promise to Beth to drop the subject of dreaming hadn't been made for any reason other than a way to cover his ass.

Things were happening and he was struggling to understand them. His dream world and real world had begun to drift into one another and he couldn't decide if that was a good thing or a bad thing.

And then there was *Dreamware,* with the potential to teach anyone how to hack into other people's dreams. Could he actually make it happen? What would it take to create the course materials? Could he really make money from it? And most importantly, if it worked, what could be the consequences, for him and anyone who took the course?

What would it be like to live in a world where a person's dreams were no longer private but accessible?

He thought again how he had entered the dreams of two people but only by chance. He had merely done the things he'd learned to put himself into a state of readiness, a state that might or might not lead to being drawn into someone's dream if a particular person was actually dreaming about him at that moment. The chances to get the timing right were very slim but the rewards made it worth the effort.

He remembered his earlier realization that over the years any number of people who knew him must have had a dream that included him. Totally random and with no consequences, or at least that was the way it used to be.

Maybe he should stop messing with dream sharing and just get back to lucid dreaming and controlling what went on in his own head. He focused on that thought for a moment and quickly said to himself, "Oh hell, no way."

Finally his caseload worked its way back to the front of his mind and for the next few hours he was strictly Dylan Ward, Attorney at Law. The Doyle and Finch cases seemed pretty straightforward; a couple of DUI charges, a small marijuana possession case and a domestic disturbance. Nothing he hadn't handled dozen of times before.

His moonlight cases looked to be more colorful and a bit more challenging and thanks to Tommy Rizzo there were more of them coming in the near future. A referral from Dylan's stripper client, Misty, was the case of a fellow dancer who had somehow managed to misrepresent herself to a customer in a way that led to her being charged with solicitation for prostitution. From everything Dylan knew it was a simple misunderstanding but the District Attorney's office was making it a high profile case to garner political points for the Mayor in his upcoming reelection run. Dylan's biggest challenge would be to keep the case out of the headlines along with his connection to it.

There was another case, one that could potentially grow into a big one and he couldn't quite decide how to approach it. It was the case of a young man, one James "Jimmy" Arnone. Jimmy was a student at a local community college, a computer wizard and a pothead. He was also Tommy Rizzo's nephew and Godson. He had gotten himself into trouble for hacking into the school's mainframe and uploading a torrent of cannabis-related jokes and videos. He linked it all to the school's e-mail system so whenever an internal message was sent it included an attachment about pot.

There was no harm done to the system, no one was personally targeted and, from what Tommy had told Dylan, a number of people actually got a laugh out of it. When the school figured out who did it and brought charges against Jimmy their lawyer described it as the e-mail system being controlled by Cheech and Chong.

Dylan couldn't wait to meet the kid who pulled it off and find out more.

He also had another reason he wanted to talk to Jimmy. *Dreamware* seemed ready to become something more than a three-ring binder full of notes and instructions, something that could be worth money. Jimmy's computer skills and internet knowledge might be the key to taking the next step.

The next few days were the typical juggling act that had become Dylan's life. Juggle his schedule to accommodate the hearings and legwork for his Doyle and Finch clients. Juggle all the phone calls and e-mails that kept his moonlight clients moving through the legal system without requiring his presence in court. And juggle the activities of a personal life that once again seemed to include Beth.

In the midst of everything he had to do he managed, not without effort, to arrange a meeting with Jimmy Arnone. Tommy had warned Dylan that his fun loving nephew wasn't exactly easy to reach. The kid didn't like to use a phone for conversation and instead used texts and e-mails almost exclusively. After half a dozen texts and even more e-mails Dylan had convinced Jimmy that a face-to-face meeting was the only way to handle the start-up of the case. They arranged to meet at Dylan's house the following evening.

It turned out to be another long work day and a busier than planned evening. A simple dinner and the usual glasses of bourbon bracketed several hours of looking over case files. He found that by the time his head hit the pillow he was too tired to even try to float in the pre-sleep state that allowed dream sharing. As much as he wanted to visit someone else's mind he also wanted to spend the night just dreaming like he'd always done before, before he'd started experimenting with it. Normal dreaming, no more and no less.

His resistance to a night of dream sharing lasted all of five minutes. He moved himself into the sleep posture he'd developed, began the proper, rhythmic breathing technique and began to clear his mind. He saw the little white flower and concentrated on it and nothing else. Before long he had once again reached the state between wakefulness and sleep.

FADE IN
INTERIOR – BACKSTAGE AREA OF THE SAN DIEGO STATE UNIVERSITY STUDENT CENTER – EVENING

Three young men are sitting in a cramped practice room behind the main stage. A short, skinny man with a large mustache is clutching a bass guitar, slowly plucking its strings and trying to complete the rest of a song that the other two men don't recognize.

MARK BRANDON: Okay, man, we have like an hour and a half before we go on stage. We have just the one shot to play one song and impress one judge, and I have no fucking idea what that was you just played.

CRAIG LESSIG: It was *Post Acid* by Wavves. I thought it might be cool to play one of their songs since they're local and have a lot of fans here.

LAMAR HICKS: Yeah, they're local but there's no way we can do that song without it being a total fuck up.

CRAIG: Why do you say that? We can make it work.

MARK: Well, for one thing they have two singers to get the harmony and I'm the only guy who does vocals here. I can make my keyboard fill in for some of the sound but I can't make it sing.

LAMAR: And there's also the fact they go with two electric guitars and a mountain of electronics. We have one electric and one acoustic. And my drum set is like half the size of their guy's set.

CRAIG: So if you don't want to do that one give me a better pick.

The heavy, acoustic-lined door swings open and a flash of light from the corridor sweeps across the room. A lanky, bearded man carrying a guitar walks in.

LAMAR: Hey, Dylan, just the man we need. There seems to be a difference of opinion on the song we're gonna do tonight.

DYLAN: So, what did I miss?

MARK: Craig wants a Wavves song.

DYLAN: Nah, they're too heavy, almost acid rock. And we don't have the equipment to pull it off.

CRAIG: So what do you have in mind that's better?

DYLAN: I was thinking *Photograph* by Nickelback. We've all messed around with their stuff in the past and we know their sound.

LAMAR: But we'd still need a second vocal to make it work.

DYLAN: Well, it just so happens I decided to come out of my shell and see if I have the pipes to be a rock star.

The men all laugh and shake their heads. Dylan sits on a folding chair and takes his guitar from the case along with a small stack of sheet music. He passes it around to the other men and they look it over in silence. One by one they sit with their instruments, sheet music on easels in front of them and begin to do separate runs through their parts. Ten minutes go by.

MARK: You know, guys, this just might work.

LAMAR: I agree, it's not too far off from our own sound and if Dylan thinks he can sing and keep up with Mark maybe we'll have a shot at this.

The four men start from the beginning and work on the instrumentals only. They adjust the sound levels on their amps and control board several times before they feel comfortable with the mix. They do one final instrumental run-through.

DYLAN: Okay, I think we're there. Now if you guys are ready I'd like to introduce you to the smoothest voice this side of Nashville.

A ceiling light reflects off the shiny, lacquered surface of Dylan's guitar and flashes across his face. He tries to hide his slightly dizzy feeling.

FADE OUT

CHAPTER 12

May I return to the beginning? The light is dimming
and the dream is too. The world and I, we are still
waiting, still hesitating. Any dream will do.

From the song *Any Dream Will Do* by Jason Donovan

FOR THE PAST FEW MONTHS nights of normal dreaming had been few and far between for Dylan. Not because the number of dreams had shrunken but because he had become so hooked on dream sharing he couldn't stop trying it. As he laid in bed looking up at the ceiling he felt the same rush of excitement he'd felt after the first two shared dreams. But this one was different because he'd broken into the dreams of a person he hadn't seen or spoken to in several years. He and Mark Brandon had been close friends but drifted apart the way friends do when college is over and the real world takes over. But despite that separation Mark had had a dream and it included Dylan, and Dylan had prepared himself to barge in and take over.

It was his third shared dream and the first evidence that he could be brought into the dreams of anyone who happened to be thinking of him, even someone from long ago, as long as he was lying in bed and in a ready state. And the same dizziness at the end of the dream was how he got out of the person's mind.

It was evidence that the number of possible dream adventures had just increased exponentially. And once again he couldn't decide if that was a good thing or a bad thing.

By the time he'd arrived at his office, sat down at his desk and turned on his computer he already felt like he was behind schedule. His Doyle and

Finch caseload was manageable and if things went according to plan he would have them wrapped up within a week. His moonlight work would me more of a challenge and more time consuming.

Except for a quick but enjoyable lunch with Beth he spent the entire day in his office with the door closed or in his truck on the phone. It was the same daily balancing act he'd been struggling to manage and he was getting better at it. As five o'clock came and went the pile of paperwork on his desk had shrunk to almost nothing. He shut down his computer, texted a quick and, to his mind, a romantic message to Beth and then headed home for his meeting with Jimmy Arnone.

After he changed into jeans and a polo shirt and wolfed down a sandwich he went through the house straightening up anything that looked out of place. As he went from room to room he thought about how rare it was for him to have visitors. What had been passing for a social life had played out in bars, restaurants or someone else's house but rarely his own. And it seemed strange that he should be concerned about the neatness of his house when it was doubtful a pot smoking college kid would even notice.

The doorbell rang at seven o'clock and when Dylan opened the door he did a quiet double-take. Jimmy Arnone was a short, scruffy looking young man with black hair, dark, sunken eyes and a few days -worth of beard and stubble. The tip of a flame tattoo protruded up his neck above the collar of his shirt and a golden nose ring glistened in the shine of the porchlight. Dylan had never considered himself to be old but suddenly, looking at Jimmy, the generation gap felt like a canyon.

"Jimmy, hi, I'm Dylan, it's nice to meet you," he said, extending his right hand.

"Yeah, same here," Jimmy answered, reaching for Dylan's hand. The limpness of Jimmy's grip made Dylan wonder if it was the kid's very first adult handshake.

Dylan stepped back and said, "Come on in." He led Jimmy into the dining room where the notes and files of his case were neatly stacked. Jimmy laid his laptop down and took a chair at the end of the table. Dylan slid the pile of papers in front of the chair closest to Jimmy and sat down. He was surprised when the young man started the conversation.

"So what do we do here? Do you know all the stuff about my case? My Uncle Tommy said he filled you in."

"Yes, he told me the basics, and this stack of papers here are the charging documents and the notes and comments your uncle got from some of the people involved. I gotta be honest with you, Jimmy, you're in some real trouble here."

Jimmy nodded in agreement but his face didn't reveal the slightest bit of concern. "That's what they tell me but Uncle Tommy says you're good so I'm not too worried."

Dylan studied Jimmy's face, trying to figure out if the kid was clueless about his predicament or truly confident in his lawyer's abilities. "Well let me just tell you something I tell all of my clients. I tell them no case is easy and no case is a sure thing. You never know what a judge or a plaintiff will say or do, and until a not guilty verdict is actually declared you better be careful and worried."

"But you can get me out of this, can't you?"

"Jimmy, let's slow down here. I just started getting my head into this and we'll both have to do everything possible to get you off the hook. As I see it right now we'll have to do two things. One is to convince the court that you did the hack as a joke and at no time did you mean to cause any harm to the school or its computer system." He paused and looked at Jimmy.

The kid's face still didn't show any hint of seriousness. "And what's number two?" he asked.

Dylan sighed. "Number two is kind of a peace offering. You'll have to show them you're willing and able to work with their IT staff and come up with a way to make sure no one else can do what you did in the future. You can do that, can't you?"

"Piece of cake. I keep a notebook of things I learn about computers and networks and I already have a patch to fix the school's network, which is a piece of shit by the way."

For the next hour Dylan explained to Jimmy the charges that were filed against him, what the possible penalties could be and the line of defense he wanted to use for each of them. He talked slowly and gave Jimmy every opportunity to interrupt him or ask questions but the kid did nothing but nod his head.

Finally, when Dylan could take no more of a client without concern or curiosity, he stopped and asked, "So, Jimmy, what do you think about everything I've been laying out here?"

Jimmy sniffed and rubbed the back of his hand across his nose ring. "How much do you charge for this kind of thing?"

Dylan fought the urge to roll his eyes, sigh or give the kid any kind of hint that he was already frustrated with him. "Well, all I can give you is a range for now until we enter a plea and I have a better idea of what we'll be up against. In a case like this I usually ask for a thousand dollar retainer in advance."

Jimmy's face seemed to go blank and for a moment he said nothing. Then he took a deep breath and said, "Man, a thousand dollars. I can ask my mother for some money but I don't know if she has that much on hand." He paused and added, "And the rest of your fee won't be easy for me to pay no matter how much it is."

Dylan purposely gave the kid a few moments to ponder his situation and then said, "Jimmy, I think I have a way for you to pay me that you'll go for, a kind of trade of services between the two of us."

"A trade, what do you mean?"

"I mean you need the kind of services I provide and I need help with something that you know how to do and I don't. So instead of any money changing hands we just work together and help each other out."

Jimmy's face showed a definite uptick in enthusiasm. "So what do you need my help with?"

Dylan paused a moment, unsure of how to explain to a stranger his obsession with controlling dreams and finding a way to sell it to others. Every time he thought about it the whole idea sounded stranger and riskier. "Well, I have an idea for a small, online business, more like teaching a class, really. I have the course material written but I need someone like you to help me turn it into a podcast or a website or some way to get it into the public's eye."

"I'm on the staff of the school's website, or at least I used to be until, well, until I got in trouble. And I helped a couple of people design their websites to sell stuff and I showed them how to link it all to social media and stuff."

Dylan was struck by the kid's abrupt change of mood from seeming boredom to near excitement. "It sounds like you can do what I need you to do, but we'll have to keep it on a business level. I'm used to tracking and documenting my hours so I can show a client why I'm charging him what the invoice says. I want you to do the same thing."

Jimmy seemed to be confused. "So do you want me to show you how many hours or dollars or what?"

"From the moment you start working on my online class or podcast or website or whatever it becomes, I want you to write down, each and every day, how many hours you spent working on it. I have some blank forms I can give you to use."

"And if I do that you won't charge me anything to handle my case?"

"That's right. Do we have a deal?"

The look of relief on Jimmy's face was almost comical. "Oh, hell yeah, we got a deal!"

Over the course of another half hour Dylan grilled Jimmy on everything he'd said and did related to the school's charges against him. How did he get past the school's internet firewall? How did he decide whose mail to target? Had he ever had any kinds of arguments or problems with any of the targeted people? While he was working on his little scheme did he read or alter any e-mails or documents? It was important to determine if there was any kind of damage done to the reputations of any of the people who were on the receiving end of his prank.

At about eight forty-five the conversation seemed to have reached a logical stopping point. Dylan had enough information to begin building a defense. And he'd also noticed that Jimmy was losing his focus.

"Well, Jimmy, I think I have enough for now. Give me a few days to go over my notes and I'll get back to you."

Jimmy leaned back in his chair and nodded. He brushed away a clump of hair that was hanging in his eyes and said, "Okay, so you're gonna work on my case now. You said you had something for me to do but you didn't say exactly what it was."

Dylan felt a sheepish embarrassment. For the first time he had to describe to another person his idea to teach people how to invade other people's dreams. He had ducked and dodged the subject with Beth but he knew if he was going to make *Dreamware* a reality he'd have to share with Jimmy everything he'd been doing, everything he'd learned and everything he hoped to accomplish.

His obsession with dreaming was about to move outside of his own head and into the real world. It felt both exciting and scary, and even a little embarrassing. He was entering some strange new territory.

"Okay," he started, knowing the need to be careful with his words, "I've been working on an idea about dreaming. I dream a lot and I've done a lot of research about it and I've learned some interesting things."

He waited a moment to gauge Jimmy's interest or at the very least his level of concentration. So far the kid hadn't changed his expression at all. Dylan continued. "Here's the thing. Everybody dreams. You, me, your Uncle Tommy, your mother, everyone dreams. I have developed a method to control what happens in my dreams and I want to teach it to others."

Jimmy seemed to be paying attention but there was no change in his expression and no comment.

"And besides controlling my dreams I've come up with a way to put myself smack in the middle of other people's dreams as well."

That was the statement, or more accurately the admission that had been making Dylan nervous and it drew an immediate response from Jimmy.

"Holy shit, are you serious? You can actually get into people's dreams, like into their heads?"

It was as though Jimmy's face had finally lit up into something resembling enthusiasm. His mouth was hanging open and his eyes were wide. He leaned forward and Dylan knew that, at last, he had the kid's total attention.

"Yes, I can do that. Like I said before I've been doing some research and a lot of experimenting and practicing and I finally figured out how to do it."

Jimmy still seemed to be transfixed on what he was hearing and to Dylan it was a kind of proof that anyone else who heard about *Dreamware* would be just as interested. The kid's simple and inelegant response convinced Dylan there was reason to commercialize his dreaming obsession.

Jimmy's enthusiasm was obvious. "So you want me to help you come up with a website or what? You're going to try and sell this idea, right?"

"Yeah, but I don't know if a website can do it or if I need something else. I need to turn this into an online course, like I was teaching it at your school or somewhere else."

Jimmy looked down at the table. "You mean my former school."

"Well, for now it's your former school but maybe I can help you change it back to being your school again. So what do you think, are you interested?"

There was no hesitation from Jimmy. "Oh hell yeah. When do we start?"

"Well, I guess we can start in the next day or so. I'll have to turn my notes into a kind of script for me to read. I'll be like the narrator, like a teacher that you only hear but don't see."

"I have some video equipment if you want me to tape you. A friend of mine is pretty good with it too."

"No, I'd prefer to stay sort of anonymous with this, because of my job and some other things."

"Gotcha, but if you need anybody to appear in the video I can get some people."

"Well, I'm trying to keep my costs in line. This is strictly a side venture for me. But now that you mention it I'll probably need to show somebody in a bed sleeping and dreaming."

Jimmy's face was beaming. "I owe my friend Josh a few bucks and this could be my way to pay him back. He's a Theater Arts major and he's always looking for ways to build his resume for when he graduates. He could be the guy in the video, the guy who's dreaming. He's a pretty good actor by the way."

"So he'd do it for free then?"

"Yeah, I think I can talk him into it. You might have to buy him some beer or something like that but he'll do it for the experience and for his resume."

Dylan nodded, trying to hold back a smile that might give away his excitement. "Okay, talk to him and get back to me." He paused for a moment and then added, "And if you have a female friend who'd be willing to do the same thing let me know. I think it would make the video better to have both a male and female in it."

"Oh man, my girlfriend would love to do it. Her name is Sheila and she wants to do modeling and TV commercials."

Dylan nodded, wondering if the young woman shared her boyfriend's penchant for tattoos and piercings. "Okay, sounds good."

When Jimmy finally left Dylan poured himself a glass of bourbon and sat back in his favorite chair. He resisted the urge to turn on the television and instead stared at the ceiling. There was so much to think about and so much to do. His Doyle and Finch caseload was smaller than it had been for months and none of his moonlight work was on any kind of urgent timeline.

It seemed like the perfect time to launch *Dreamware*. His dreams had become more than a distraction to his day to day life and the thought that they could actually lead to income was something that was hard to get his head around. So far he hadn't made much of a name for himself as a lawyer. Could his dreaming make up for that? He sat there trying to enjoy the upside of his little creation but the downside kept pushing its way into his thoughts. What would Beth think of his strange, new venture?"

By the time he turned in for the night he'd decided to take a few days of PTO so he could concentrate on *Dreamware*. He hadn't taken a vacation or sick day in over a year and if any of his clients needed him they knew how to reach him via e-mail. He'd decide at the moment if he was in the mood to reply to them. Jimmy Arnone would be both his work-related focus and his only automatic personal call response, except for Beth.

With so much to think about he laid in bed trying to decide if sleep should be his priority or if he should allow a dream to intervene in his slumber, especially if it was someone else's dream. It really wasn't much of a decision to make. As usual the dream won the argument.

FADE IN
INTERIOR – A HOME OUTSIDE OF SACRAMENTO – DAY

A plump, gray-haired woman is sitting in a wicker chair on the expansive front porch of her home. She is reading a magazine and occasionally glances up and down her quiet street. From time to time she lays the magazine in her lap and sips from a glass of red wine that sits on a small wicker table beside her.

She finishes her reading but before she can stand up to walk inside movement on the street catches her eye. She sees a man about halfway down the block. He is walking on the sidewalk across the street and moving in her direction.

Something about him looks familiar and she finds herself staring at him. When he is directly opposite her house he stops and turns toward her. As he waits for a car to pass the late afternoon sun reflects in the windshield and into his eyes. When the car has passed he steps off the sidewalk and begins a slow walk to cross the street.

When he reaches the sidewalk at the edge of her front yard he stops, looking up at her. She looks at him and her eyes widen as he walks closer.

DYLAN: Hi, Mom.

SANDRA WARD: Oh my God, Dylan. Dylan.

DYLAN: I'm surprised you still recognize me.

SANDRA: Well of course I recognize you.

He climbs the porch steps and stands off to the left of her chair. He waits for her to say something more but she just stares at him in silence.

DYLAN: How are you?

SANDRA: Oh, I'm okay I guess. I was thinking about you today. Last night I cleaned out some boxes in the attic and found your high school yearbooks and I looked through them.

DYLAN: Yeah, it was right after that I went away to college and you didn't have to worry about me being around anymore.

Sandra looks at him and then lowers her gaze to the porch floor.

SANDRA: What are you doing here?

DYLAN: I came to see Dad.

SANDRA: You know your father isn't here. You know he's, you know he's gone.

Dylan steps around her and walks through the front door. He stands inside, looking around the living room. His mother turns and watches him for a moment and then stands up from her chair, turns and enters the house. She stops in her tracks, looking around the room and then directly at Dylan. The look of shock on her face is evident.

SANDRA: Oh my God, what is this? What happened here?

DYLAN: What do you mean, Mom?

SANDRA: I mean this room. What happened to this room? It looks old, it looks like it used to, back when you were, back when you were here.

DYLAN: I don't know what you're talking about, Mom. It looks normal to me. It looks like it's supposed to look.

Sandra notices a framed photograph on the fireplace mantel. It's a photo of Dylan, his father and her on a beach vacation. She stares at it and then looks down at the floor. Dylan slowly walks into the dining room and Sandra follows him, the shocked expression still frozen on her face as she scans the room. The dining table is set for dinner, with three place settings and a large vase of fresh flowers at the center of the table.

DYLAN: What's for dinner?

Sandra's look of shock has now turned to one of total confusion. Before she can answer the sound of a car pulling into the driveway interrupts their conversation. Dylan looks out the window and sees a dark green

Pontiac come to a stop beside the back porch. A moment later the driver's side door opens and the late day sun reflects in the side view mirror of the car, flashing into Dylan's eyes. A tall, slender man gets out of the car.

DYLAN: Dad's home.

Sandra looks at Dylan, her expression a combination of disbelief and terror. She seems afraid to speak.

DYLAN: What's for dinner, Mom?

Sandra continues to stare at Dylan and then finally turns away. She doesn't notice him grab hold of a dining chair to keep his balance.

FADE OUT

CHAPTER 13

You can see the change you want to be. What you want
to be when you get a head. A head full of dreams.

From the song *A Head Full of Dreams* by Coldplay

FROM THE MOMENT HE HAD awakened, through the entirety
of his normal morning get-ready-for-work ritual and his commute
to the office, Dylan couldn't shake thoughts of his mother. For
years he'd tried to keep thoughts of her at bay. They'd long ago forged
a sort of long distance stand-off, a sort of pretense that they were family
but without any real and regular communication. It was token birthday
cards, maybe a Christmas card and nothing more. They were family in
name only.

Being brought into her dream had unnerved him. Up until now his
dreams and the dreams of those he'd invaded had been based upon people
and events that were a regular part of his life or at least people who'd been
close to him.

Now he'd been made a part of something totally unexpected. Suddenly
dream sharing had come with an emotional punch that he didn't like. He
couldn't help but wonder if his mother had felt the same punch.

When he got to his office he turned on his computer and went down
the hall for his first cup of Monday coffee. His plan was to gather his files
for the few, near-term cases he was dealing with and then talk to Marie in
human resources about his need to take some time away from the office.
By ten o'clock he'd accomplished his goals. As he was heading toward the
door for more coffee Beth walked in.

"Morning," she said, before puckering her lips and making a kissing sound.

"Good morning," he answered. "I was just heading to the lounge for coffee, do you want some?"

"No thanks, I have to sit in on a meeting in fifteen minutes for that Lincoln Equity merger. They'll have coffee there and it's a good thing because I'll need it to stay awake. That shit is so boring."

"Yeah, I know what you mean." He sat back down at his desk and Beth sat in the lone visitor chair in front of him. He shifted his weight in his chair and Beth immediately read his body language.

"What's the matter?" she asked. "You seem nervous or something."

"Oh, I'm just trying to get some things wrapped up here. I decided to take a few days off and I have to make sure I have everything here covered."

"I'm glad. You haven't taken any time off since forever and you can probably use a break." She paused a moment and then asked, "So what are you going to do with the time?"

He knew that question would come eventually but he still was nervous about answering it. "Well, I was going to tell you about it when the time was right but since you asked." He took a breath and then said, "I'm going to work on my idea to write a course on dreaming. It'll be an online thing and it's just something I thought I could do to maybe make some extra money."

Beth didn't respond for what seemed to Dylan an uncomfortably long time. Her face showed a mix of surprise and bewilderment. Finally she said, "So it's your dreams again."

Dylan had been expecting her less than enthusiastic response and he'd even thought of several ways to answer them. "Yes, it's my dreams again and I'm pretty excited about this whole thing. Everybody dreams and I think if I do this right I can tap into a lot of interest, a lot of people who'd like to be more involved in what goes on in their heads at night."

Beth's expression didn't change. "Well, I have to say this isn't really a surprise, but I'm wondering why you can't just have your dreams and your lucid stuff and let it go at that. Why do you want to bring other people into it?"

Her question was at the core of his idea. While he saw the potential to market *Dreamware* and maybe make some money there was a larger reason behind his plan. "I see this as a good thing, a way to help people explore their imaginations and maybe find some fun and pleasure in the process."

It sounded good. It sounded believable, reasonable and positive. But he was only beginning to realize that the way he was controlling his dreams was a part of something else, something darker.

She still didn't know the specifics of his dream sharing and he'd planned to put off that part of the conversation for as long as possible. If he had a choice she'd never find out what it was all about. But all she'd have to do is look at *Dreamware* to know what he'd created.

She let out a little sigh and said, "Well, I guess you know what you're doing. Just be careful with it, okay?"

Even knowing that it would lead to a conversation he didn't want to have he went ahead and asked, "Why are you so negative about my dreaming?"

"I don't mean to sound negative but I just think there's potential for some kind of problem getting involved with other people and their dreams."

"You sound like someone who spends too much time around lawyers." He meant the comment to lighten the tone and it seemed to work.

"Yeah, I guess I do. Sorry." She paused a moment and then asked, "Is there any way I can help you?"

"Actually, there is something you can do for me. The course will include video footage of people sleeping and it'll be taped in my bedroom." He immediately realized his comment could be taken as inappropriate so before Beth could react he added, "Tommy Rizzo's nephew is doing the online work and has a couple of his friends lined up to portray the sleepers."

Beth replied slowly, "So, okay, then what is it you want my help with?"

My bedroom is a little, oh what's the word, outdated, and I want to paint it and maybe hang a couple of framed pieces of art and maybe get a new bedspread, that kind of thing. I need a photogenic bedroom that people can relate to."

"Well, okay, I'd be glad to help you pick some things out."

"I was hoping you'd just go ahead and do it for me. I like your taste in things, like your apartment and the way you furnished it. It's very cool."

Beth smiled and nodded. "Okay, I'll do some looking around after work. What's your budget?

"Keep it cheap. This whole thing is a crap shoot for me."

"I better get to my meeting," she said as she stood up. She blew him another kiss and said, "Call me tonight."

By noon Dylan had gathered everything he'd need to work from home. He typed up an out-of-office message on his e-mail and then headed for his truck. Except for Jimmy Arnone's case he planned to spend a week being Dylan Ward, Dreamer rather than Dylan Ward, Attorney.

By the time five o'clock rolled around he had finished transforming his notes on *Dreamware* into a fairly workable script for the narration of the course. His voice would lead the dream students through the podcast training with Jimmy's friends appearing as average, everyday people getting ready for bed and ready to learn how to navigate their own dream world.

He grabbed a beer from the fridge and then sat down on his sofa, his laptop on the coffee table in front of him while he alternately sipped and reviewed what he'd written. He wanted it to sound more like a play or performance than something instructional. Every now and then in the text he injected a bit of subtle humor to keep things from getting too heavy. He also was careful about references to alcohol or pot as sleep inducers, instead just encouraging the dreamer to partake of whatever helped him or her relax before bed.

The next day was a juggling of Jimmy's case and *Dreamware*. Beth had selected a Celadon green paint for the bedroom walls and arranged for a painter to do the work immediately. She bought a new bedspread, a bedside lamp and two framed landscapes. When the makeover was finished Jimmy stopped by with his video camera to start framing the shots he'd be taking. Dylan had even done a simple storyboarding exercise to create the order of the training sections and video sequences.

Dreamware was coming to life and Dylan's excitement was building. The only thing that took the edge of his enthusiasm was his gnawing concern for what Beth would think when she finally knew about his dream sharing.

When he really thought about it he wondered what everyone who'd find out about it would think.

After getting things underway on Jimmy's case Dylan had reached the conclusion the kid wasn't in quite the mess they'd both assumed that first evening they'd met at Dylan's house. While Jimmy had most certainly breached the school's computer security there was no clear evidence that any harm had been done. The school's struggle to clean out Jimmy's uploads were more a matter of the staff's ineptitude than the prank's level of sophistication.

An hour and a half of review of the *California Computer Crime Statutes* seemed to support Dylan's position. He wanted to talk with an old friend at San Diego State who worked in their computer services department to clarify the details but the case looked very winnable.

After a quick dinner and a long phone conversation with Beth he once again sat down with his laptop. For two hours he read his script out loud, rehearsing every word, trying for just the right tone and inflection. *Dreamware* would be presented as a podcast in four separate segments: *Dream Legends, Why We Dream, Lucid Dreaming* and finally *Dream Sharing*.

Each segment would include visuals, either still photos from his dream legend book or video of Josh or Sheila in the bedroom going through the breathing and relaxation techniques and then in feigned sleep. He realized watching a video of someone sleeping wouldn't be exciting but he had a feeling his script would make up for it.

Since he wasn't a currently enrolled student and didn't have a job Jimmy responded quickly when Dylan e-mailed him an update on the progress of the bedroom upgrades along with the outline for *Dreamware*. It wasn't a lengthy comment, just "Very cool, when do we start?"

A quick exchange of several more e-mails led to them setting up a meeting for ten o'clock the next morning. Jimmy and Sheila would come to Dylan's house prepared to shoot about an hour's worth of video in the bedroom. They would also do some basic sound checks, photograph some still images from Dylan's dream book and then record his narration of *Dream Legends*.

To keep all of his duties on track the next day's activities would also include discussion on Jimmy's case and what Dylan had in mind for a defense. A quick follow up review of the computer crime statutes only reinforced Dylan's feeling that the school's case against the bright but unfocused kid was less than airtight.

So *Dreamware* was just hours from its birth and Dylan tried to imagine what the public's response would be. Telling people they'd soon have more fun and adventure in their dreams would hold their attention. Telling them they could invade the dreams of others would have them glued to their screens.

At about ten-thirty Dylan caught himself starting to doze off on the sofa. He shut off his laptop and then went through his bedtime routine. It was the same routine he'd followed every night but now it felt strangely different. His bedtime ritual and the dreaming that followed it would no longer be his personal property. They would now be for sale.

FADE IN
INTERIOR – McHALE'S BAR - NIGHT

The main bar room is surprisingly quiet. Only a few customers are scattered among the tables and one lone man is sitting at the bar. A young woman tending bar is taking beer glasses from a glass washer and carefully placing them on a nearby shelf. Another young woman approaches her from behind the bar. The woman tending bar turns toward her.

KELLY: Can you believe how dead it is in here? We aren't gonna be rolling in big tip money tonight.

HANNAH: Yeah, I've only been working here for a couple of months but this is the slowest I've ever seen it.

KELLY: Maybe we can talk Dave into cutting the floor. I have an English Lit exam tomorrow and I still have a lot of reading to do.

HANNAH: You might as well go. Why hang around here cleaning glasses if there's nobody using them?

KELLY: I think he's in his office. Would you do me a favor and go see what he thinks?

Hannah nods and then turns and walks toward the back of the building. Kelly turns back to the glass washer to finish her restocking. She hears the front door bell chime. Her hands full of clean glasses, she turns toward the sound as the door closes and a man walks toward her. She smiles as he reaches the bar. The overhead bar lights reflect off the glasses and across the man's face.

KELLY: Hey, stranger, where have you been lately?

DYLAN: Oh, it's been a busy couple of weeks. I decided I needed a break and I thought to myself, "Why not head to McHales for a beer?"

KELLY: Well, it's nice to see you again. Hang on a second while I put these away.

She turns her back to him while she places the glasses on the shelf and he takes a moment to enjoy the view of her from head to toe. A moment later she turns and faces him again, still smiling.

DYLAN: Wow, where is everybody? I've been coming here for years and I never saw so many empty stools and chairs, especially when you're on duty.

KELLY: I have no idea. It's way too early for it to be this quiet, and I'm sure it has nothing to do with my being here or not.

DYLAN: You sell yourself short. Guys can buy a beer anywhere but you happen to work here.

She pauses for a moment then puts her hands on the bar and leans closer to him. Her smile has turned from friendly to something more.

KELLY: So let me guess. You're usually an IPA guy but something tells me you're in the mood for something special.

She pauses, studying his face for a reaction to her comment.

KELLY: So what are you in the mood for, a bourbon or something else?

He hesitates before answering, trying to decide if there is any hidden meaning to her question. She seems to be eager for his answer. Before he can respond Hannah walks back to the bar and taps Kelly on the shoulder. Kelly turns toward her

HANNAH: Dave says since it's so deadzo tonight you can leave if you want.

KELLY: Thanks, I'll just take care of this gentleman first.

Kelly waits for Hannah to walk away and out of earshot, the turns back to Dylan.

KELLY: So what would you like tonight?

Once again Dylan waits to answer her, still not sure if there is more to her question than she is letting on. She is still leaning on the bar, her face close to his and her smile still seeming to be more than friendly.

DYLAN: If I told you just a bourbon what would you say?

KELLY: I'd say I was disappointed.

DYLAN: How many times, including tonight, have I come in here when you were behind the bar and I'd try to hit on you?

KELLY: Oh, geez, like maybe a hundred.

DYLAN: And how many times did you smile and send me the message you weren't interested?

KELLY: If you're including tonight, ninety-nine.

Dylan smiles and reaches for her hands. He looks into her eyes and starts shaking his head.

DYLAN: So I think this is where fantasy meets reality.

KELLY: What, you've had fantasies about me?

DYLAN: Only about a thousand times.

KELLY: So what do you mean about meeting reality?

Dylan pauses and stares into her beautiful dark eyes. He feels her squeezing his hands. He struggles to find the words to answer her question. Finally he lifts her hands toward him and kisses them.

DYLAN: Fantasy is just another name for a dream, and you've been a big part of my dreams.

KELLY: Your dreams but not your reality?

DYLAN: I'm afraid not.

A customer opens the side exit door on his way out and the headlights of a car flash briefly into Dylan's eyes. He leans against the edge of the bar to steady himself.

FADE OUT

CHAPTER 14

A dream you dream alone is only a dream. A
dream you dream together is a reality.

A quote from John Lennon

NOT HAVING TO GO INTO the office that morning was
a huge relief for Dylan. The extra time he could spend in bed
staring at the ceiling, trying to understand his dream made it
easier to face the day ahead. Once again he had hacked another person's
dream and this time it was Kelly Alvarez.

On the one hand it was flattering to know an attractive young woman
had had a dream about him but he couldn't help but wonder what might
have happened in the dream if he hadn't been lucid and controlling it.
Would it have been romantic? Would they have ended up in bed together?
How would she have felt about it if they had?

He decided there probably couldn't have been any outcome in her
dream that wouldn't produce some degree of discomfort the next time he
saw her. If he'd followed his lustful impulses the dream would have made
her feel one way. His turning away her flirtation made her feel another. He
had a feeling that most dream sharing would turn out to be a "damned if
you do, damned if you don't" situation.

And the dream only reinforced his uneasiness that dream sharing
could lead people into all kinds of trouble. That was both the fear and the
appeal. After all, didn't forbidden fruit always taste better? But he finally
decided that the dizzy-headed exit she gave him had been a good thing.

Jimmy and Sheila showed up half an hour late. Dylan wasn't surprised
by their tardiness but he was surprised by the fact Sheila didn't look

anything like what he'd expected. He had envisioned a female version of Jimmy but she was very pretty and very normal looking. She was a brunette with a great smile and no piercings or visible tattoos. She'd make a perfect actor in the series of little, one-act plays in the podcast. He hoped Josh would look just as normal.

The three of them agreed to work on the podcast until noon, break for lunch and then talk about Jimmy's case after that. Sheila used a digital camera to photograph the images from the *Dream Legends* book while Jimmy and Dylan established the range and framing for the video work. They had enough time to shoot a short scene of a pajama-clad Sheila adjusting the window shades and climbing into bed and another one of her practicing her breathing routine. Dylan would do the voice-over narration later.

Around noon they shared a couple of deli sandwiches that Dylan had picked up earlier and talked about Jimmy's case. Dylan was careful to balance his optimism with a healthy dose of reality. His plan was to negotiate with the school's lawyers outside of court but he knew nothing about them or their firm. He always preferred knowing some background on the opposing team before he sat down across the table from them.

It was going to be an interesting and challenging negotiation to get Jimmy back in school and, hopefully, pointed in the right direction.

They managed to get two more video clips finished after lunch. Jimmy agreed to download the still photos and clean them up in *Photoshop*. Before they left, Jimmy and Sheila agreed to come back the next day with Josh and work until they completed the rest of the video segments Dylan had storyboarded. Jimmy left behind a DVD that contained all of the videos and a small microphone. He showed Dylan how to use his own laptop to overdub the narration.

A late afternoon text from Beth altered his evening plans for working on *Dreamware*. He'd been so wrapped up in his project and Jimmy's case that he'd been neglecting her and he knew he had to fix that. He called her on her cellphone and they arranged to meet for happy hour. She suggested McHale's but given his previous night's dream he figured he should stay away from there for a while.

The day's work on the podcast had been exciting and on his drive to The Goat and Vine he could think of nothing else. He wondered if it would be the main topic of conversation over their wine. He decided to downplay his enthusiasm a bit so Beth wouldn't ask too many questions even though he knew it would only postpone the inevitable. Once she saw the podcast and the segment on dream sharing she'd put two and two together.

Then he'd have to explain what really happened with his dream about Max and the one about her. And then explain much more.

When he walked into the café Beth was already sitting at a small high-top table by the back window. "Hey," she said as she reached the table, "I've missed you." She smiled as he leaned down and kissed her before he sat down.

"I've missed you too," he said, "and I'm sorry I've been so preoccupied. I just want to pack as much as I can into my time off so I can pare down my to-do list."

"It sounds like you're busier on vacation than you are when you're at work."

"Well, I just want to get my podcast finished or at least mostly finished, and I set up a meeting for tomorrow afternoon to see if I can negotiate a settlement of some kind that'll get Jimmy off the hook."

A young man in a black shirt and black apron approached the table and they listened as he went through the wine offerings and happy hour deals. They chose to split a shrimp appetizer and share a bottle of Chardonnay. He couldn't help but feel like a cheapskate.

When the man was out of earshot Beth leaned forward and asked, "So I want to hear your plan for Jimmy's defense but first tell me about *Dreamware*." The look on her face showed him she was more than a little interested.

"Well, I got things set up as Dreamware, LLC and created a *Pay Pal* account for payments. I figured that would be the easiest and safest way to be paid. Jimmy also helped me set up a *Facebook* page for it and he already got a bunch of his friends to like it.

"Okay, that's the business part. What about the taping, all the dream scenes and things in the bedroom?"

"We had a pretty productive day today, taping some of the breathing techniques, some sleep scenes and getting the dream legend still shots.

Jimmy is like a genius with media and computers and he's already come up with some cool ideas."

"Like what?"

"Like using a blurring technique to show how Sheila and Josh, the guy he's bringing tomorrow, are slowly falling asleep. He also has this big camera boom, I have no idea where he got it. It's like something straight from Hollywood and it lets him take the shot from above the bed, like you're looking straight down from the ceiling. And tomorrow morning we're going to sample some music to use in the background. The kid is really into my project."

"Wow, it sounds like this idea of yours is really turning into something."

"Yeah, it's exciting. I still have to do the voice-over part but we think we can have it pretty well done by Saturday."

"So when do I get to see it?"

He hoped his face didn't show any sign of the nervousness her question brought him. "Oh, sometime next week I guess. I want to make sure it's ready for prime time before I show it to you."

The server returned with their wine and Dylan was relieved that it interrupted the topic at hand. "It took a few minutes for the server to pour and for them to take a first sip. It seemed like a good time to change the subject.

"I think I have a good angle on Jimmy's defense. I've been pouring over computer crime case law and from what I've found so far this is like a case of "no harm, no foul".

But didn't Jimmy's little prank disrupt the computers and e-mail system?"

"Not really. I guess that's the key word here, disrupt. There was minor disruption but no damage and no intent to do harm. And he didn't profit from it in any way. In my opinion his only crime was to embarrass the school's computer department."

"That's probably why they brought the charges, to save face."

"That's my take on it too, and that isn't going to get them very far if this thing makes it to trial."

For the next hour and a half they were just two people in love, making small talk, drinking wine and enjoying being together. As they walked to the parking lot afterward they agreed that Beth would come to his house late Saturday afternoon and spend the night. It would be their first intimacy since they reconnected that wasn't part of a dream. He hoped the reality would be as satisfying as the dream.

That evening Dylan focused on nothing but the voice-over work and he was surprised when he noticed the clock on his computer said it was after midnight. He shut things down, stood up and stretched. Barring any technical glitches he figured his part of the project would be done by mid-morning the next day. He'd turn things over to Jimmy to tweak and finalize the production by sometime on Saturday. The only interruption for both of them would be the meeting with the school's legal team.

Jimmy had been so caught up in his side of their bargain that he'd barely mentioned the trouble he was in. Given his age and personality Dylan wasn't exactly surprised by that. Jimmy's demographic was totally foreign to Dylan; millennial and without a clear direction in life. He just hoped his defense strategy would work in the kid's favor.

Without his usual pre-sleep bourbon or a few tokes on a joint he found himself lying in bed and feeling the way most people probably felt when they turned in for the night. A strange thought came to his mind: Was alcohol or pot essential to making the techniques in *Dreamware* work? Either way, he had no intention to change anything.

Before he fell asleep he'd come up with a way to revise his voice-over script to subtly suggest ways to enhance a dreamlike state, legal or otherwise.

CHAPTER 15

As certain as it seems, I think you might agree. Well, is this real
life or is this just another dream? Yeah, it's just another dream.

From the song *A Head Full of Dreams* by Coldplay

IT SEEMED ODD TO DYLAN to lie in bed in the morning without
having a head full of emotions about the theater of the previous night's
dreams. He'd had several mundane and almost forgettable dreams for
a change. They hadn't brought him any drama, no angst or guilt, just the
normal playing out of events like everyone else experiences during sleep.

He couldn't help but wonder if it was due to the lack of alcohol or
just an unexpected return to normalcy, or at least normalcy for him. But
he also decided that his dream explorations were far more enjoyable than
anything that suggested normal.

A quick cup of coffee and a microwaved breakfast burrito followed by
the fastest shower he'd ever taken gave him more time to get back to his
computer and make a few minor edits to his script. He'd no sooner finished
when the doorbell rang. Jimmy and Sheila stood there on the porch smiling
while a tall, handsome young man with thick blonde hair stood a few yards
back on the sidewalk.

"Morning, Mr. Ward, uh, Dylan."

"Good morning," Dylan replied as he looked toward the other
young man.

"Dylan, this is my friend, Josh."

Dylan nodded in the young man's direction. "Hey, Josh, nice to
meet you."

Dylan stepped back from the door as the trio walked in. He did a quick and he hoped unnoticed scan of Josh and saw no tattoos, piercings, weird hair style or anything that would indicate to viewers of the podcast that the young man was anything but mainstream.

Jimmy was dressed in a crisp white shirt and a sport coat like Dylan had instructed. A tie would come later in hopes it would help to hide Jimmy's neck tattoo. They would go the three o'clock negotiation directly from Dylan's house.

Jimmy was carrying his usual assortment of camera and equipment bags, Sheila had a backpack and Josh had a small suitcase. When he saw that Dylan was looking at it he said, "It's just my wardrobe and some stage make-up."

Jimmy rolled his eyes, looked at Dylan and said, "Remember, he's a Theater Arts major."

Dylan led the group into the bedroom. While Jimmy unpacked his equipment Sheila set up two small, portable lights. Josh took his suitcase into the bathroom and closed the door. About ten minutes later Jimmy said, "Okay, I think we're ready. Where do you want to start?" He'd no sooner asked the question when the bathroom door opened.

Josh stepped into the bedroom and all Dylan could do was stare at him. In ten minutes the young theater major had transformed from a slender, blonde twenty-something into a slightly paunchy, middle-aged, balding man with a mustache.

Before Dylan could respond to the sight, Josh said matter-of-factly, "Sheila will speak to the younger demographic but we think you also need this to reach the older, middle-aged audience."

Dylan hesitated, still surprised by the kid's transformation, and said, "Yeah, I guess you're right. We want to reach a big audience."

For the next several hours they taped the rest of the sleep scenes from Dylan's storyboard. Each time Dylan walked them through the script and explained what was going on with the dream and the particular segment of the podcast. They each did a good job of conveying that something was going on in their minds while they slept. Josh had really gotten engaged in the whole thing and even convinced Dylan to let him do a costume change and become another character, a 30-something man who looked like an executive with a lot on his mind when he turned in at night. It could have been Dylan.

When the taping was done Josh changed back into his street clothes. Before he left Dylan agreed to let him have taped copies of his scenes for his resume and then handed the kid a check for a hundred dollars. He acted like it was a thousand.

Sheila plugged two small speakers into the laptop and they spent half an hour selecting the music for each scene. It ranged from soft, romantic instrumentals to harder-edged, up-tempo jazz riffs. Each one linked perfectly to its respective dream scene; slow and easy backgrounds for the sleep scenes that gently eased into more energetic suggestions of what the sleeper was dreaming. *Dreamware* felt like its own little movie.

By about two o'clock they'd reached a point where, to Dylan's mind, the project felt like it was finished. Jimmy would fine tune the entire video on Saturday and send it back to Dylan for review. When Dylan was comfortable with everything Jimmy would upload it to the internet and link it to the *Facebook* page.

It didn't take long to pack up all the equipment and stuff it into Jimmy's well-worn Nissan. Sheila kissed Jimmy and drove away.

"Come on," Dylan said, "I'll throw on my suit and we can rehearse our plan on the way to the meeting."

Jimmy shrugged and said, "Whatever."

They got to the Harris and Lamb offices with ten minutes to spare. Before they got out of the car Dylan had to remind Jimmy to remove his nose ring. Until they had walked through the front door Jimmy had acted as though he was unconcerned about what might lie ahead. Standing in the posh and meticulously decorated lobby seemed to be a wake-up call for him. He stood there in silence, looking intimidated by the surroundings.

Dylan walked over to the receptionist. "Dylan Ward and James Arnone, here for our three o'clock with Mary Stuart."

The young woman behind the counter smiled and said, "Please have a seat and I'll tell her you're here."

As they walked toward a cluster of chairs nearby they passed a man sitting alone and staring at them as they sat down.

Jimmy leaned toward Dylan and said quietly, "That guy's from the school. I think he's the main computer guy."

Dylan looked over at the man who was still staring and nodded in his direction. The man looked away.

Dylan whispered to Jimmy about letting him do the talking and only answer questions when asked. He also reminded the kid be polite, sit up straight and to try not to be nervous.

Finally, the receptionist stood up and walked around to the front of her desk. "Gentlemen, Attorney Stuart is ready for you now, please follow me."

The group walked in silence to a small conference room not far from the lobby. There were bottles of water sitting in front of each chair. The three men sat down as the receptionist left. Dylan decided to take the initiative and reached across the table to the man from the school.

Hi, I'm Dylan Ward, attorney for Mr. Arnone here."

The man offered a timid smile and shook Dylan's hand. "Nice to meet you, I'm Roger Marshall. I'm the school's Director of Technology."

Mary Stuart's entrance into the room made any attempt at small talk unnecessary. She shook hands with Dylan first and when she shook Jimmy's hand she stared directly into his eyes. Dylan immediately noticed the nervous look on Jimmy's face.

She sat down, looked at Dylan and then said in a flat, all business kind of tone. "I just started looking into the school's case when I got your message about wanting to meet. This conversation should be considered as very preliminary."

"I agree," Dylan replied as he glanced down at his notes.

After a moment of hesitation Stuart started the conversation. "Mr. Ward, since you were the one who requested this meeting why don't you start with telling us your client's position on this case?"

"Certainly," he replied. He looked at her then turned and looked at Marshall. "We fully understand the school's concern for the security and integrity of their computer system. We all read and hear things daily about hacking and security breaches that end up putting people's information at risk. But after reading the details of the charges brought against Mr. Arnone and conducting a very careful review of the California statutes on computer crime I can only reach one conclusion."

He paused, looked over at Jimmy and then back to Stuart. "The facts simply don't justify the charges."

Stuart glanced down at her notes and then looked at Dylan with a surprised expression. "Do you mean you don't believe your client broke the law?" That's hard to swallow."

"I mean the charges filed by your office on the school's behalf don't meet the specific criteria for a Class B misdemeanor as you have charged."

Marshall finally spoke. "The kid managed to get around our firewall and hack our system. That's a fact."

Dylan nodded. "Yes, Mr. Arnone did that. He accessed your system without authorization. But that, in and of itself, isn't enough to convict him."

Marshall seemed to be irritated. "He hacked our system!" he said in a much louder voice.

"Here," Dylan began. "Let me ask you a few basic questions. First, did Mr. Arnone obtain any data, services or benefits from the intrusion?"

"Well no, not that we're aware of."

"Second, did his intrusion cause any degradation or damage to your system?"

"No, there was no damage."

"Was there any indication that Mr. Arnone intended to profit from the intrusion, like did he ask for money or anything of value?"

"No." Marshall's voice had grown softer with each response.

Stuart interrupted. "There was a disruption to the operation. Mr. Marshall and his people had to shut down their e-mail server while they looked for problems."

"Mr. Arnone uploaded harmless, humorous items that became e-mail attachments. They were harmless, no viruses or malware involved, and all the recipient had to do was hit delete. That doesn't even reach the minimum Class Five threshold of five hundred dollars of damage"

Marshall's voice rose once again. "It took my assistant and me and entire day to check out everything in the system and run tests after we flushed the e-mails.

Dylan stopped and sorted through his notes and then pulled one sheet from the pile. He glanced down at it for a moment and then said, "I did some checking and because your school receives funding reimbursements from the City of San Diego the salaries of all administration and faculty are a matter of public record."

Stuart interrupted again. "Where are you going with this, Mr. Ward?"

"Well, Mr. Marshall's annual salary is sixty-two thousand three hundred dollars and his highest paid assistant makes forty-thousand four-hundred and sixty. Allowing for two weeks of vacation per year they each work one thousand nine hundred and sixty hours per year. When you divide their salaries by the number of hours you get an hourly rate. Multiply that times an eight hour day and their combined salary cost to the school for that day of checking the system comes to four hundred and five dollars and forty cents."

Both Stuart and Marshall sat in silence. Dylan continued, "For my client's intrusion to meet the requirements for even a Fifth Degree level of misdemeanor the damages or costs to the plaintiff have to be at least five hundred dollars."

"So," Stuart asked, "is your argument that there was not a sufficient amount of damage done to the system?"

"Yes, that's part of it, and by an amount of ninety-four dollars and sixty cents."

Marshall's face had turned red and he was looking straight at Stuart. "Is he right?" he asked," Is this kind of hair splitting legal?"

When Dylan had first reviewed the charges and statutes he'd assumed that the school's lawyers would know the case was on shaky ground but when Stuart had said she'd just started reviewing it and then let him kick off the conversation, he knew he was already a step ahead of them.

Before Stuart could answer the question Dylan said, "Mr. Marshall, I realize it probably sounds like I'm trivializing things but the California statutes about this are pretty specific."

Stuart nodded her head but said nothing.

Dylan continued, "My client had no intention of doing harm. He has an odd sense of humor perhaps, and he expressed it in an inappropriate way but that's all."

Before Dylan could say more Jimmy surprised him by interrupting. "Mr. Marshall, I sincerely apologize for what I did. It was just supposed to be a joke. I didn't mean anything by it."

"You hacked us and caused a whole lot of trouble and confusion."

"Yeah, I know I did but to be honest sir, you sure made it easy. It only took me about five minutes to get behind your firewall."

Jimmy couldn't have done a better job of setting things up for Dylan.

"My client just made a point that I believe could put an end to this situation and turn it into a win for both sides."

Marshall sat in silence, looked over at Stuart and then asked, "So what do you have in mind?"

"My client's prank exposed a major vulnerability in your system. He did no harm but he's a very sharp young man and if he could get in so could someone else, maybe someone who'd do more than leave behind funny attachments." He looked at Stuart and added, "If you and the school agree, I propose that in exchange for you dropping all charges and reinstating Mr. Arnone as a full-time student he will, free of charge, work with you and your staff to expose potential vulnerabilities, help you fix them and maybe even help you improve the way it works."

The four people looked around at each other's reactions but no one said a word. Finally Stuart leaned toward Marshall and said, "Roger, it sounds reasonable to me. Given the circumstances I think you should agree."

Marshall leaned back in his chair and let out a deep sigh. "Well, I'll have to check with the Dean but I guess it's okay with me." He looked at Jimmy and added, "This should be interesting."

The rest of Dylan's day was spent picking up groceries, wine and, on an impulse, fresh cut flowers. With Beth arriving the next afternoon to spend the weekend with him his domestic side, a side he hadn't tapped into in a long time seemed to be showing itself again. Except for the night he'd hacked her dream it would be the first time in nearly six months that they'd share a bed, It was an enticing situation that he should be dominating his thoughts but he couldn't seem to go more than five minutes without thinking of *Dreamware*.

With Jimmy in control of the final tweaks to the podcast there wasn't much more Dylan could do on his new venture. After a quick dinner of supermarket take-out deli food he poured himself a bourbon and sat down at his computer. He'd received a few e-mails including one from Lamar that included a reminder the two friends hadn't gotten together in a long time.

The message reminded him that it had been Lamar who'd led him to the idea of *Dreamware*. That evening when they'd met a McHale's and Lamar had told him about lucid dreaming was the first step toward taking his nighttime hobby to a higher level.

Lamar's simple comment, tossed out easily over drinks in a bar had turned a hobby into an obsession. And that obsession had now become the beginnings of a business.

He sent Lamar a reply that simply said, "Yeah, it's been way too long. What the hell is wrong with us? I have much to tell you, will call this weekend."

Sleep that evening was back to being the way it was before lucid dreaming and dream sharing and anything other than what came naturally. There were a few simple dreams that he barely remembered when he woke up Saturday morning. There was no need to stare at the ceiling analyzing what they meant. They were nothing he'd think about later in the day.

In a way he felt relieved.

Beth pulled into his driveway shortly after noon and between then and Sunday evening they were just a couple, two people who cared about each other and enjoyed being together. They shared meals, drank wine and made love. When he watched her drive away on Sunday he stood in his driveway thinking back to the past day and a half.

The thing that struck him most was the fact that, at long last, he'd finally spent a weekend like his friends probably had, a weekend where he wasn't alone and where he didn't feel the need to retreat into his dream world.

Despite the warm feeling of the moment he knew himself well enough to know he'd be back enjoying the world of *Dreamware* very soon. And that he couldn't keep the details from Beth much longer.

CHAPTER 16

I have a dream, a fantasy to help me through reality,
and my destination makes it worth the while.

From the song *I Have a Dream* by ABBA

MONDAY MORNING WAS DYLAN'S FIRST day back at the office after his brief but enjoyable reprieve from being a lawyer. It started out with enough rain to slow his commute but not enough to dampen his eagerness to engage John Finch. This wouldn't be just another frustrating Monday. Their stand-off had lasted six years and that was long enough. Dylan felt invigorated from his time away from Doyle and Finch. It wasn't just from all of the work on *Dreamware*. He was ready to state his case and get his career out of neutral for once and for all.

When he walked into his office there was a light blue envelope on his desk; and in it a card that said "Good Luck" printed in big blue letters on the outside and "Stand up for yourself, you deserve this" handwritten in blue. At the bottom was a large hand-drawn heart and "Beth". Once again she had done some small thing that brightened his day.

Fifty-nine emails on his computer, eleven text messages on his phone and a stack of files on his desk weren't enough to take his mind off his ten o'clock meeting with Finch. Somehow he managed to focus enough to get a few things done but at five minutes to ten he stood up, straightened his tie, picked up two sets of stapled pages of notes and details he'd compiled as his talking points and headed down the corridor. Every step seemed to embolden him and strengthen his resolve. It was D-day, Dylan's Day.

When he reached Finch's office the door was partially closed. He knocked three times and heard Finch say in a flat tone, "Yes, come in."

"Good morning, John. Are you ready for me? Dylan hoped his tone was the appropriate mix of warmth and professional respect.

"Yes, I'm ready, have a seat. I don't think this will take too long."

The words sounded both ominous and insulting and Dylan had no idea what to say in response. He sat down in front of Finch's desk and crossed his legs, his notes on his lap. He thought about making small talk or throwing out some gesture of camaraderie but decided to let Finch make the first move. As usual Finch had yet to make eye contact and spent a few minutes sifting through paperwork. Finally he leaned back, adjusted his glasses and finally looked straight at Dylan.

"So here we are, Mr. Ward. Another year has gone by and once again you have been asked to present your case for partnership."

"Yeah, here we are again only this time it's just you and me. I'm still curious as to why the Partner's Committee isn't involved in this like they have been every other time."

Finch's stiff expression revealed nothing in the way of emotion or even common courtesy. "It was my decision to do this review on my own. I didn't believe the partners needed to take time away from their clients just to rehash the same points we have discussed so many times."

Dylan's earlier confidence was slipping and he sensed that Finch's decision had already been made. The same resentment he'd felt every other time he'd dealt with the man started to surface. Something inside him, a feeling he got on a regular basis, told him he should go on offense.

He took a breath and said, "Well despite your opinion that we are only here to rehash the past I have six pages of facts and figures here that say otherwise and I assume I'll be given the chance to present them." With that he laid a set of his notes on the desk. Finch glanced down at them but made no move to pick them up.

Dylan knew he had to make some kind of effort to keep the conversation going in a way that would benefit him. "If you care to read along with me that's fine," he said, "but if not I'll just run down this spreadsheet for you. It's a three-year summary that lists the clients I have represented, the fees generated, the firm's overhead in each case and lastly the verdicts. The last few pages are comments and thanks from a variety of clients who appreciated my work and what I did for them. That includes several members of the Makris family."

Dylan noticed the way Finch's left eyebrow went up when he'd said the word "Makris" and how the old man finally saw fit to pick up the notes and flip through the pages. There was silence as Dylan watched Finch read through the packet. The old man's face showed no hint of emotion, even while he read through the clients' comments. As far as Dylan was concerned his report was everything he needed to finally clear the last hurdle to partnership. The thought was nice while it lasted, until Finch quashed whatever confidence Dylan was clinging to.

"Your report is very well organized and very detailed," he said as he tossed the pages back on to his desk, "but I'm not sure it's a compelling argument for becoming a principal."

Dylan felt his stomach tightening and a feeling of anger bordering on rage coming over him. If ever there was a time to maintain his self-control he knew this was it. "John, I've been in the profession and with this firm long enough to know how people make it to partner. They work hard, satisfy their clients and earn their trust and in doing so they make a profit for the firm. The summary I just gave you proves that I have accomplished all of that for at least three years."

Finch sat back in his chair and stared at Dylan with the same blank, emotionless expression. "There is more to being a lawyer than numbers." He was silent after that, as if daring Dylan to challenge him.

Dylan's mind was a swirl of thoughts; about his report, about his moonlight work and about his history of clashes with Finch. He slid his chair closer to the desk and leaned forward, almost as a way of telling Finch he wasn't about to back down.

"Well then, since you made the decision to control my future without the committee's involvement, suppose you tell me what the magic formula is." It was sarcastic and borderline rude but Dylan felt good in saying the words, words that put the ball squarely in Finch's court. Dylan waited, the only sound in the room the ticking of a brass-framed clock on the desk.

Finch finally sat up straight then leaned forward, his face no more than a foot from Dylan's and his coffee-tinged breath noticeable. He cleared his throat and said, "The magic formula also includes looking and acting professional at all times. There have been times when your methods have been somewhat less than that."

Somehow Dylan held his position and his self-control. "The kind of cases I deal with sometimes demand different methods than you have ever had to use in business law. You can't measure them, or me, by the same yardstick that you use to measure anyone else in this firm. If you were to ask my clients their opinion of my methods I'm sure they'd say they don't care as long as I get them off the hook." He paused for a moment and then said, "Take a minute to read the Makris brothers' comments and see if they give a rat's ass about my methods."

Once again he had gone out on a limb with his words and once again he sat there both satisfied and upset with himself. And once again he was feeling the high he got from confrontation.

Finch's emotionless face had slowly changed. He looked flushed and angry but, surprisingly, he didn't respond the way Dylan had expected. Instead, he leaned back and let out a long, slow breath. He ran a hand over his chin and, looking down at the desk, said, "I'll have an answer for you on Friday morning."

Dylan was surprised that such an important discussion could be so brief and come to such an abrupt ending. Given the contentious nature of the conversation he decided it was time to back off and let things play out. As far as he was concerned he had made his case and now it was up to Finch to make his decision.

"Okay," he said as he straightened the stack of papers in his hands and stood up. He hesitated for a moment, tempted to extend his hand to Finch in a gesture of professional courtesy but when Finch just sat there looking down at the desk it was clear this annual review was over.

"Thank you for your time, John," he said, then turned and walked out.

When he sat back down in his own office it occurred to him that he didn't even remember the walk down the corridor or if he had passed anyone along the way. He felt numb and confused. "What the fuck just happened?" he asked himself. He had been so confident about arguing his case with Finch but the old man's negativity was like a punch in the stomach. And it dawned on him that using a term like *rat's ass* in a serious discussion about his future had probably been a mistake. "Geez," he thought, "I don't have a good feeling about what that son of a bitch is going to do."

It was just before noon when his computer chimed with an urgent e-mail message tone. He scrolled down and saw a message from Beth that read "Hey, how did it go? Are you back in your office? Call me." He thought for a moment and then replied, "Much to figure out. How about lunch?"

Fortunately the crowd at *Dominick's* was light, probably because it was a Monday, and they got their salads and pizza slices fairly quickly. Despite the fact he was planning to return to the office Dylan ordered a bottle of beer with his lunch and figured the usual dosage of breath mints would hide the smell.

They grabbed a table that was out of the line of traffic so a conversation couldn't be easily overheard and had no sooner sat down when Beth said, "Okay, from what you said on the way over things went fast and you didn't get an answer, so what in the hell do you think is going on? Do you think Finch already had his mind made up before you met?"

"That's what I thought at first but I kind of got in his face and showed him my summary and he kind of pulled back. But you know how he is, he never shows any emotion. He just talks to you in his "I'm the boss and you're not" tone and leaves you guessing what's on his mind."

"I read every word of your report and when I finished all I could think was, "Holy shit, this is one great argument for becoming a partner."

"Thanks, and I thought so too. But from day one there's been something about me that asshole just doesn't like. It's my appearance or my attitude or my methods or something that makes him think I'm not worthy."

"Well, just keep your cool and be careful what you say for the rest of the day. If Finch is on the fence about his decision you don't want to do anything to push him off."

It was as relaxing an hour as Dylan could expect given that his conversation with Finch was playing over and over again in his head. When they got back to the office they walked through the front door together with the knowledge that some tongues would be wagging before they made it halfway down the corridor. Beth had already made evening plans with two friends so they agreed to have lunch the next day.

After the meeting with Finch and an afternoon full of dealing with his caseloads both in and out of the office Dylan looked forward to sampling a new bottle of bourbon he'd purchased and finally, after a long hiatus, getting back into his dream world.

A take-out Mexican dinner, two beers, an ample serving of bourbon and enough television to block out the stress of the day put him into a comfortable frame of mind. His intricate bedtime ritual had become second nature to him and it felt good to finally find himself floating on the edge of sleep again.

FADE IN
EXTERIOR – DECK OF A SWIMMING POOL BEHIND AN ELEGANT STONE HOUSE – DAYTIME

A gray-haired man, clad in slacks and a polo shirt sits in a chair, alternately reading a newspaper and looking at his cellphone. A glass of iced tea sits on a small table beside him. He is interrupted when a woman wearing golf attire opens the back door of the house and walks toward him.

SANDRA FINCH: John, dear, I'm heading out now to pick up Nancy. We had to change our tee-time to one-thirty so I have to hurry.

JOHN FINCH: Alright. What about dinner?

SANDRA: I should be back in time to fix us something unless you'd like to go out somewhere.

JOHN: No, I'm not in the mood for crowds or bad service. Let's stay home.

SANDRA: We haven't eaten out in weeks. I thought the idea might appeal to you.

JOHN: Well, it doesn't.

Sandra sighs and stands there for a moment, just staring at her husband. Then she turns to leave.

SANDRA: Goodbye.

Finch continues his reading, stopping occasionally to sip his tea. He is interrupted again when he hears the squeaking of the pool gate and he turns to see a young man walking through it.

FINCH: Mr. Ward, what are you doing here? I don't recall inviting you.

Dylan sees a flash of sunlight glinting off the surface of the pool as he approaches Finch.

DYLAN: Well, John, whether you realize it or not you invited me.

FINCH: I have no idea what you're talking about and I want you to leave.

Ignoring Finch's instruction Dylan takes a seat at the other table-side chair. He leans back, squinting in the sun and looking at Finch with a faint smile.

DYLAN: So this is where you live. Pretty impressive. I've heard from some people at the office that you live in a mansion and they weren't exaggerating. I'm betting every single partner has been here before, sitting and sipping tea or something.

FINCH: I'm asking you again to please leave, and leave now.

DYLAN: So why is it you never invited me to your parties, John? I know I'm not a partner yet but I've been with the firm long enough to merit a little socializing. You should invite me some time, I'm a real party kind of guy.

FINCH: You don't get it, do you? I simply don't like you. I never have.

Dylan's smile disappears and his expression changes to noticeable anger. He sits forward and leans toward Finch. The old man appears to be nervous and leans back, trying to keep his distance from Dylan.

DYLAN: I've never given you any reason to dislike me.

FINCH: On the contrary, you have given me any number of reasons. There's your casual approach to the firm's rules. That beard that makes you look more like a bum than a lawyer. And there's your propensity to appear in a courtroom and conduct yourself in a manner that can only be described as loose and reckless.

With that comment Finch stands up and looks down at Dylan.

FINCH: For the last time I'm asking you to leave. If you don't I'll phone the police and ask them to escort you to the curb.

Dylan stands and steps toward Finch. His face is a mere foot away from Finch's and his anger is obvious.

DYLAN: Look, John, I can handle your dislike for me but what I can't handle is your condescending attitude. It's been so long since you had your fat ass was in a courtroom you don't remember what it's like. You're all about the bottom line and nothing else. You're just a fucking businessman. I'm a lawyer and a good one and I know what it takes to help my clients.

FINCH: They're not *your* clients they're *Doyle and Finch's* clients. They come through our door because they know our reputation, not to meet the great and wonderful Dylan Ward.

With every word Finch's face becomes redder and his breath comes in short bursts. He reaches for the back of his chair to steady himself and then Dylan uses his left leg to kick the chair away. Finch falls to the pool deck and stares up at Dylan. The old man tries to regain his composure and starts to stand up. As he does his right shoe slips on the curbing of the pool edge. His arms flail in an attempt to keep his balance but he falls backward into the pool.

FINCH: Ward, help me!

The old man thrashes around in the water, struggling to stay afloat. Dylan stands at the edge of the pool, smiling and watching the man's struggles but makes no effort to help him. Finally Dylan turns just as a reflection from the water flashes across his face. He walks back out through the gate, feeling dizzy and steadying himself for a moment against the frame. He is gone before the man slips beneath the surface.

FADE OUT

CHAPTER 17

We all are living in a dream, but life ain't what
it seems. Oh, everything's a mess.

From the song *Dream* by Imagine Dragons

AS DYLAN SAT ON THE edge of his bed that Tuesday morning details of the previous night's dream filled his head. It was the sixth dream that belonged to someone else that he'd been drawn into by using his dream hacking techniques. John Finch had had a dream that had probably been triggered by his thoughts of his contentious meeting with Dylan earlier in the day. At least that was the only possible explanation that made any sense. Being drawn into the dream was a surprise beyond description and Dylan wondered why he'd said and done the things he had.

It was as though in a dream or real life, conflict between the two men was inevitable.

He laid back down and stared at the ceiling, trying to conjure up a replay of the dream. He hoped it might lead him to an answer about his behavior in the dream of the man who held the key to his future.

This dream was definitely troubling. It was different from the other five. When he'd hacked into Max's dream he'd enjoyed playing the role of a troublemaker for a man he disliked so intensely. It seemed like harmless fun even though it had resulted in problems for Max. When Beth's dream drew him in the result was a deep and sensual reconnection with the woman he loved. Both dreams had been varying degrees of invasions into someone else's life.

When he invaded Mark's dream it was just old friends getting back together and having the kind of fun they'd had all through college. His mother's dream, as unsettling as it was for him, was still just a simple story based upon old memories. And he couldn't begin to figure out what Kelly's dream might have meant. But none of those dreams felt even close to what happened after he'd entered Finch's mind.

Finch's dream had felt like reality.

The chime signal on his phone brought him back to the present. He rolled on to his side and picked it up from the nightstand. It was a text message from Beth, a reminder that he'd asked her to lunch and that they could decide on a place and time when they got to the office. He felt a strange sense of relief. Beth had always been the only person who could take his mind off whatever it was he was thinking at any given moment. Her timing was perfect. He knew he had to stop dwelling on his dream and get into the day, a day that would include the woman who had once again filled an empty spot in his life.

The rush hour traffic was heavier than usual and he got to the office about twenty minutes late. He didn't encounter anyone on his walk to his office which was fine with him. Then came the daily routine of laying his computer case on the desk, hanging his suitcoat on the hook on the back of his doo r and setting up his laptop. He was ready to head down the corridor for a cup of coffee when he heard the ping of an incoming email. It was Beth and the message read, "Are you in yet? We have to talk now!"

"He typed back, "Just got here, come on over." He wondered if he was just imagining the urgent tone to her message. The look on Beth's face when she walked in told him his hunch was right.

"What's the matter?" he asked. "Your message sounded like you were kind of stressed."

"Something has happened. It's terrible." she said, her voice soft and unsteady.

Dylan closed the door behind her and waited for her to say or do something to explain her obvious distress. She took a deep breath and said, "I just was talking with Sarah. She was talking to Anne Carter who got a call from John Finch's wife this morning." She paused and her voice seemed to crack when she said, "John Finch died last night in his sleep."

Dylan didn't say a word. He couldn't tell if he was feeling surprise, shock, grief or a strange sense of satisfaction. The sour, old man who had stood in his way for six years was no longer an obstacle. He stood there as the dream came rushing back. He saw Finch fall into the pool. He heard the man's cry for help. And he did nothing to help him. Then it dawned on him. Finch was a sick, old man with a bad heart. Did the struggle with Dylan in the dream trigger the man's death?

"Dylan, did you hear what I said? Finch is dead."

It took him a few more seconds to pull himself together and then he finally said, "Yeah, I heard you I just don't know what to make of it. I guess I should feel some kind of sadness but I don't. On his best day Finch could barely scrape together even basic courtesy toward me. I guess I can say I'm surprised but sorry, I'm not sad."

Beth looked at him almost as if she was studying his face, looking for something. "I guess I know how you feel but it's still such a shock." Her expression didn't change. "The story from his wife is that he was kind of tossing and turning in his sleep, like he was having a nightmare, and it kept her awake. He was mumbling and she said it sounded like "Lord, help me. Then he reached over and grabbed her arm and then fell back.""

Once again Dylan just stood there, staring at Beth without hearing her and replaying the dream in his mind. He remembered every word and every sound, Finch's anger, his face and the sight of him struggling in the water. Dylan's silence lasted long enough for Beth to once again interrupt his thoughts.

"Dylan, are you listening? Where is your head?

"I heard what you said," he lied. He took a deep breath and tried to focus on Beth instead of his own thoughts but it wasn't easy. "This Friday was when he was supposed to tell me about the partnership. Our meeting yesterday didn't go well but I had my fingers crossed that it was finally going to happen. Now it looks like things are back to square one."

Beth's expression didn't change. She stared into his eyes and started, "I'm going to say something here and I'm not sure how you'll feel about it. I'm not even sure what to think but here goes." She paused and said, "When I was talking to Sarah and I found out that this thing with Finch seemed to involve a dream I automatically thought of you. It's like another situation where someone has a dream and then something happens. First it was Max and then me and now Finch. And it was the night after he had a meeting with you."

Dylan wanted to reach for her even though he wasn't sure why but he held back. "I'm not sure what you're implying but I don't think I like it."

"I'm not sure if I'm implying something or just wondering out loud but there are just too many questions and coincidences with everything that's going on."

She leaned back in her chair and let out a long sigh. Dylan leaned forward in his. Neither of them spoke for an uncomfortably long time until Beth said, "Dylan, it's like I said, there seem to be a lot of coincidences here. I mean it's like your dreams are part of what's happening in your life and that's kind of weird."

Dylan squirmed in his chair and struggled to act like last night's dream had never happened. A man had died while dreaming a dream that Dylan controlled. How could he possibly block it from his mind? He tried to maintain eye contact with Beth and hold an expression on his face that didn't convey anything more than interest in her comment. "So you're thinking my dreaming is somehow different than yours or anyone else's."

Beth leaned toward him and he couldn't begin to read the mixed message her face was showing. "Dylan, I know your dreaming is different than most people's, hell maybe everyone's. You dream a lot and you enjoy it and that's okay. But somehow I have this feeling it's gotten out of control."

And what's that supposed to mean?"

"I'm not totally sure what I mean or what I'm feeling about all this. Look, sleep is something that's supposed to be totally private, the one thing you're guaranteed is your own. If you have a dream it belongs only to you. No one else needs to know what it was about. No one needs to know what you did or what happened."

"And you're telling me this because you think I disagree with that?"

Her expression was still impossible to read and she hesitated before she replied. Finally she sighed and answered, "That book I gave you, the one about dream legends, you told me you read about something called dream sharing, about a belief that a person could get into another person's dreams. Have you tried to do that, I mean get into someone's dream?"

He hesitated, thinking again how he didn't want her to see the part of *Dreamware* that involved dream sharing. He struggled for the right words and finally answered, "Beth, it's a legend, a story. Dream sharing is something people have talked about for years and that's why it's in that book. And remember, the book is about dream legends and nothing more." He hoped that would be enough of an answer to change her line of questioning but it wasn't.

"I looked through that book a little before I gave it to you and I got the impression that some of those things were real enough that people believed them. They were more than just stories. People actually did some of those things. Now I'm wishing I'd never given it to you."

"Yeah, I know but still most of the stuff in that book is just legend. It's just superstition that's fun to think about and nothing more." He waited for a reply that didn't come and then said, "You know, I can't believe we're having this conversation."

"Well I don't like talking this way either but a man died in his sleep last night, probably while he was dreaming and he had a connection to you. How can I help but think about that?"

"Look, I can't say I'm surprised that the whole dream thing popped into your head but you have to just take it for what it is and nothing more."

"Okay, so go ahead and tell me what it is."

It was clear that Beth wasn't going to let go of her uncertainty about the facts of Finch's death. As usual she was like a dog on a bone and he had to think of some way to make her drop it. He looked her straight in the eye hoping his words wouldn't sound angry or defensive. "Look, I've been a dreamer all my life and to me it's just normal. When I go to sleep at night I don't know any other kind of experience except dreaming and dreaming a lot. It's not something I can stop even if I wanted to.

"Yeah, that's all well and good but..."

"Wait, let me finish. Everyone has dreams and they usually involve people and things that are part of their lives. That's what my dreams are made of and the fact they intertwine with things that are really going on makes perfect sense to me."

Beth hesitated before she replied, "I have never had a dream that affected what happened in my life or anyone else's life either. When my dreams are over I wake up and they're forgotten and I go on with things in the real world but your dreams don't seem to end and they don't seem to have any boundaries."

Dylan sat there in silence and finally he was able to read the expression on her face. It was fear. Suddenly he had the most uncomfortable feeling he'd ever had with her. Could the woman he loved actually be afraid of him?

"Okay," he started, trying to choose his words carefully, "this is obviously a very strange situation. I can tell you're upset and so am I. When you told me about Finch I have to say I was surprised but not shocked. Given his health history I figured his days were numbered but you seem to have read something more into the situation. Maybe we should just bag our lunch plans and retreat to neutral corners."

"You make it sound as though we're fighting about this."

"Well, aren't we?"

"No, I don't see it that way. I'm just trying to figure out what's going on."

"You mean with my dreams."

"Yeah, with your dreams and with you. I'm just trying to connect the dots."

Despite Beth's calm and measured tone Dylan couldn't help but feel he was on the defensive. She had always taken a light hearted and bemused view of his dreaming but now that seemed to have changed. She was the only one who knew what had been going on with his recent dreams and the things that had happened as a result of them.

He hesitated a moment and then said, "There are no dots to connect. It's like you said before, this is all just a few coincidences but I think you better go before this conversation takes a turn I don't want it to take."

"I confess I'm not in the mood for lunch or anything else right now and I'll probably cancel my plans with Sarah later. She'll just want to talk about Finch and that's the last thing I want to think about."

Dylan stood up and then Beth did too. He took two steps toward her and thought about kissing her. She seemed to stiffen so he stepped back.

"I'll call you later," he said. He followed her to the door and when she looked back at him as she left her expression hadn't changed.

He knew that fear and romance didn't mix.

He slowly eased into the strangest workday he'd ever experienced. The official news of Finch's death appeared as a firm-wide email sent from the partner's committee. It was the expected mix of solemn words of sympathy to Finch's family and praise for his years of leadership in guiding the firm.

There was a strange silence around the office. A few small groups of people stood talking very quietly but for the most part everyone seemed focused on their work. The usual office banter was missing. If anyone was feeling grief he couldn't detect it.

Dylan read the partner's message over and over. He was in a fog of confusion and emotion unlike anything he'd ever felt before. The more he'd thought about the circumstances of Finch's death the more he felt it was his doing. Finch had unknowingly drawn Dylan into his dream and Dylan, once in, was in control. There was any number of way's he could have conducted himself during the dream. Why had he chosen to be confrontational? Why had he stepped toward the old man and forced him to back up into the pool? And most of all when the man cried out for help why had Dylan turned his back and allowed the man to drown?

Within the boundaries of the dream that was probably what triggered a heart attack or some kind of coronary episode. If Dylan had rescued Finch from the imaginary pool would the man still be alive?

Dylan picked up his cellphone and started to punch in Beth's number but then he stopped and hit cancel. What would he say to her to make her feel any different from the way she felt less than an hour ago? Unlike the other people in his life who joked about his dreams she'd always been mildly interested in them. She knew about his lucid dreaming and never criticized him for it. But it was obvious his interest in dream sharing smelled odd to her. She was too smart to buy his story that everything was a series of coincidences.

Too much had happened to too many people in too short a period of time and the common denominator was Dylan and his dreaming.

He knew he had to get away from the office for a while so just before noon he slipped out a side door and headed to his truck. The only lunch place that came to mind was McHale's. He got there fairly quickly and just sat in the parking lot for a while, still trying to clear his head.

When he finally went inside and sat down at the bar he was glad to see that Kelly wasn't working. It had only been a few days since he'd invaded her dream and there was no way to know if the sexual encounter they'd come close to having would have faded away from her memory. And if she approached him with her dazzling smile there was no way he could make small talk or pretend his life was normal.

He ordered his lunch and a beer and ate in silence, staring at the highlights of a college football game on the big screen without caring who the teams were.

People who are responsible for someone's death find it hard to focus on small things.

The rest of the day was made up of staring at his computer without actually working, starting and stopping a dozen calls to Beth and reaching into his desk drawer for his flask. He knew that drinking bourbon in the afternoon was wrong on so many levels but he did it anyway.

If Finch hadn't died he knew that he and Beth would have made plans for happy hour but on this day he never called her to arrange it and neither had she. After a longer than normal commute he pulled into his driveway without remembering the drive.

He never got around to making dinner and by eight o'clock going to bed seemed like the logical next step. But somehow it felt different. Something he'd always looked forward to now made him feel strangely nervous. Sleep led to dreams and dreams led to adventure, or at least they used to. Maybe Beth was right to be afraid of him. Maybe he should be afraid of himself.

When he finally staggered into bed he had made the decision to just fall asleep. No breathing ritual, no special position in the bed and no attempt at controlling what happened once he was asleep. He figured he'd have a dream or two like nearly every night of his life but tonight would be just that and that only. The last two inches of bourbon in his bottle sped up the process.

FADE IN
EXTERIOR – ALBERTSON'S GROCERY STORE – NIGHT

A man walks toward the front entrance of the store and enters through the automatic doors. He pulls a shopping cart from the rack and walks down the first aisle. The store appears to be crowded for that time of night. The man notices that the other shoppers have carts and baskets full of groceries but he is shocked when he sees that every shelf in the store is empty. He steps toward a heavy set young woman who is standing beside her cart as she looks through her purse.

DYLAN: Excuse me, miss, but where did you get all the stuff in your cart? The shelves are all empty. It looks like the whole store is empty.

WOMAN: Well, it wasn't empty when I got here.

The woman turns and walks away and Dylan is confused about what he sees around him. He turns to his left and pushes his cart toward the checkout aisles but when he looks ahead he sees that every register light is turned off and there are no cashiers. Customers are walking through the lanes with full carts but not stopping to pay. He parks his cart beside an empty display case and walks down the main cross aisle. He turns his head to the right and looks down every aisle and sees the same empty shelves and customers with full carts all heading for the front of the store. Finally he spots a man in a black work apron and nametag and walks over to him.

DYLAN: What in the hell is going on here? No merchandise left and nobody paying for what they got off the shelves.

MAN: Sir, we'll be closing in five minutes. I suggest you find what you came for quickly.

DYLAN: There's nothing to find! Your store is empty, man, it's fucking empty.

The man gives Dylan an unfriendly look and walks away. Starting at the back of the store the lights begin to shut off. By the time Dylan makes it back to the main door the customers are gone and all of the lights are off. He walks back through the automatic door and hears it click and lock as it closes behind him. Except for two pole lights the parking lot is dark. There are no cars or people and even his truck is gone.

DYLAN: What the fuck is going on?

Feeling near panic he runs to the nearer pole light and looks down the alley beside the store. He sees a small security light on the wall at the rear corner. The light is just bright enough to illuminate two men standing nearby, the glow from their cigarettes visible in the shadows. Dylan quickly walks toward them. When he is about twenty feet away he shouts to them.

DYLAN: Hey, do you guys work here at the store?

TALL MAN: Yeah, who's askin'?

DYLAN: I'm just a customer and when I went inside the whole place was emptied out and people were pushing carts and went through the lines without paying. And now everyone's gone and so is my truck.

FAT MAN: I guess you better call somebody.

Dylan noticed that when the men spoke he couldn't see their lips moving. He pulled his cellphone from his pocket and saw the power readout showed no bars. There was no way he could call anyone. He turned and looked across the rear delivery area behind the store. He saw a glow of light and the outlines of two people.

DYLAN: Thanks for nothing.

He hurried toward the light and the two figures. When he was closer he once again saw the glow of two cigarettes in the darkness. When he was about twenty feet away he stopped, his heart pounding. It was the same two men he had just talked to.

DYLAN: Do you work here? What the fuck is going on?

TALL MAN: Yeah, who's askin'?

DISSOLVE TO:
INTERIOR – VIBRATIONS GENTLEMEN'S CLUB – NIGHT

A man walks through the front door and approaches the hostess stand. A slender, once-beautiful woman greets him.

WOMAN: Welcome to Vibrations.

DYLAN: Thanks. I'm here for the ten o'clock show.

WOMAN: Sure. You just pay that man right there in the pay booth.

Dylan walks over to the wire-screened booth where a grizzled looking old man wearing jeans and a black tee-shirt stands by a cash register. He looks at Dylan with a stiff expression.

OLD MAN: Can I help you?

DYLAN: Yeah, I'm here for the ten o'clock show. How much is it?

OLD MAN: I take it you're not one of our regulars.

DYLAN: No, I'm not. I just wanted to come and see Misty.

OLD MAN: Well, you can see her all you want but that's all. If there's any touching or grabbing or foul language that large man with the tattoos over there will help you find your way out the door.

DYLAN: Don't worry, I'm her lawyer.

OLD MAN: You don't look like no lawyer.

DYLAN: Thank you for that. Now how much do I owe you?

OLD MAN: It's ten bucks to get in for the show on the main stage. Private shows in the back rooms are a hundred bucks an hour. You can get yourself a lap dance out here in the main room for free but there's a ten dollar minimum tip.

DYLAN: Oh, I guess I'll just go for the admission for the main stage.

The old man sneered and shook his head as Dylan slid a ten dollar bill under the edge of the cage.

OLD MAN: How about drinks? You can buy a bar pass in ten dollar increments or just pay as you go. A girl will come around for your order.

DYLAN: I'll pay as I go.

OLD MAN: You'll be needing singles to tip the girls. I can give you change in ten dollar increments.

DYLAN: That's okay, I already have some in my wallet.

OLD MAN: Boy you sure are a big spender aren't you?

Dylan takes his admission stub from the man and looks at the tables clustered around the main stage. There are still a fair number of empty tables so he heads toward the bar to order a drink. A bear-like middle aged man with gray hair and a nose piercing is tending bar.

BARTENDER: Hey, man, what can I get you?

DYLAN: I'll have a bourbon with one ice cube.

The bartender walks to the back bar and prepares the drink while Dylan looks around the room. He sees Misty standing near the entrance curtain to the stage. She's talking to another dancer and a man in a gray suit. The bartender returns and slides a half-full pint glass toward him. Dylan looks at it in surprise.

DYLAN: No, I didn't want a beer I wanted bourbon.

BARTENDER: That is bourbon. I gave you a good pour.

DYLAN: That's a pint glass. I can't drink all that.

BARTENDER: You never know until you try. This way you won't have to take your eyes off the girls every time you want a refill. And here's some gum so nobody'll know you was drinkin'. That'll be ten bucks.

Dylan hands the man a ten and a five dollar bill.

DYLAN: Keep the change.

Dylan finds himself a small table in the front row just a few feet from the stage. He sits and looks around the room, not sure if he's feeling embarrassed for being there. After a few minutes Misty spots him and walks over to him. She is still wearing street clothes but looks every bit as sexy as he remembered her in full costume.

MISTY: Hi, Dylan, what are you doing here?

DYLAN: Oh, I had a free evening for a change and it occurred to me that you're a client but I've never seen you work.

MISTY: Oh, okay, I just never took you for someone who'd come to a place like this.

DYLAN: Don't say it like that. You're here so it must be a nice place.

MISTY: That's sweet of you to put it like that but come on, it is what it is.

She hesitates and looks at him, suddenly seeming nervous. She looks down at the floor and then back at him.

MISTY: Dylan, you're a really nice guy and I really like you but you're also my lawyer and I don't think it would be right for you to be stuffing dollar bills in my thong.

Dylan is surprised by the comment and it takes him a moment to respond.

DYLAN: Don't worry, I promise I'll just watch.

Misty walks away and steps through the curtain behind the stage. Dylan sips his huge glass of bourbon as every table and chair is soon filled. At exactly ten o'clock the house lights go down, the pink and blue stage lights come up, what passes for sexy music comes up on the sound system and Misty steps through the shiny red curtain. For the next half hour Dylan sits in the darkness and watches her dance, strut, bend over and smile provocatively at every man in the room except him. He's not sure how to feel about it.

FADE OUT

CHAPTER 18

Restless sleep, the mind's in turmoil. One nightmare
ends, another fertile. It's getting to me, so scared to
sleep but scared to wake now, in too deep.

From the song *"Infinite Dreams"* by Iron Maiden

HOW DO PEOPLE STAY GROUNDED in reality? What are the things that the average person clings to that help to keep the crazy at bay? Is it family, friends, religion or maybe just a simple day-to-day routine that doesn't ever change? How do people block out the things that work to take them in the wrong direction while still trying to stay engaged in the world around them?

Dylan found himself spending yet another morning staring at his ceiling, one more morning of reconstructing the events of his life and the events in his dreams. It was how he'd started countless mornings in the past but this one felt very different. Last night's dreams were like the mundane ones he'd had all of his life. No lucid dream awareness and control over the events. No major excitement. For the first time in a while they were his dreams and not someone else's.

Given the events of the previous day with Beth and everything that had happened, his decision to avoid the preparation techniques to take his dreams to a higher level had made sense before he'd climbed into bed. But now in hindsight the ordinariness of them made him feel he'd been shortchanged. He wanted more.

Dream sharing had become his obsession.

A dozen times on Wednesday he picked up his phone to call Beth but every time he did it he changed his mind and put it down. He felt like his life was in total limbo. His newly rebuilt relationship with her was strained to say the least. His hopes for making partner were definitely stalled with no clear idea of what would come next. That meant that his moonlight work would probably have to continue so he could maintain the income he'd gotten used to.

But most of all he was uncertain about where things were going with his dreaming. He'd seen how Beth seemed afraid of what his dreams had brought about and no matter how much he tried to deny it he couldn't help but share her fear. And now that *Dreamware* had gone live he wondered if he'd be able to manage what might lie ahead.

The day drifted along without him feeling the need to leave the office. He somehow got caught up on his Doyle and Finch cases and the three moonlight cases he was juggling. There were several firm-wide e-mails with details of Finch's funeral on Saturday. Scheduling it for a weekend seemed exactly what Finch would have wanted: Don't waste a workday when everyone should be putting in billable hours.

As much as we wanted to avoid it he knew he had to play the loyal employee and be there to feign grief. And when he showed up, how would Beth respond?

Somehow during the course of the day he'd even found time to sneak a peek at the new *Dreamware Facebook* page and was surprised to find that, thanks to Jimmy and his friends spreading the word, he already had nearly fifty people following him. Many of them had left comments like "OMG, this looks so cool!" and "I am absolutely going to check out this podcast." And a man named Morgan Prishak from Los Angeles said, "Wow, if this dream sharing thing really works I've already got a list of people I plan to dream-visit, including my ex-wife."

Dylan couldn't help but think how that last comment had an undercurrent of menace to it.

One of the other people who commented was a woman named Stephanie Parrish. She was the co-host of a local TV talk show and she asked for contact information for whoever created *Dreamware*. She wanted to arrange for an on-air interview and a simulcast with their Los Angeles sister-station. Without hesitation he left *Facebook* and then *Googled* the TV station. He found her profile and contact information and sent her a message with the items she requested along with a comment that he would only be available on Monday to tape an interview. For a moment, greed had overcome any sense of guilt or fear.

His little side venture seemed to have some momentum and he knew that many online businesses grew exponentially. He felt a mixture of excitement and nervousness, knowing full well that the part of *Dreamware* that excited people the most was the part that Beth would absolutely hate.

He left for home early and the two hours of remaining daylight were filled with the routine chores of laundry, cleaning and yard work. It gave him brief a respite from thinking about his problems but only for minutes at a time.

After he went back inside he tried playing his guitar and even singing while he played. He tried to find something, anything on TV that would take his mind off everything that was going on. Nothing seemed to work. He kept checking his phone screen, hoping there was a text or voicemail from Beth but it was blank.

He also checked his e-mail and was surprised to see a message from Stephanie Parrish. Apparently she was a workaholic who even kept busy in the evening. The message said she wanted to tape a ten minute long segment with him to talk about *Dreamware,* how the project came about and where did he think it would lead. She asked him if Monday at 9:00 AM would work with his schedule. Without even checking his calendar he committed to the appointment.

It felt like a risk but he figured that no one but housewives and unemployed people watched morning talk shows, at least that's what he hoped. He felt fairly confident that no one from Doyle and Finch would see it.

When darkness finally came there was nothing left to distract him or occupy his mind. He knew sleep would be coming soon and so would a dream. And when he awoke it would be Thursday, the third day at the office without John Finch.

After his nighttime grooming ritual was finished he opened a new bottle of bourbon. The second glass told him it was time for bed. He laid down and pulled the covers up to his waist, not sure of what to do next. He had trained himself to use lucid dream techniques that had led him into his own little world of slumbering adventure and he'd gotten used to the freedom and control it gave him.

But it was the other technique that he was nervous about trying again. That technique seemed to come with a power that was almost intoxicating. And he now knew it also came with consequences for everyone involved in the dream.

When he finally closed his eyes his memory conjured up a picture of Beth's expression on Tuesday morning. Loving a woman who seemed afraid of him brought him an aching he'd never felt before. His near addiction to controlling his dream world wrestled with his hunger for some kind of normalcy in his real world. A few minutes later he decided that tonight would not bring a dream of power but just a dream. A dream that he hoped would be harmless.

FADE IN
EXTERIOR – A SMALL ROADSIDE DINER – DAYTIME

A man drives slowly through the parking lot of a small diner on the outskirts of a town in farm country. It's just after noon and his eyes scan left and right for a parking space in the crowded lot. Finally he sees a place at the far edge of the asphalt that appears to be big enough to park his truck. With some effort and maneuvering he parks it and walks toward the entrance. Before opening the door he stops to take in the view of green fields, rolling hills beyond and a perfect, almost cloudless blue sky. He hears the jingle of a bell above him as he opens the door and steps inside. What he sees stops him in his tracks. Except for a heavy-set, young woman standing behind the counter the place is empty. But what is more startling to him is that as he looks around the place the entire view is in black and white. It resembles an old black and white movie. He stops, turns and looks out the front window and the view of the countryside is in full color.

DYLAN: Excuse me, what's going on here? Where are all the people driving all those cars outside?

WAITRESS: What cars? We've been so slow lately I was real glad to see you come through the door.

DYLAN: Then who's driving all those cars? I had to park half in the grass to find room.

He pauses and before she can answer he shakes his head and offers another question.

DYLAN: This is so weird, everything is in black and white in this place but it's all in color outside. What's going on?

WAITRESS: Look, mister, I don't know what you're talkin' about or what you think you're seein'. If you'd like to take a seat I'd be glad to show you the menu. Folks say our food is the best in twenty miles.

Dylan looks at her in bewilderment. He looks out the window again and sees his truck at the end of a long row of vehicles and all in full color. He looks back toward her and then up at the menu mounted on the wall behind her. Uncertain what to think or what to do he drops on to a counter stool, his back to the window. His hands are shaking as he pulls a menu from the rack on the counter. The waitress walks into the kitchen while he looks over the menu. He hears the sound of the entry bell again as a frail looking old man enters through the door. Dylan glances over as the man sits down on the stool at the end of the counter. Like everything else in the diner the man appears in black and white.

DYLAN: Excuse me, sir. I hope this doesn't sound strange but what color is my shirt?

The old man looks at Dylan with an annoyed expression, shaking his head.

OLD MAN: Well, since you asked, it's gray.

DYLAN: And my Pants?

OLD MAN: Dark gray and your shoes are black and so is your hair. Now leave me alone.

Feeling even more confused and nervous Dylan swivels his stool and faces the man who still looks annoyed.

DYLAN: One last question. What color is that SUV there by the window, the Jeep?

The man swivels and looks out the window.

OLD MAN: It's red, and the car next to it is brown and the sky is blue. What is it with you and colors?

DYLAN: Don't you think it's strange that everything in this place is in black and white and everything outside is in color?

OLD MAN: I don't think about it one way or another now how about leavin' me alone.

The waitress returns from the kitchen and walks over to the old man. They chat while Dylan pulls his cellphone from his pocket. When he looks down at the screen his uneasiness grows stronger. The normally full color screen is in black and white. He looks up when he notices the waitress standing in front of him.

WAITRESS: So have you decided what you want?

DYLAN: Uh, yeah I guess so. I'll have the patty melt and fries, and can I have extra pickles?

The waitress rolls her eyes and shrugs.

WAITRESS: Uh, yeah I guess so.

Dylan scrolls through his phone to check his messages and is surprised to see there are no text or voice messages. He checks his e-mail messages and there are none. The signal strength indicator shows no bars and he realizes he is disconnected from his normal routine and everything familiar. A few minutes later the waitress returns and sets his order in front of him.

WAITRESS: Enjoy.

Dylan looks down at the plate and like everything else in the diner the food appears in black and white. He sees steam rising from the food but when he picks up a French fry it feels like it's at room temperature. He puts it in his mouth and there is no flavor whatsoever. He can feel the fry in his mouth but there is no flavor. He picks up the sandwich and takes a large bite. Again he can feel the food in his mouth at room temperature and with no detectable flavor. The waitress walks over to the old man.

WAITRESS: So how's the barbeque today, Earl?

OLD MAN: As tasty as ever, that's why I keep comin' back.

She walks toward Dylan and then stands over him with a look of feigned interest.

WAITRESS: And how about you, how's that patty melt taste to ya'?

Dylan looks up at her and hesitates, trying to find a response that reflects the bizarre situation in which he finds himself.

DYLAN: It's everything I imagined.

FADE OUT

CHAPTER 19

You're living in dreamtime, baby, it's time to wake up.
You're living in dreamtime, baby, it's time to shape up.

From the song *"Dreamtime"* By Daryl Hall

THE REMAINDER OF HIS WORKWEEK seemed to play out in slow motion. Thursday was spent mostly in his office and a big part of Friday was spent filing motions at the courthouse and having a long lunch with Tommy Rizzo. There had been an odd vibe around the office and he got through it by minimizing his contact with his coworkers.

Saturday mornings were usually an opportunity to decompress from all of the stress but this one was different. The church was crowded by the time Dylan walked through the tall mahogany doors. He hadn't been inside a church since his high school years. Even when he was Best-Man at Lamar and Tamara's wedding he did his duty standing barefoot at their beachfront service. He stood inside the doorway for a moment, looking around and taking in the view of all the figures, imagery and details that typified a large Catholic church. The organist played softly, the music as somber as the occasion required.

He glanced to his right at the rows of pews and in the row second from the rear he saw Beth sitting alone. He hesitated, took a breath and slowly walked toward her. She didn't notice him until he dropped to the seat beside her. She turned toward him. Her smile was faint but it was still a smile and he returned it.

"I'm glad you're with me for this," he said quietly.

She hesitated and then reached over and put her hand on his. "Me too," she replied.

In a matter of ten minutes the last remaining seats had filled in and the service had begun. Dylan could tell that Beth felt the same awkwardness when the crowd rose to sing hymns and speak their memorized parts of the Catholic funeral mass. He couldn't help wondering how much genuine grief was being conveyed.

When their pew emptied as people walked to the communion rail he leaned toward her and asked, "Holy cow, do you feel as conspicuous as I do?"

She nodded and said, "Yeah, I hope it's over soon."

They sat quietly as the rituals and eulogies dragged on. Finally, the ornate, gray and brass casket bearing Finch's body was wheeled from its place in front of the altar, down the long aisle and out the doors to the waiting hearse and procession.

When the organist began the recessional hymn the crowd stood as if on cue. Dylan watched as people exited from the back pews and then he stepped into the aisle to let Beth step in front of him.

When they were outside they stood off to the side of the large gathering of cars and people. Dylan let out an audible sigh and said, "I'm glad that's over with."

Beth looked at him and asked, "Are you going to the cemetery?"

"I wasn't planning on it. How about you?"

"I'd rather not. These things are so depressing and I think just my showing up here was enough."

Since he'd first sat down next to her Dylan had been wondering what to say to her and how to act given the uncomfortable and silent work week they'd just gone through. He took a breath and finally said, "You know, I've missed you this week."

She looked up at him, nodded and said, "Yeah, I've missed you too."

He couldn't help but smile. "Since we're both all dressed up and looking like a million bucks how about going to a nice place for lunch?"

"Well, I guess we should do something to lift our spirits but I feel so overdressed for a Saturday lunch. Can you follow me to my place so I can change?"

"Sure, and I'll just ditch my suitcoat and tie."

Forty-five minutes later they were on the patio of Mission Palms, a new and elegant little bistro that Beth had mentioned on more than one occasion. They ordered a bottle of Chardonnay and told the server they were in no hurry to order food just yet. How does a person find an appetite right after attending the funeral of someone who was impossible to mourn?

The conversation was hard to start. As well as they knew each other and as close as they were, small talk was all they could muster. There was talk of the turn-out and the rituals of the church. They debated who would make up the firm's power structure without Finch. There even was talk about how many people standing outside the church after the service seemed to be in a light hearted mood.

When they had covered pretty much everything related to the funeral Beth mentioned she was having problems with her car and Dylan told her about a large tree branch that had fallen and just missed his house during Thursday night's windstorm.

Talking had always been Dylan's stock in trade but even he could tell the conversation was just circling around the subject they should really be talking about.

When their server stopped by their table it was a welcome interruption. They promised her they'd look over the menu and have their orders ready in five minutes. Despite having skipped breakfast Dylan's appetite was almost nonexistent.

"Okay," Dylan said as he picked up a menu, "we better do what we promised her."

There was a minute or two of silence as they poured over the extensive menu. Beth looked at him and asked, "How hungry are you?"

"Not very, how about you?"

"Me neither, but we came all this way and we look so good we should order something, at least to soak up the wine."

After another couple of minutes they'd each decided on something from the "Light and Easy" section of the menu. The server stopped at the table, they ordered and then they were alone again. It seemed to him that every possible bit of small talk had been traded.

There were a few minutes of sipping wine and looking around the dining room and then finally Beth said, "So it's been a whole week since you got your podcast launched. Have you checked on it lately?"

There it was. *Dreamware* and dream sharing were on the table.

"Yeah, I checked it last night and the *Facebook* page too."

"How does it look so far, I mean the traffic, the interest in it?"

"Well, I've had almost ninety paying customers and I'm up to two hundred likes on the *Facebook* page. It's really surprising for just one week."

She looked him right into his eye and said, "Get your phone and open up the *Facebook* page. I want to see what people are saying about it."

"Oh, looking at *Facebook* on a little screen is a pain in the ass. We can look at it later on a computer."

Once again she read his facial expression and tone of voice. "Come on, humor me. I'm tired of waiting. It's like you don't want me to see it after being so excited about it in the first place."

Somehow it felt like an ultimatum. He picked up his phone and slowly started to open up the page, all the while struggling to find the words he'd use to explain what he knew would be her shock about dream sharing.

He finally opened the page, took a breath and handed her the phone. "Remember," he said, "this is still a work in progress."

He sat in silence as she looked at the page. He leaned forward in an attempt to see what she was looking at but she was holding the phone on an angle that prevented that. Judging from her finger movements he figured she was looking at the images and scrolling through the likes and comments. He tried but failed to read her expression.

For a while he let her look without interruption. Any further attempt to delay or distract her would only look deliberate. It was all of ten minutes before she laid the phone on the table and leaned back in her chair.

She looked at him with the same, unreadable expression. "Well, based on the comments I just read about dream sharing I guess we can stop using the word "coincidence". She said the last word very succinctly.

He swallowed hard and felt like a guilty little boy who'd been caught doing something bad. "What do you mean by that?"

"I mean that it's clear what these people are most excited about and that's getting inside someone else's head. I haven't even seen the podcast but just from reading the words of people who have taken the course it's obvious they believe they can really do that."

"Babe, for the last few weeks you've been focused on just that one part of the course but you have to look at this as multiple parts of a bigger thing."

She picked up the phone and scrolled through the still open page. "Here it is. The next podcast is scheduled for today at five o'clock our time. I think I'll check it out."

Dylan knew the sinking feeling in his stomach would be coming eventually and now it would only get worse knowing Beth would be watching or even studying his dream project. All of it would be out in the open with him having no chance to spin it or offer excuses.

He didn't want that to happen. He watched her for a moment, still trying to interpret her mood, then said, "If you want I'll watch it with you in case you have any questions."

"Nope, I want to experience it like all these people who took the course and commented, on my own and in private."

The server delivered their food, topped off their wine glasses and then turned and left. Dylan wished the interruption would have been longer.

He took a sip of wine and said, "So I guess this means we won't be getting together tonight until after you finish the podcast."

She took a deep breath. "Tell me, babe," she said, "this *Dreamware* project is a very personal thing for you but now you've gone and shared it with the world. And yet somehow I can't help feeling you aren't sure you want to share it with me."

"Well, you're sort of right. The people who commented don't know me or anything about me. I purposely left my name off of the podcast and the *Facebook* page. All it says is *DreamWare LLC*. I guess it's the lawyer in me. So that makes you the only person who knows me and how this all came about. That makes me feel kind of vulnerable."

"Dylan, think about all these people who commented, who want to invade other people's dreams. Their friends and people they know are the ones who should feel vulnerable. The whole idea just feels so terribly wrong and even dangerous."

He just sat there, looking at her and not knowing how to respond. "Shit," he thought to himself, "why did I use a loaded word like vulnerable?"

They ate in silence for a while until Beth made a comment on her shrimp salad. The rest of the meal was mixed with uncomfortable small talk about going back to work on Monday and that Beth was thinking of getting a cat. When the server brought the check it was a welcome relief.

The drive back to Beth's apartment was as quiet as their lunch had been. He walked her to the door and they both seemed to know there was no point in spending the afternoon together. They kissed and before Beth went inside Dylan said, "Hey, after you're done with the podcast give me a call. I want to know what you think."

She smiled and softly said, "Okay."

It was far from the best Saturday night Dylan had had. He checked the podcast reservation list and saw that nearly a hundred more people had signed up. He did a quick mental calculation of the fees and how much of the money would go into his pocket. The *Facebook* page was full of more comments from excited and curious people from around the country. Dream sharing was the main topic of discussion and the comments seemed to have a dark undertone. A dark undertone that was going viral.

It looked like *Dreamware* was catching fire. But there was only one viewer he cared about and as of eight o'clock he hadn't heard a word from her.

Around eleven thirty, as he finished a toke and one last sip of bourbon and with Beth still not responding to her viewing of the podcast, all he could conclude was that the dream sharing segment frightened her the way he'd suspected it would. Her fear of what he'd created worried him. And it gave him a sense of guilt that made him question his idea for the first time.

Given the situation he decided to just lie back and fall asleep in a normal way. Before he drifted off he made the decision to give Beth one more day to get in touch with him. He hoped that Sunday would be the day that everything got resolved.

As unsettling as his Saturday had been Sunday seemed even worse. He found it almost impossible to think about anything but Beth. Every little household chore was performed in a fog of thoughts about her. His lunch at McHale's lasted just an hour but it felt like three. By ten o'clock in the evening there was still no call from her. His mind was already fuzzy from a day of very little food and more than his usual alcohol. He fell asleep on the sofa and slept there through the night.

CHAPTER 20

Suffocation, waking in a sweat. Scared to fall asleep
again in case the dream begins again. What a dream,
when will it end and will it transcend?

From the song *"Infinite Dreams"* by Iron Maiden

F OR MOST PEOPLE WEEKENDS SEEM to fly by, finished
too soon and five days until the next one. But Dylan had just
gotten through the longest, strangest week of his life followed by a
weekend full of questions, self-doubt and worry, mostly about Beth.

For the first time in memory he was eager for Monday even though
he had no clear idea of what the day would bring.

This morning there was no staring at the ceiling to relive his dream.
Guilt made that unnecessary. His fear of what might happen if he tried to
hack another person's slumber had kept him locked into the regular world
of normal and spontaneous dreaming. He wondered how long that fear
would last before he was drawn back into the amazing nighttime world
he'd only begun to sample.

But his newly found fame as a dream expert crowded its way into
his thoughts. The TV interview already felt like a double-edged sword;
something both exciting and risky.

He left home a full hour earlier than usual. Morning traffic was lighter
than usual and the drive through a Starbuck's take-out window only took
a few minutes for a change. Even with the interview, maybe this would
be an easier Monday than he usually endured. When he walked through
the front door of the office the usual throng of people that filled the
lobby and corridor was much smaller due to the early hour, but there was

a still a strange vibe and a silence that was palpable. As he walked down the corridor to his office he didn't get any sense that his colleagues were in mourning. There were no smiles and no banter but also nothing that indicated even a hint of sadness.

After unpacking and turning on his laptop and taking off his suit coat he sat down and waited for his e-mail to come up on the screen. His decision to stop for coffee meant that he wouldn't have to walk to the lunchroom and try to make small talk about Finch's funeral. He couldn't help but wonder how many other people in the office were feeling the same way.

A long list of messages appeared on his screen. His first thought was, "Jesus, don't you people know what a fucking weekend is all about?" The third message from the top was a firm-wide note from Will Sutton announcing that, according to the succession plan the firm had already worked out he would replace Finch as Managing Partner. Everyone else on the Management Committee moved up a notch.

Almost like another eulogy, there was the expected tribute to Finch's hard work and vision that created the firm and the lawyer-speak that was meant to buoy the staff's spirits as they dealt with a perceived but probably nonexistent grief. At the very least Dylan knew who he would have to talk with about his future with the firm.

He was certain that Finch's death had come as no great surprise to the people in the firm. The man's health issues had been obvious for some time and Dylan once had a macabre thought that the staff should start a pool and bet on the day the son of a bitch finally kicked the bucket. He'd even come up with a name for it, "The Finch Farewell Tour", and if he ever would have actually done it he guessed the turnout would have been huge and the betting heavy.

Sutton ended his message with thanks to those who'd attended the funeral service and the sappy, not so subtle statement, "I'm sure John was looking down and feeling proud and grateful."

Dylan thought back to the service and thought he'd done a pretty good job of feigning respect for the hour or so he'd been at the church. John Finch was finally out of his life and fake sadness had been Dylan's form of celebration.

The TV station was within walking distance of Dylan's office and he got there a few minutes before nine. An attractive young women escorted him down a long hallway, through a small cluster of workstations and finally into a make-up room. It only took a few minutes to powder his forehead, nose and cheeks and then he was led on to the stage. Stephanie Parrish greeted him with a big smile and a genuinely enthusiastic interest in *Dreamware.*

She handed him a sheet of paper and walked him through the contents; a sort of bullet point script of questions and topics. He couldn't help but notice that the part about dream sharing was in bold face type and all caps. He knew right then what the focus of the interview would be.

The ten minute segment took nearly fifteen minutes to tape and Stephanie told him they would edit it down to the precise amount of time. The interview included a large projection on the green screen behind their chairs. It was the photo art for the podcast and seeing it on a screen that was easily eight feet high made Dylan feel almost overwhelmed by what he'd created.

All in all Dylan thought it was a reasonably balanced approach to his dream project and when it was over and the cameras went to a commercial he felt himself exhaling with relief. Stephanie stood up, shook his hand and told him that, with the Los Angeles simulcast included, *Dreamware* would be introduced to about half a million people. It would be broadcast on Wednesday morning.

Dylan knew he was smiling when she told him the number but while he walked back to his office every step seemed like punctuation to a story that still had no clear ending. He wondered if he'd let his ego get out of hand by doing the TV interview. Another half million people would soon know about lucid dreaming and dream sharing. He thought again of his unshakeable feeling that Beth was afraid of what *Dreamware* could lead to. Exposing so many more people to its possible consequences might have been the worst thing he could have done.

He had set something in motion and only time would tell exactly what it was.

Back at the office, concentrating on his caseload proved almost impossible. Thoughts of what happened at the TV station were quickly drowned out by the louder than normal office buzz. He was reminded of his connection to Finch's death with every conversation he overhead in the hallway outside his door and with every e-mail from someone in the firm. But more than that, it was the fact the morning had nearly passed and he hadn't heard a word from Beth. She usually stopped by to say good morning and share some little thing about her weekend but not today. Not after delving into the world of dream sharing.

He decided to end the waiting and wondering and sent her a short e-mail message that asked, "Didn't hear from you yesterday, can we talk?" About twenty minutes later her reply popped up on the screen. "Okay, your office?" He sent back, "How about my truck at noon?" Her answer said simply, "Okay." Her minimal number of words and the lack of her usual light hearted emoji seemed to confirm that her mood hadn't changed since Saturday afternoon.

He'd hoped that their Saturday conversation, as tense as it was, along with a relaxing Sunday had helped her get over what he was still certain was fear of him. And he'd already decided not to mention the TV interview. He wanted to take things one step at a time.

He was sitting in his truck checking messages on his cellphone when Beth opened the passenger door and climbed in. "Hi," he said with a nervous smile.

"Hi," she answered. She closed the door and then added, "How was your Sunday?"

He hesitated before he replied, "Oh, it was strange. It was lonely and quiet but mostly it was strange. How about yours?"

"That pretty much describes mine too."

He tried and failed to interpret her mood. "I thought about calling you a hundred times but decided to give you some space."

She nodded slightly. "That was a good idea. I kept expecting my phone to ring but when it didn't I figured it was just as well."

"Beth, I'm not sure what I can say that I didn't say on Saturday but all I know is you're the most important thing in my life and this dream thing has become a big wall between us."

There was an uncomfortable silence before she said, "It's all I've been thinking about for days. I just don't know what it all means."

"Suddenly I feel like tainted goods, like I'm stuck with some kind of affliction."

"Dylan, your dreaming used to be so different. It was always just something you did but now it seems to be who you are and it scares me."

There it was, in her own words. "Do you mean my dreaming scares you or I scare you?"

She looked out the window and it took her a moment to answer. "I'm not sure anymore how to separate the two. At first I thought it was kind of fun hearing about the things you dreamt but now it's like you're obsessed with it. It's not really your dreaming anymore, it's more like your reality."

Dylan noticed a woman getting into her car parked just a few feet from Beth's open window. He waited for the woman to get inside and close her door before he replied. "Beth, I've said this before and I have to say it again so you'll understand. Dreaming is a part of everyone's reality including yours. People dream about other people. They dreams about things in their lives. Maybe my mistake is that I've talked about it too much. Maybe I've given people the idea that it's way more important to me than it really is." He knew he was lying and he hoped she wouldn't detect it.

She was silent, looking out the side window. He wondered if he should keep talking but finally she said, "Okay, let's cut to the chase. Maybe this thing with Finch is just coincidence, a fluke like you say. Maybe I'm just imagining something that isn't true or that isn't even possible. This dream sharing thing has sounded so far-fetched it's been hard for me to believe." She paused and then said, "I watched the podcast and when I saw the part about dream sharing and I heard your voice talking about it I got chills. You sounded so different, like you weren't just explaining what to do but like you were inviting people into some kind of strange place."

Dylan sat there, waiting to see if she had more to say and struggling to come up with the words that could somehow quell her fears. After a few more seconds of her silence he said, "First of all, I hope you used the password I gave you so you watched it for free."

She nodded that she had.

"Good. Now as far as my voice is concerned, I guess I was trying to make it sound soothing so the viewer would feel be relaxed and thinking about sleep. I didn't mean for it to sound scary."

She nodded slightly as he continued. "I want you to tell me exactly what it is you think I've done wrong here."

She looked out the windshield and then all around her to make sure no one was within earshot. "I'm not saying you did anything wrong, at least not intentionally."

"What in the hell does that mean?"

"I just mean I think you probably went into this project thinking of just your own experiences and not about how other people are different from you. Dylan, there were comments from people who clearly wanted to do harm to someone in their dreams. It's like *Dreamware* has unleashed the dogs or something and there's no way to call them off."

She paused and then added, "I mean, who knows what's already gone on out there with some of these people and all the other people's dreams they might have hacked? Maybe there's already been another John Finch who's died in his sleep or another Max Dewart who's lost his job. What if someone hacked into some politician's dream and tried to influence his opinion about a bill? When you really think about the possibilities, some guy could even stalk someone in their dreams."

Her words sounded like an accusation.

Dylan felt a mix of emotions; a big concern for her feelings toward him and just as big a feeling that he needed to defend everything he'd created. He took a breath and said, "Or maybe there was a couple who made love after being apart for a long time."

His comment seemed to surprise her. She was silent for a moment before saying, "Okay, I agree there are two sides to this thing. She leaned toward him and put her hand on his shoulder. "Babe, all I want you to do is keep an eye on things. Read the viewer comments and watch for anything that looks menacing or weird. Make *Dreamware* something good, something you can be proud of and not something evil."

"Deal," he said, unsure of his desire or ability to go along with her request. His *Dreamware* followers would use the information any way they wanted. Given the privacy of dreams he knew there would probably be as much or more evil going on as good.

He leaned over and kissed her and this time he felt her kissing back.

The rest of the workday flew by, a mixture of Doyle and Flynn cases with a few simpler but more colorful moonlight cases. Tommy Rizzo had steered two people Dylan's way and they'd become two of the more unusual clients he'd ever had. One was a cross-dressing tattoo artist who'd been asked to relocate his business because his landlord felt it was drawing undesirable people to the neighborhood. The other one was a woman who made her living as a street musician and had run afoul of the law by not having an entertainment license to perform her loud and lengthy violin concertos on the sidewalk. Tommy seemed to be a magnet for oddballs and more and more of them were sticking to Dylan as well.

That evening's bedtime routine was a struggle to decide if he would comply with Beth's request to monitor *Dreamware*. His quick agreement had been a lie and he wasn't proud of it. But he was strangely protective of his creation and was as eager as he'd ever been to share it with the world.

As he held the glass in his hand and stared at the last, long sip of bourbon in it, he saw it as a reward for his week-long sacrifice of avoiding his dream skills. Despite his promise to Beth tonight would be different. Tonight would find him back in his world of exploring the dreams of others.

FADE IN:

INTERIOR – A HOME OUTSIDE OF SACRAMENTO - NIGHT

A small, gray haired woman carefully removes dishes from a dishwasher and places them into the overhead cupboards of her kitchen. A cold breeze lifts the curtains of the window over the sink and she stops to close it. When she is finished unloading the dishwasher she closes it, looks around the room and slowly walks into the living room. She is no sooner settled into a large, cushioned chair when she hears a knock on her front door. She stands up, her nervousness obvious and walks toward it. She cautiously pulls the privacy shade aside and looks out. A faint smile comes to her face and after a brief hesitation she unlocks and opens the door.

SANDRA WARD: Dylan what are you doing here?

DYLAN: I had some business down at the capitol today and I thought I'd stop by

She steps away from the door as Dylan steps inside. He is holding a small overnight bag in his left hand. As he takes the door from her and starts to close it the reflection of the front porch light flashes across his face.

SANDRA: It's so late. I assume you're staying over here in town and not planning to make that long drive back home in the dark.

DYLAN: Yeah, that was my plan but somehow my hotel reservation got screwed up and they were all booked up for the night.

Sandra puts her hands together and holds them against her chest. She looks confused.

SANDRA: So what are you going to do?

DYLAN: Well, Mom, I was hoping I could stay here, in my old room. My bed is still there, isn't it?

SANDRA: Of course it is, it's exactly the way it was when you left. I try to keep it clean and dusted like I always did.

Neither of them speaks. Sandra looks straight at Dylan and he looks down at the floor. Finally he clears his throat and looks at her.

DYLAN: Well, that's great. It's been a long day and I'm really bushed.

SANDRA: Do you want anything to eat or drink?

DYLAN: No thanks, I had a quick burger and beer at the hotel bar before I left. Actually, even though it's early I was thinking of turning in so I can get an early start back in the morning.

SANDRA: Can't we sit up and talk for a while?

DYLAN: Sorry, Mom, but I'm really beat. I feel like I'm falling asleep just standing here.

The disappointment on Sandra's face is obvious as she sighs and starts walking down the hallway. She stops by the door to his old room and he steps inside and tosses his bag on to the bed. He turns on the overhead light and takes a quick look around the room. There is an uneasy pause as they look at each other in silence.

DYLAN: Well, good night, Mom.

SANDRA: Good night, son. Sleep tight.

Dylan closes the door. After undressing he turns off the overhead light and climbs into bed. He lays back and stares at the old, familiar ceiling. He hears the door of his mother's bedroom squeak as it closes and then hears the click of the latch. He lies in the darkness for an hour, trying to fall asleep. Finally, sleep comes.

CHAPTER 21

I had a dream my life would be so different from this
hell I'm living. So different now from what it seemed.
Now life has killed the dream I dreamed.

From the song *I Dreamed a Dream* by Anne Hathaway

NO MATTER HOW MODERN OR well-furnished a
hospital waiting room might be it can't do much to help a
person overcome the nervousness and stress that the activities
surrounding it bring. Emergency department waiting rooms are the worst.
Beth tried to stay seated but she found herself pacing and staring blankly
out the large windows. Her cup of coffee from the vending machine
had been cold for half an hour and finally she dropped it into a nearby
trash can.

A man's voice behind her brought her back into the moment. "Excuse
me, are you Miss Chilcotte?"

Beth turned, looked at the man. He was stocky and Middle Eastern in
appearance with a low voice and a thick accent. "Yes. Are you his doctor?"

"Well, I'm one of the one of the doctors who has looked at him since
they brought him in. I'm Dr. Shamil." He motioned to her to step away
from the line of traffic walking past them and led her over to a small
nurses station. "Okay," he started. "You were the one who found him this
morning. What can you tell me?"

Beth was struggling to keep her composure. Her eyes were swollen
and red and she was shaking as she answered, "Well, he hasn't been to
the office for two days and they said he never called in sick or anything.
I called him a couple of times yesterday and all last night. He's my, well,

he's my boyfriend so when he didn't return my calls I figured something was wrong."

"Do you know if he's been sick lately? Has he complained about any kind of pain or not feeling well?"

"Nothing, nothing at all. He's always been healthy and active."

"So how was he when you found him this morning?"

"Well, I drove to his house and let myself in. I have a key. I called his name and looked around his house and found him in his bed. I thought he was sleeping so I sat on the bed and shook him and said his name but he didn't move. He didn't wake up or anything." Her eyes filled with tears as she looked at Shamil. "What's wrong with him?" she asked, her voice cracking.

"Like I said, I'm just one of the doctors who have looked at him. I'm a neurologist. When an apparently healthy person comes to us and there are no signs of injury and no trace of drugs in his system, although we did find alcohol, we start to look elsewhere. You told the admitting nurse that Mr. Ward was sleeping when you found him but couldn't wake him up. That tells us it might be a brain issue of some kind."

Beth let out a sigh that sounded painful. "His brain, did you test him? What is it?"

"We don't know yet. My preliminary brain scan tells me there's no apparent tissue trauma or obvious malady. The readings are identical to those of a man who is simply asleep and in a dreamlike state."

Shamil's comment hit her like a punch in the stomach. "Well, what can you do? Is there some way you can wake him up?

"It's too soon to know exactly what's going on. We don't want to jump to conclusions and do anything that might make things worse. For now we're just going to observe him. He doesn't appear to be in any pain, his heartrate is normal and his breathing is regular. For now we'll just have to wait."

Beth began to cry and Shamil put his hand on her shoulder. A nurse sitting at the station stood up, reached over and handed her a tissue. Beth wiped her eyes and cheeks and then asked, "Can I see him?"

"Sure, we have him in an exam room right now. If you can give the nurse here some information, if you know it, she can contact his employer about his healthcare coverage. I'll let her know when we have him moved into a patient room and she can tell you how to find him."

Twenty minutes later Beth walked into a small, private room. She stopped at the bedside and looked down at Dylan. Except for a saline drip and a wristband attached to a heart monitor, he looked as though he was sound asleep. She pulled a chair over close to the bed and sat there holding his hand.

Twenty minutes went by and a nurse stopped by to check the drip bag and then left without saying anything. Ten more minutes went by and Beth glanced at her reflection in a mirror near the bathroom door. Her eyes were still red and she didn't try to wipe away a tear that slipped down her cheek.

The ringing of a cellphone in her purse interrupted her thoughts. It was Dylan's phone. Without really giving it much thought she'd grabbed it when the EMTs were wheeling Dylan out of the bedroom at his house. When she pulled it out of her purse she didn't recognize the number on the screen but swiped the answer key anyway.

"Hello" she said, trying to sound steady and clear when she felt anything but.

"Uh, yes," a woman's voice started. "I'm calling for Dylan Ward and this is the number I have for him."

"This is his phone. I'm Beth Chilcotte. I'm, well I'm his girlfriend."

"I'm Marjorie Sax, I'm a friend of Dylan's mother, Sandra. May I speak with him?"

Beth looked over at Dylan and her eyes filled with tears. "I'm afraid he can't talk right now. Can I take a message?" Her voice was starting to crack.

The woman cleared her throat. "Well, I'm afraid I have some bad news for him. His mother is in the hospital. She had some kind of seizure in her sleep on Monday night and she's in a coma."

Beth's gasp was audible and Marjorie said, "Oh, I'm sorry to have to give you such bad news." She waited a moment and then asked, "Are you okay?"

Beth hesitated with the phone held tightly against her chest while she took a deep breath and tried to maintain her composure. She slowly exhaled and put the phone back to her ear. "Um, how bad is she? I mean what does her doctor say?"

"Well, so far they don't know much. She's had some health issues lately but when I talked to her on Monday evening she just said she was tired and wanted to go to bed. They told me this morning she appears to be comfortable, like she's just sleeping but they have no idea if and when she'll come out of it."

"You mean there's a chance she won't wake up?"

"Yes, they said there's that chance. That's why it's so important Dylan knows what's going on. Can you tell him, or can you have him call me?"

Beth started to shake, first her hands and then her entire body. "Uh, yes, I will. Thank you for calling," she said, choking back tears as she suddenly ended the call.

She laid the phone on the bed and grasped Dylan's hand again. Her shoulders slumped as she bent down to kiss it, her tears dropping on to the thin white sheet that covered him to his chest. She thought how peaceful his face looked. She placed his hand across his chest, let go of it and then slowly ran her fingers over his face. "Oh, Dylan, where are you?"

THE END

Printed in the United States
By Bookmasters